The BAD MOTHER'S HOLIDAY

SUZY K QUINN

Lightning
Books

Published by
Lightning Books Ltd
Imprint of EyeStorm Media
312 Uxbridge Road
Rickmansworth
Hertfordshire
WD3 8YL

www.lightning-books.com

British Library Cataloguing in Publication Data
A catalogue record for this book is available from the British Library

Printed by CPI Group (UK) Ltd, Croydon CR0 4YY

ISBN 9781785631597

Author's note
I still cant believe so many people read my books.
Each and every day, I am grateful for you, dear reader.
Thank you so much.
If you want to ask me any questions about the books
or chat about anything at all, get in touch:

Happy reading,
Suzy xxx

Email: suzykquinn@devoted-ebooks.com
Facebook.com/suzykquinn
(You can friend request me. I like friends.)
Twitter: @suzykquinn
Website: suzykquinn.com

Monday, 1st January

New Year's Day

How do you measure a life in a year?

+ 416 fish fingers cooked for Daisy, but mostly eaten by me.
+ 244 loads of washing.
+ One stone lost, one gained.
+ Seven bottles of Calpol.
+ 364 nights of disturbed sleep.
+ Said 'no' approx. 5000 times, told no 50,000 times.
+ Two calls to 999 (Daisy glo-stick chewing incident and freaky green poo two days after).
+ One unexpected pregnancy.
+ One marriage proposal.
+ Told Daisy 'I love you' more times than I can possibly count.

This year? I would like fewer:

+ Custody battles with Nick, Daisy's feckless, irresponsible father.
+ Relationship uncertainties with Alex.
+ Stressful house renovations.
+Mortgage, credit card and utility bills.

Finances are an uncomfortable subject right now.

I'd planned to get a proper grown-up job in London this year, but commuting will be tough now I'm pregnant.

I know employers aren't supposed to discriminate, but pregnancy mimics hangover symptoms – tiredness, sickness, bad memory, etc. – and lasts all day, every day. There's no afternoon respite after a restorative Big Mac.

Frankly, I wouldn't hire me.

Alex has offered to pay my bills during the pregnancy, but told him 'no thank you'.

Maybe I'm being an idiot, but it would just be too weird. Yes – we're having a baby together, but our relationship is extremely uncertain.

Have asked Alex to give me thinking space, re: his marriage proposal. I think he's a bit offended. Am imagining him drinking an expensive Southbank latte, watching the Thames, black hair romantically tousled, dark eyes flashing.

'Another coffee, Mr Dalton?'

'No thank you. I'm too furious.'

Tuesday 2nd January

It's only been four days since the positive pregnancy test result.

Four years wouldn't be enough to digest this information.

Two children.

How will I do it?

Have booked in to see Dr Slaughter tomorrow.

Called Alex to let him know.

Alex was silent for a moment, then said, 'Juliette – a very good doctor and family friend has agreed to see us too. I spoke to him this morning. He's called Dr Rupert Snape and has promised to take very good care of you.'

'I've known Dr Slaughter since I was a little girl,' I said. 'He's wonderful. Why would I see anyone else? Look, you don't have to come. First appointments are just routine, anyway. All they do is log you on the system and tell you not to eat Stilton.'

'Dr Snape also mentioned sushi,' said Alex.

Told Alex I don't like sushi, so Dr Snape's premium advice would be useless in my case.

Alex asked where I'd eaten sushi.

'Marks and Spencer,' I said.

Alex said Marks and Spencer doesn't do real sushi, because it's made from cooked tuna, mayonnaise and seafood sticks. Then he asked me to move into his Chelsea apartment.

'I can't move to London,' I said. 'I have a job here and a house. And a family.'

'If we're committing to a life together,' said Alex, 'we have to make compromises.'

'OK, Alex,' I said. 'Why don't you stop working a fourteen-hour day and move back to Great Oakley?'

Alex said moving out of London was impossible right now.

'I hate the city, but it's where the money is,' he said.

'You're obsessed with earning money,' I replied. 'Babies only need a cot, clothes and nappies. Most of the other baby gadgets I wasted my money on never got used. And you can get a lot of free stuff second-hand – people are always getting rid of baby things. Your business earns millions.'

Alex said that company profit and personal income were not the same, and anyone who said different didn't pay enough tax.

Told Alex he reminded me of an anorexic girl who thinks she's fat.

Alex didn't seem to understand the comparison, citing the fluctuating diet industry as an excellent example of boom and bust.

'And children are expensive,' Alex insisted. 'They need schooling, healthcare, good-quality ski equipment… The list is endless.'

'That's what you're working for?' I asked. 'Ski equipment?'

'Every child needs ski equipment,' said Alex.

It was another reminder that we're from different worlds.

'So are you coming with me tomorrow?' I asked.

'Yes, of course,' said Alex. 'I'll see this NHS doctor with you.'

I felt he said the word 'NHS' in a derisive tone.

'You'd better not be snobby about private healthcare if you come along,' I said. 'Dr Slaughter doesn't suffer fools gladly. He's one of the few people who's shouted at my mum and lived to tell the tale.'

'What did he shout at your mother for?' Alex asked.

'He caught her buying twelve custard-filled doughnuts in the Co-op,' I explained. 'The day after she'd been diagnosed with diabetes.'

Wednesday 3rd January

Appointment with Dr Slaughter.

Alex drove me to the doctor's surgery in his shiny MG.

It was unnecessary to be driven there, since the doctor's surgery is a five-minute walk from my house, but I think Alex wanted to feel useful.

Felt a bit conspicuous, getting out of Alex's fancy sports car.

It didn't help that Alex looks a bit like James Bond – black tailored suit, clean-shaven jaw, dark eyes scanning the surroundings for snipers.

An old lady, hobbling past on a Zimmer frame, whispered, 'Tosser'.

'This is the doctor's surgery?' Alex asked, looking over our village health centre. 'The medical facility where you'll be cared for? It looks like an insane old lady's house.'

It's true – our doctor's surgery is essentially a bungalow, complete with moss-covered roof and orange curtains. But it's very cosy inside, except for the damp.

We waited the usual half an hour (Dr Slaughter is always late, except for the rare occasions when I'm late, in which case he's always right on time and I miss my slot).

'This is unacceptable,' Alex announced, when we were finally called into Dr Slaughter's office. 'Juliette is pregnant. She's had to wait over thirty minutes.'

Dr Slaughter said it was impossible to run an over-stretched NHS medical facility on time.

'Most problems exceed the ten-minute appointment slot,' he explained. 'And the older patients like a bit of a chat.'

'Is this a health facility or a community centre for the elderly?' Alex challenged.

Dr Slaughter considered this for a moment, then replied, 'I suppose it's a little bit of both. Are we congratulating or commiserating?'

'Congratulating,' Alex barked.

'Wonderful,' said Dr Slaughter, pulling out a box of mint-chocolate sticks. 'Well help yourself to the leftover Christmas spoils. Since we're celebrating.'

Alex declined the chocolate, muttering something about purified water and hand-cut vegetable platters at Dr Rupert Snape's surgery.

'You've done all this maternity stuff before, Juliette,' said Dr Slaughter, munching on a mint chocolate stick. 'You know the drill. Don't eat Stilton. Stay away from raw egg. We'll do a glucose test next time you come in. Buy yourself a bottle of Lucozade and drink it one hour before.' Then he handed me a Bounty pack of maternity information and said, 'The midwife will see you from now on. I'd make the appointment today if I were you – she's booked up solid until March.'

'You're not going to carry out a pregnancy test?' Alex asked.

'A home test is sufficient,' said Dr Slaughter. 'You have done the wee on a stick test, haven't you Juliette?'

'Yes,' I said. 'I bought a kit from Boots.'

'But what about a proper pregnancy test?' said Alex.

'Pregnancy tests are all much of a muchness these days,' said Dr Slaughter. 'It's just absorbent paper at the end of the day. The home tests are no different from the NHS ones. If anything, they're more accurate.'

'Juliette.' Alex took my hands. 'I really think we should see Dr Rupert Snape.' Then he turned to Dr Slaughter, eyes blazing, and said, 'You haven't even mentioned sushi.'

Thursday 4th January

The morning sickness hit today – a sort of low-level, travel-sickness feeling.

Did watery, spitty sick in the toilet when I woke up and now feel both sick and starving hungry.

Long, curly hair is no friend of the nauseous, so I've tied it up in one of those messy top buns that make me look like a sumo wrestler.

Have spent the morning watching kids' TV with Daisy, delicately sipping teaspoons of Heinz Tomato Soup. We watched a *Mickey Mouse's Club House* episode all about hot dogs, which finished with the usual 'Hot Diggity Dog' song. It made me feel simultaneously sick and in need of a hot dog.

Phoned Mum for sympathy.

'Will you come over and help with Daisy?' I pleaded. 'I feel awful.'

Mum refused, telling me to walk or drive to the pub.

Told Mum I couldn't face getting Daisy dressed.

'Why not?' Mum asked.

Explained that dressing Daisy, now she's a wilful two-year-old, involves half an hour of stressful negotiating. Doing her hair is equally challenging, since she either refuses to have it brushed or asks for some elaborate Disney princess hairstyle that I can't do.

'Why don't you just leave her hair?' Mum asked.

'I can't do that,' I said. 'Daisy's hair grows forward over her face now. She looks like a Yeti cave girl until I get a hairband on her.'

Then I moaned some more about feeling hungry and sick.

'How about something light to eat?' Mum suggested. 'Like a nice thick slice of buttered toast with jam? You want to get some calories into you.'

The thought of anything buttered made me vomit into Daisy's half-eaten bowl of Shreddies.

Mum took pity on me then. 'Dad will come get you,' she decided. 'Let me shout at him a bit and he'll be on his way.'

Dad arrived twenty minutes later on his bicycle, wearing waterproofs, cycle clips and a red reflector pinned to the back of his green bobble hat. With his neatly clipped white beard and the single white curl escaping onto his forehead, Dad looked like a special-edition cyclist gnome. There was a cushion strapped to his bike rack with hooked elastic.

'Hop on love,' said Dad. 'I'll pedal you up the road. Daisy can sit on your lap.'

'I thought you'd be in the car,' I said. 'I can't sit on the back of your bike with Daisy. It's dangerous.'

'As if I'd waste the petrol on a three-minute journey!' Dad chortled. 'There's nothing dangerous about this bike – I've just given it a full service.'

Told Dad my instructions had been miscommunicated, and I required a nice, warm motor vehicle.

Dad said I was getting spoiled, and relayed (again) the story of his own father pedalling him and his brothers to school on his bicycle crossbar with no cushion or padding of any kind.

'Our testicles were black and blue by the time we reached the school gates,' Dad announced. 'But it toughened us up. Taught us not to complain about minor discomforts.'

Ended up walking to the pub with Daisy, while Dad pushed his bike.

The ten-minute walk took half an hour, because Daisy needed to investigate every leaf, bramble and potential dog poo.

Am now at Mum and Dad's, taking yet more delicate sips of Heinz tomato soup from a mug shaped like a pair of boobs.

Mum keeps trying to force Guinness on me, believing it to be some sort of health tonic for pregnant women.

Phoned Alex to complain about how sick I felt.

Alex suggested taking me to Accident and Emergency. I hope he's not going to be this paranoid for the whole pregnancy.

Friday 5th January

Still at the pub.

KEEP being sick. The only foods I can keep down are bland, yellow processed foods.

Thank god my cousin John Boy is staying at the pub. He's stocked up on white bread, Super Noodles and Monster Munch crisps.

It's incredible John Boy has such a muscular physique on an unbelievably crap diet. But he's some sort of genetic oddity. Apparently, he lived off corned beef, biscuits and vodka in the army and didn't put on an ounce of fat.

Maybe it comes down to exercise. Even with his prosthetic leg, John Boy does squat jumps, ten-mile runs and one-handed press ups – the latter with Callum on his back.

'What happened to your weird pencil moustache?' I asked John Boy. 'You've let it go all straggly. And are you growing your hair out too?'

John Boy explained that he is cultivating one of those overly long, fashionable beards and a man bun.

Mum keeps asking why he wants to look like the back-end of a Crufts champion. But she isn't one to talk about succumbing to silly fashions. In the 1980s, her hair was bleached, permed and feathered. She also still wears lots of neon Lycra, animal prints and lace, often together, and shops in New Look, Top Shop and Forever 21.

Nice being back at the pub.

Dad has made the bathroom a bit more fun, putting magazines, crossword puzzles and a radio in there, plus a vase containing hazel catkins he picked from the woods.

Alex has asked to come see me, but I don't want visitors while I'm pale and throwing up. This has put into stark relief the uncertain nature of our relationship, and the fact I don't know him well enough to be sick in front of him.

The undesirable effects of pregnancy are yet another reason to be in a proper relationship before you get knocked up.

Saturday 6th January

Still at the pub.

Saw my tired, pale face this morning, coupled with a giant mess of frizzy curly hair, and realised there's no way I can go home yet.

Having morning sickness with Daisy running around is impossible.

Toddlers have no respect for illness. While I'm vomiting into the toilet bowl, Daisy prods me and shouts 'cuddle, cuddle'.

Realised, between vomits, that Daisy looks more like Nick these days. Her fluffy blonde hair is brown and straight at the roots, her eyebrows are darkening and her eyes are bright blue.

I wonder whose nose Daisy will get – my roundy, squishy one, or Nick's long, straight, actor nose? Hard to know what to hope for. Nick's nose does look striking in his headshots, but extremely evil on his mother.

I suppose it doesn't matter if Daisy looks like Nick, as long as his selfishness isn't genetic.

Afternoon

It's nice being looked after at the pub, but Mum can't get her head around me feeling sick. She is certain she can 'cure' me with the right meal.

Today Mum bought a range of 'get-well food' from the Cash and Carry: a catering-sized 24-slice pepperoni pizza, a 2ft garlic baguette and 50 chocolate-covered profiteroles. She unloaded this nauseatingly calorific assortment onto the kitchen table and said, 'There you go love – there must be something in that lot you fancy.'

Tried to ignore the tower of cream-filled chocolate puffs and cheesy, oily pizza, but Dad drew attention to it by starting an argument.

'You've bought enough food for twenty people, Shirley,' Dad complained, wagging the Guinness pencil he was using for Sudoku. 'It's a waste.'

'Jules and Daisy are here,' said Mum. 'We need a bit extra.'

'Juliette is feeling nauseous,' Dad insisted. 'A huge garlic baguette dripping with greasy butter is hardly going to settle her stomach. Nor is a pizza with all that gelatinous, bright-yellow cheese and fatty sausage on top. And she won't want a dessert, filled with whipped double cream and covered in rich, chocolate sauce.'

Slunk off to be sick then, but could still hear the argument about 'oil' and 'grease' through the toilet door.

'How are we ever going to eat a pizza that size in two days?' Dad finally demanded.

'Oh, stop going on,' said Mum. 'If there's any food left over, I'll bring it downstairs for the regulars.'

Dad took out his calculator and totted up the cost of leftover food Mum brought down to the pub last year. He estimated at least three-hundred pounds worth of food had been 'lavished' on Yorkie and Mick the Hat. He also pointed out that Yorkie is always too drunk to appreciate what he's eating and thinks smoked salmon is ham.

Mum snatched the calculator and added up Yorkie and Mick the Hat's bar bills last year. They worked out at over £10,000.

Dad sloped off to his office, muttering about 'dubious calculation methods' and 'imprecise measures'.

After lunch, Alex rang. 'How are you feeling?' he asked.

'Like I'm on a bumpy, winding road in an old, petrol-reeking truck,' I replied.

'I'm sorry to hear that,' said Alex. 'I was hoping you'd be feeling better. And that I could see you.'

Said I still didn't feel up to visitors.

'I'm not just a visitor,' said Alex. 'I'm the father of your child.'

Relented, and said Alex could come over for tea, which he calls 'supper'.

Told Alex not to bring any food.

'Not even a dessert?' said Alex.

'Especially not a dessert,' I said. 'Absolutely nothing contained whipped double cream or rich chocolate sauce.'

Evening

Alex just left. He brought me fifty red roses and a large bottle of Perrier (his mother told him sparkling water was good for morning sickness).

Things were a bit awkward, with Alex giving me a very formal peck on the cheek, then embracing me like I was made of china.

'Are you OK?' he whispered. 'How is the nausea?'

'Honestly, I'm fine,' I insisted. 'Just not too up for physical contact.'

Alex nodded sagely, a concerned expression on his handsome face. 'Perhaps we could see Dr Rupert Snape after all. He could tell us if this sickness is anything to worry about.'

'Almost everyone gets morning sickness,' I said. 'It's more common in healthy pregnancies. The extra hormones are there to prevent miscarriage.'

Alex struggled to get his head around this biological design flaw. 'But if the baby is healthy, why would the human body create illness?'

'You want to know why women throw up, wee themselves and get indigestion, sciatica, constipation, migraines and brain-fuddling tiredness during pregnancy?' I asked. 'It's simple. Mother Nature is a psychopathic old hag.'

Asked Alex about his Christmas, and whether he'd got to see much of his family.

'Yes,' said Alex. 'I stayed with Anya in Kensington.'

Asked who Anya was.

'My mother,' said Alex.

Remembered that Anya is the Hungarian word for mother. Felt guilty for forgetting.

'She would have been alone otherwise,' Alex continued. 'Carlos went back to Spain.'

'So it was just the two of you on Christmas day?' I asked.

'Yes,' said Alex. 'Very quiet. I imagine your Christmas day was somewhat busier. Listen. Juliette – have you thought any more about moving to London?'

'I don't want to move to London,' I said. 'Daisy is two-and-a-half. She likes parks and swings and woods. London isn't the place for her.'

Alex claimed London had 'some of the best parks in the world'.

'But Daisy has grandparents here,' I said. 'They love her. They want to be with her.'

Mum bellowed from the kitchen: 'I assume you're talking about your father, not me. The best thing about being a grandparent is giving the kids back at the end of a long day.'

I closed the door, and Alex and I chatted about family versus hired childcare.

'Whatever Mum says, she truly cares about Daisy,' I insisted.

Alex conceded that one of his nannies, Tiggy Carmichael, smoked forty cigarettes a day, stole cigars from his father and encouraged Alex and Zach to smoke, telling them that the Marlborough cowboy never caught a cold. 'But we loved her, nonetheless.'

'I'm happy in Great Oakley,' I said. 'I'm not moving.'

Alex sighed, knelt down to my stomach and kissed my woolly jumper. 'Little one, your mother is very stubborn,' he said. 'But we'll make it work somehow.'

It was a sweet thing to say, but actually having Alex's hands on my stomach made me feel quite nauseous.

Sunday 7th January

Still at the pub.

Woke up this morning to find John Boy red-eyed and quiet, automatically spooning Frosties into his mouth between swigs from a giant tea mug.

John Boy's teeth were a weird grey-purple colour and he smelt like an old tramp. His attempted man bun was straggling over his face.

Daisy said, 'On Boy. Smelly like wee.'

Asked John Boy why he smelt of stale booze and had teeth like a Victorian chimney sweep.

John Boy said his new girlfriend, Gwen, had dumped him.

I learned the whole story, through big swigs of sugary tea.

Gwen texted John Boy yesterday and said she was seeing

someone else – a mature student at her university.

John Boy called Gwen over twenty times, but she wouldn't answer her phone. Heartbroken, he bought a £4.99 bottle of King's Oak Crème sherry, drank the whole thing and fell asleep on a park bench.

The cheap, red sherry explained John Boy's purple teeth.

I put my arm around John Boy and told him it would be alright. Couldn't think of anything else to say, so opted for the cliché, 'There are plenty more fish in the sea.'

John Boy said he hated fish. He spent the morning watching Rocky I, II and III back-to-back, then strapped his prosthetic leg on and said he was off to the shops.

An hour later, John Boy returned with two bottles of King's Oak Crème, a huge bag of pick and mix sweets for Daisy and a Liverpool football kit for Callum.

Callum was delighted with the football kit, declaring it 'well ace' and borrowing my phone to take selfies. The age six-to-seven kit was a bit big for Callum, because he's small for his age, but Callum declared his baggy appearance to be, 'Growing room, innit? That's better value.'

Nice that he listens to Dad sometimes.

Callum admired his selfies, believing he looked like Jamie Foxx from the new Annie movie.

John Boy put him straight. 'You're just not black enough, mate. You're more a sort of milky tea colour.'

Callum was disappointed. 'But I've sort of got an afro, haven't I?'

'No, mate,' said John Boy. 'Having tramlines shaved on your head is not the same as an afro.'

Callum looked sad about that. His dad (whom he never sees) is mixed race – half Caribbean, half Norwich – and Callum has always hoped to become a black football player.

John Boy put jelly rings on Daisy's fingers and laced up Callum's football boots, saying, 'You kids are the only things keeping me going right now. If it weren't for you two, I'd never smile again.'

Felt hurt by this. After all, I'd comforted him earlier and made that caring 'plenty of fish in the sea' comment.

Evening

Popped out to the Co-op after tea for more cream crackers and tomato soup, while Mum and Dad watched Daisy.

While I was at the Co-op, Mum phoned with a 'bright idea' for curing morning sickness – an all-inclusive holiday to Greece.

'I've found a cracking deal for May,' Mum told me. 'The Teletext people are on the other line right now, ready to book us all in. Your Dad and I will pay. It's cheap as chips – only £180 per person, including flights. That's less than it costs to live at home.'

'How will an all-inclusive holiday help my morning sickness?' I asked.

'All the food,' said Mum. 'You get so much choice on those all-inclusive buffets. Fruit, cheese – the lot. You're bound to find something you can eat.'

'You can't cure morning sickness with food,' I said. 'Food is what makes me feel sick.'

'Well, a few Coca Colas in the sunshine won't hurt,' Mum reasoned. 'And it's something to look forward to. Pregnancy is so miserable. And at the end of it, all you get is a screaming baby.'

'All-inclusive holidays aren't the place for a pregnant person,' I said. 'I can't eat at normal capacity. I can't drink alcohol. It just isn't cost effective. I don't want to sit around, being big and pregnant, watching everyone else get pissed and enjoy themselves.'

Mum told me I was being 'bloody miserable'.

She's right. I am bloody miserable. But that's pregnancy for you.

The moment Mum hung up, I regretted my grumpy, snap decision. A holiday would be nice, even if I can't drink alcohol or overeat, and it's very generous of Mum to pay for me.

Phoned Mum back, but the line was engaged. By the time I got through, Mum had already booked the holiday for the rest of the family.

'It's fully booked now, love,' said Mum. 'There's always next year. Of course, by then you'll have a baby and a toddler. And don't forget you'll have to pay full whack for Daisy's flight when she turns three. But never mind.'

Dad came on the line and said, 'It's not all bad news, love. Your Mum has agreed to a family camping trip at the end of June. So you can have a lovely break with the Duffy clan in the great outdoors.'

'I have not bloody agreed,' Mum shouted in the background. 'It is very manipulative of you to say that, Bob. All I did was mention the dry-rot in the caravan.'

Thanked Dad for trying to cheer me up, but there's no way I'm going camping. And from Mum's shouting and swearing in the background, there's no way she's going either.

When I got back from the Co-op, Brandi and Mum were colouring their hair in the kitchen.

They were both wearing dressing gowns – Brandi's skinny figure and push-up bra were wrapped in monogrammed Barbie pink. Mum's bulging bosom and stomach sported her favoured leopard print.

Brandi had foils all over her head and a full face of makeup, including creamy foundation, thick false eyelashes, flashes of black eyeliner and matte red lipstick.

'Do you want me to give you some more blonde highlights?' Brandi asked me. 'Your roots are nearly an inch long. It looks like Daisy felt-tipped the top of your head.'

Thanked her, but I've learned from past mistakes. Brandi always gives me white-blonde hair, no matter what tasteful, subtle blonde shade I request.

I asked why Brandi was painting a pink colour onto Mum's foils, rather than the usual bluey-white peroxide.

'Mum fancied a change,' said Brandi. 'And pastel-toned blonde is very in this year.'

When Brandi had finished, Mum was delighted with her new pinky-blonde hair.

'I look like one of those Real Orange Housewives,' said Mum.

I was too kind to say she looked like a stick of candyfloss.

Monday 8th January

John Boy's mum, Aunty Trina, phoned at 3 am this morning.

'I've just seen it on Facebook,' Aunty Trina screeched, in her lovely Irish accent. 'He's not with that Gwen any more. His profile thingy says he's single. I'm worried about my boy. He can't be without a woman taking care of him. He doesn't know the first thing about bacteria.'

'He's got people taking care of him, Aunty Trina,' I reassured her. 'He's at the pub with Mum and Dad.'

Aunty Trina screeched. 'His leg dressings need washing and ironing every day. Who will do it, if he doesn't have a girlfriend?'

At this point, Mum marched out of the bedroom, blonde-pink hair sticking up all over the place, and snatched the phone.

'For Christ's sake, Trina, it's 3 am,' she roared. 'Let us all get some rest.'

Then Mum slammed the phone down and stomped back to bed.

Tuesday 9th January

Woke this morning to hear Aunty Trina banging on the front door.

Mum stomped downstairs, shouting and swearing.

I heard the door open, and Aunty Trina shouting and swearing back.

Then Mum and Aunty Trina had a screaming match on the doorstep.

I heard references to Mum's pink hair and Aunty Trina's '80s leather jacket.

Dad pleaded with both women to stay calm and not hit each other.

After ten minutes of shouting, Mum said, 'Come in for a bacon sandwich then, Trina. Bob will help with your luggage.'

Stumbled out of my bedroom to find Dad hauling three floral suitcases upstairs.

Aunty Trina was already in the kitchen, washing the cupboard doors with vinegar and baking soda solution.

There were three Aldi shopping bags on the table filled with sugary cereal and biscuits.

Aunty Trina's birds' nest of peroxided hair was stiff and unmoving as she vigorously scrubbed kitchen cupboards.

'Trina's going to stay with us for a bit,' Mum announced. 'She and John Boy can have some quality time.'

A few minutes later, John Boy sloped out of his bedroom in combat trousers, with Callum clinging to his good leg.

John Boy didn't seem at all surprised to see Aunty Trina in the kitchen and greeted her with a casual, 'Hello, Ma.'

'You've had another tattoo,' said Aunty Trina, hitting John Boy about the head with a kitchen roll. 'And your beard is too long. You look like a terrorist.'

John Boy, oblivious to the beating, poured himself a bowl of Sugar Puffs.

Aunty Trina looked worried then. 'Won't you have a proper breakfast, son? You can't just have cereal, you'll waste away. I've bought black pudding and two dozen eggs.'

John Boy admitted he'd had 'a few beers' last night, so wasn't quite up to a full English.

Aunty Trina hit him around the head again, then demanded to know if he'd been cleaning his leg properly.

'*Yes*,' said John Boy in a tired voice, adding three sugars to his Sugar Puffs.

'You need to change those dressings *every* day,' said Trina, aggressively prodding John Boy's shoulder. Then she had an inquisitive sniff of his thigh area and said, 'Those sleeves need a good wash. *And* those underpants.'

She sent John Boy back to his bedroom to change.

'Has he been eating all right, Shirley?' Aunty Trina asked, eyes wild with worry as she spooned ten sugars into the teapot.

Mum reassured her about the 'cracking pork butchers' down the road.

'He's had a hot pie or pasty every day,' said Mum. 'And all the sausages he wants for breakfast.'

Mum's nutritional views are from the 1960s, when meat was regarded as a health food.

I'm not happy about this new development, re Aunty Trina staying with us. But I can't really complain, since I'm a sickly interloper.

Will just have to get used to the smell of bleach and Shake 'n' Vac.

Evening

Alex just phoned.

He'd finished work (at 7 pm!) and thought he might pop over for an 'early' supper.

Told him I was already in bed, feeling pregnant, weak and exhausted.

Given our conflicting sleeping/working schedules, it might be a while until we see each other.

Wednesday 10th January

My nausea was a bit better this morning, so visited Laura and baby Bear in London.

It was probably a mistake to take Daisy on the train. She's OK as long as I constantly talk/distract/read stories, but it's like sitting beside a hand grenade, praying it won't go off. The moment I relax and enjoy the scenery...boom!

Laura greeted me at the door of her Bloomsbury townhouse, looking like one of those girls in *Stylist* magazine.

My beautiful big sister has already got her figure back (no surprise, since she was out jogging five days after the birth), and was gorgeous in loose, turn-up jeans, white plimsolls and a soft, pink-cashmere jumper artfully draped off one shoulder.

Her shiny, natural blonde hair hung straight down her back, and her soft, lovely face smiled with kindness and love.

Baby Bear wore a little shirt and trousers, and looked like a miniature, balding executive, boss-eyed and drunk after a boozy lunch.

Laura made us tea from herbs and fruits she'd dried herself in her new dehydrating machine. She apologised that Zach couldn't join us, but he's busy with his new wind turbine business.

Laura, Daisy and I watched baby Bear dribble and chew at things, then vomit white sick over his nice clothes.

'Just think,' said Laura, her eyes going soft. 'You'll have another one of these soon.'

'I know,' I said. 'How will I cope?'

'You'll cope,' said Laura.

My sister is so serene. A natural at motherhood, and everything else she turns her hand to.

We're so not alike.

Thursday 11th January

Callum did a bad thing today.

He poured all the toiletries into the bathtub: my whitening toothpaste, a bottle of Mr Matey bubble bath, Dad's pine-scented Radox, Mum's Wash and Go shampoo and Aunty Trina's rose-scented talcum powder. He sprayed the mixture with John Boy's Lynx Africa deodorant and added Brandi's peroxide powder and other dangerous beautician's chemicals.

Dad and I discovered him in the bathroom, toilet brush in hand, stirring a fizzing, gelatinous pool of orange liquid.

Callum's eyebrows had turned bright white, which I suppose was some strange reaction to the peroxide fumes.

'Callum,' said Dad, in his sternest voice. 'Kindly explain *what* you are doing.'

'I'm doing science,' Callum replied.

Dad was incensed. 'This isn't *science*,' he said. 'Where is your hypothesis? Where are your measuring instruments? *This* is just making a mess.'

Callum did have a hypothesis of sorts – he believed his concoction, if fed to Sambuca the cat, would create a mega super-feline 'the likes of which the world has never seen'.

It turns out they're reading *George's Marvellous Medicine* at Callum's school.

Dad doled out his favourite sort of punishment – a learning experience. He made Callum turn the mess into a 'proper scientific experiment'.

I walked past the bathroom an hour later and saw a sorry-looking Callum measuring and recording everything he'd wasted.

Callum was even more upset when he finally saw his eyebrows in the hallway mirror.

'How am I going to charm the babes looking like this?' he wailed.

Friday 12th January

HEADACHE.

This is another forgotten symptom of early pregnancy – the random migraines that sweep you into bed for hours on end.

Head is *pounding*, but I don't think I should take painkillers. Not while I'm pregnant.

Mum says I'm being too cautious.

'I knocked back aspirin like there was no tomorrow when I was expecting you and your sisters,' said Mum. 'And you turned out just fine.'

On the positive side, my morning sickness is getting better so I should be heading home soon. Now Aunty Trina is here, it really is time to make a move.

Woke up this morning to find her vigorously scrubbing plates with bleach.

Aunty Trina and Mum are getting on well, so it looks like Trina could be staying a while. They've found a common topic they can agree on – how useless men are.

Dad stays in his office room most of the day now, looking sorry for himself.

Poked my head in this afternoon, and found Dad re-reading *Lord of the Rings*, an aloof, hurt expression on his bearded face.

'I may not be perfect,' he said, in a stiff, wounded voice. 'But it would take a *scientist* to work out that remote control.'

Afternoon

Headache getting worse.

Some idiot (Yorkie, I think) taught Callum to sing 'Ten Bottles of Beer on the Wall'. Callum has 'pimped up' the song, changing it to '200 Bottles of Beer on the Wall'.

Callum's long serenade seemed especially heart-felt, because he has cut up a joke shop moustache and glued it over his bleached-blonde eyebrows.

I should be working in the pub tonight, but if this headache doesn't pass I don't think I can manage it.

Mum and Dad are understanding and have offered me sick pay, but there's no way I'd take it.

I'm dreading going back to the cottage now – not just because I'm sick and pregnant and hate the boiler, but also because there'll be a big pile of bills at the door.

Saturday 13th January

Mum and Aunty Trina were up late last night, hooting and howling as they 'sampled' a new tequila line.

Aunty Trina had never tried tequila before and it had an interesting effect, making her even more manic than usual.

At midnight, Dad banged on the wall and asked Mum and Aunty Trina to keep their voices down.

Mum shouted back that the banging would wake up the kids.

Daisy woke up.

Then Callum woke up.

Brandi screeched something about an exam tomorrow.

Then Aunty Trina started singing 'Amazing Grace' and wouldn't stop.

In the end, Mum had to fireman's lift Aunty Trina onto the pull-out sofa.

Aunty Trina is still on the sofa this morning with a sleep mask over her eyes. I don't think she'll be cleaning today, which means she'll be double-bleaching everything tomorrow.

Time to go home, I think.

Sunday 14th January

Back at the cottage.

Big pile of bills waiting.

The financial stress brought back my morning sickness. Read the bills, whilst throwing up in my bright-yellow toilet. I didn't see toilet aesthetics as a priority before, but now realise this was short-sighted. When you're clasping a 1970s toilet bowl for most of the day, you really do wish it was a nice modern white one.

SO much still to do in the house.

It looks OK downstairs. Quite cosy. But I need a whole new boiler system, furniture for the upstairs bedrooms, new bathroom etc., and that's after I pay for basic things, like heating.

Alex has offered to pay my bills, but our situation is weird enough as it is, without making it even weirder. Everything is back-to-front, and the last thing I want is to be financially supported by yet another man I don't have a functional relationship with.

Heated up microwave macaroni and cheese for tea but couldn't eat it. Daisy wouldn't eat it either, so we both had chicken nuggets and ketchup.

While Daisy and I were eating, Alex phoned.

'How are you feeling?' he asked.

'Sick again,' I told him.

Decided to swallow my pride/vanity, re throwing up in front of Alex, and asked if he'd come and see me. Realistically, Alex will see me get big as a cow and literally shit myself during the birth. This is no time for feminine dignity.

It occurs to me that Alex and I have missed all the usual intimacy milestones (first accidental fart or burp, first non-accidental fart or burp, admitting you've just been for a poo, etc.) and leapt straight into pregnancy – the most intimate act of all.

Goodbye seductive female.

Hello humiliating body issues.

Alex told me it was impossible to leave London right now because he's negotiating a very important deal – something that could save his hotels a fortune in wasted butter.

'But come to London,' Alex suggested. 'I can have a hotel suite waiting for you, and the staff will help out with Daisy. I'll send a driver.'

I did some mental pregnant woman ranting: 'Do you think I want to be shaken around for an hour in a fucking car? And what about Daisy? TWO-YEAR-OLDS LIKE ROUTINE! Do you think she wants a stranger looking after her? I'm throwing up every five seconds. Do you think I want a stranger watching me do THAT? I want my OWN fucking toilet.'

Alex said he'd try and visit ASAP.

'No, don't try,' I said. 'Do or do not.'

That 'do or do not' thing comes from Yoda in *Star Wars*.

Everyone knows he's wise.

Monday 15th January

John Boy phoned this morning.

He's asked if he can move in with me, because Aunty Trina is driving him nuts. She's already bleached the logo off his favourite Nike joggers and won't let him watch TV past 9 pm.

John Boy has offered to babysit and pay half the bills.

It sounds like a workable plan. John Boy is great with Daisy and help with the bills will be awesome.

Phoned Alex to let him know about the new arrangement. Could feel his stony displeasure down the phone line.

'What's the problem?' I asked.

'You refuse to live with me in London,' said Alex, the words slow and hard. 'But you'll enter into some BBC-sitcom-house-share arrangement with a cousin who has offensive tattoos and a dubious moral outlook.'

'He doesn't have a dubious moral outlook,' I said. 'John Boy is one of the kindest people you could ever meet. He only ever starts fights when he's drunk.'

'Living in that *backwards* village.'

'Great Oakley is *not* backwards. The deli sells those big green olives.'

'They sell Cerignola olives,' Alex sneered. 'Any decent deli owner stocks the Castelventrano variety.'

'John Boy will help pay the bills,' I said. 'And it'll be an extra pair of hands around.'

'*I* offered to pay your bills,' Alex barked.

'And I said *no*,' I shouted back.

'I've asked you to marry me, Juliette. And you still haven't given me an answer.'

'Would you have asked me if I weren't pregnant?'

There was a pause then. A horrible, long pause.

Alex said, 'Juliette –'

But before he could say anything else, I hung up.

Tuesday 16th January

Nick just called. He asked if I'd remembered his mother's birthday.

I said there was no reason for me to remember it.

'Haven't you sent her a present?' said Nick, sounding panicked.

'Of course not,' I replied.

'Shit,' said Nick. 'She'll go mental.'

'Didn't Sadie send anything?' I asked. 'Surely mothering you is her job now.'

'Mum and Sadie aren't getting on,' said Nick. 'Things have been said. Things that can never be taken back.'

'What things?' I asked.

'Things about facelifts, weight gain and the overpowering nature of Chanel No.5,' said Nick. Then he put on his world-weary 'I just lost an audition' voice and said: 'Didn't you even send something from Daisy?'

'It's your job to send your mother a present from Daisy,' I said.

'But you're the *mum*,' Nick wheedled.

Ended the call with a simple, 'Bugger off, Nick.'

7 pm

No morning sickness today, but SUCH a bad headache again.

Decided to take painkillers and to hell with it, but didn't have anything at home.

Bundled Daisy into the car and drove to the 24-hour chemist.

It was closed.

On the way back, I realised Daisy had somehow got hold of my mobile phone. She was hammering it vigorously against the window.

'Daisy!' I shouted. 'Stop it! Put the phone down.'

But she wouldn't stop.

Realised Daisy has reached a new developmental milestone – selective hearing.

When I got home, I discovered my phone speaker wouldn't play sounds from YouTube and the torch wouldn't turn off.

Explained to Daisy that we couldn't play 'Gangnam Style' or the Hokey Cokey.

Daisy cried.

Asked her to be quiet.

Then begged her to be quiet.

In the end, I bribed Daisy to shut up with a Facetime call to Nana and Granddad – even though it was well past her bedtime.

When the call connected, Callum's grinning face filled the video screen. He wasn't wearing his fake Tom Selleck eyebrows today, and look like a crazed, bald-faced alien.

Callum tried to cheer Daisy up by singing '200 Bottles of Beer on the Wall'.

SUCH a bad headache now.

Wednesday 17th January

Morning sickness has completely gone.

It's like someone flicked a switch – I don't have even the tiniest bit of nausea.

Phoned the hospital maternity ward, just in case.

The duty midwife told me the usual sort of thing – pregnancy is an odd business, and there's no rhyme or reason to anything. She asked me about dates and suggested I could be further along than I thought.

Admitted this was a possibility.

Then the midwife asked if I was eating healthily. Was forced to admit I'm living on Kellogg's Rice Krispies, crisps, chips and basically anything yellow – with the exception of Heinz tomato soup.

The midwife lectured me about eating a balanced diet 'for baby', but *she* isn't throwing up every five minutes. If *she* had a toddler running around, would she honestly poach a salmon fillet and steam asparagus?

Still. I am feeling better today, so decided it was time to get on the healthy-eating train. Ordered some healthy-ish food from the Tesco website (hummus, fruit, etc.). Impulsively added a three-year-old birthday candle to the basket. Daisy's third birthday isn't until October, but there was a 50p saving.

John Boy is moving in tomorrow.

Part of me thinks this could be a terrible mistake.

I like my cousin, but liking and living together are two

different things.

I learned that the hard way with Nick.

Thursday 18th January

John Boy has moved in.

He turned up this morning with a rucksack as tall as Callum.

Aunty Trina was with him, dabbing teary eyes with a hanky and gabbling about cleanliness.

When Aunty Trina finally left, John Boy unpacked his bag.

It contained:

+ A giant box of Frosties.
+ Twelve tins of condensed milk.
+ Ten Mars Bars.
+ Three loaves of white sliced bread.
+ Strawberry jam.
+ Twenty tins of corned beef hash.
+ Four litres of orange squash.
+ Ten packs of chicken flavour Super Noodles.
+ Ten beef and tomato Pot Noodles.
+ Twelve cans of Stella Artois (pint-sized).
+ Combat trousers, army jumpers and underwear.
+ A Liverpool football kit and scarf.
+ A plastic Alice-band, supporting two Liverpool flags on springs.
+ A Liverpool stadium snow globe.
+ Various *Walking Dead* comics.
+ Three pairs of Nike trainers (in neon yellow, hot pink and electric blue).

As a 'thank you for letting me move in' present, John Boy gave me a combat knife with a 'secret' screw-top handle containing matches and a compass. The blade was large and sharp enough to gut a bear.

John Boy said the knife would keep me safe, but I feel safest with the knife rolled up in bubble wrap and stored on top of the wardrobe.

So far, John Boy has been very neat and tidy. He's lined up his food stuffs in the cupboard and his fluorescent Nike trainers by the back door.

Daisy is delighted to have John Boy here, because he is a ready source of orange squash and biscuits and he loves kids' TV.

While Daisy and John Boy were watching *Paw Patrol*, I overheard Daisy telling John Boy about the hideously strict diet of water, oat cakes and hummus I subject her to.

'Mummy YUCKY food. Oomus. Smoke cake. BLAH!'

Then she asked John Boy to stay 'ever and ever'.

Called Alex before bed, but he didn't answer.

Can only guess he's still unhappy about the John Boy house-move situation.

Let him be unhappy.

I'm not happy with him either.

Friday 19th January

Althea and Wolfgang visited today. Their thick, curly black hair was tied with matching leopard print scarfs, and they both wore band t-shirts: Joan Jett for Althea, Rage Against the Machine for Wolfgang.

Wolfgang had somehow ripped the sleeves off his t-shirt. He is frighteningly strong for a two-year-old. It's a shame Althea is bringing him up a pacifist, because he could be an amazing wrestler one day.

Althea brought me a cloth bag full of treats: herbal supplements for my pregnancy, plus an organic watercress and garlic smoothie.

'I'm not sure I can drink that,' I said, looking at the clear plastic flask of green matter. 'I think it could bring back my morning sickness.'

'Yeah, most people vom the first time they drink it,' Althea confirmed. 'It does taste pretty rank. But if you down this every day for the next week, you'll build up a tolerance.'

Thanked her and put the green matter in the fridge, promising to try it later.

Maybe I can give it to Dad. He's a bit like a robot when it comes to food. He can ignore the taste/texture of things if he believes in the health benefits – an example being the dense, bitter, sprouted wholemeal bread he dislikes, but eats every day.

Althea also brought us homemade carrot cake. It looked like a huge lump of red moon rock and was made with spelt flour, agave nectar, prunes and vegan margarine. She'd dusted it with probiotic powder.

Wolfgang got really excited about the cake, lurching around and grunting, 'CAKE, CAKE!' when Althea removed the glass tub from her bag. He grabbed big handfuls, shovelled them into his mouth and macerated the hard, dry lumps with his large front tooth.

Althea has done a very good job when it comes to Wolfgang's diet. He genuinely enjoys things like prunes, cauliflower pizza and gluten/sugar-free baked goods.

Daisy, on the other hand, intuitively senses healthy deception and refused the 'red red stuff cake'.

To be fair, Daisy probably lacked the dental capacity for the hard cake anyway. Althea's baking takes a lot of chewing.

Noticed that Wolfgang wasn't wearing a nappy.

'Oh yeah,' said Althea. 'I'm doing toilet training.'

Althea explained it wasn't 'formal' toilet training, because she didn't want to put Wolfgang under any stress. Instead, she is 'empowering' Wolfgang to find 'his own continence path'.

As Althea discussed her baby-led method, Wolfgang shat on the floor. She cleared up the mess with a hessian cloth and said, 'I'm used to this now. At least Wolfgang didn't run off with the poo today.'

There had been an incident at a handmade pottery fair apparently, where Wolfgang defecated on the floor and hid his poo in a handmade pot. It took Althea nearly an hour to find out which pot, during which time the cake stall ran out of vegan brownies.

Worst of all, Althea had to buy the pot Wolfgang had defiled, and it wasn't her style at all.

'He chose this bloody awful bone porcelain thing with leaf patterns,' Althea complained. 'I can't even give it away to friends. No one I know is that uncool.'

Suggested that maybe Wolfgang needed to wear nappies a little longer.

Althea said this would create conflicting philosophies and disempower Wolfgang.

'Clearing up a bit of poo is a small price to pay for his freedom,' she said.

I do admire the way Althea sticks to her hippy ideals. She still goes to Latitude every year with Wolfgang in tow, eating free lentil curry from the Hari Krishna tent and sleeping in a communal wigwam.

Told Althea about my current Alex woes re John Boy moving in, and his jealousy thereof.

'If Alex can't get on with your family, you might as well end it now,' said Althea.

It wasn't what I wanted to hear, but I have to admit she's right.

Told Althea that Alex keeps asking me to move to London. He doesn't seem to understand that I like being near my family.

'I think he'd be happy if I never saw my family again,' I said.

'Yes,' said Althea. 'I get that feeling too.'

While we were examining my weird relationship with the father of my unborn child, the Tesco delivery arrived. Stupidly, I hadn't ticked the 'no substitutions' box, so various out-of-stock items had been replaced.

'These just get better and better,' the man said, handing me the white paper delivery note.

I asked for:

+ Hash browns
+ Heinz tomato soup
+ Flash zesty lemon cleaner
+ Facial cleansing pads
+ A three-year-old birthday candle

I received:

+ A kilo of baking potatoes
+ Sundried tomatoes
+ A net bag of lemons
+ Brillo pads
+ A four-year-old birthday candle

Was particularly incensed about the birthday candle. 'Who on earth authorised that replacement?' I raged. 'What three-year-old would require a four-year-old candle? Why not just give me a box of normal cake candles so I can count out three?'

The delivery man was unrepentant, telling me I should have ticked the right box.

Althea was smug about the substitutions, saying, 'My local vegan deli would never have done that. They *care* about the planet *and* their customers.' Then she accused the delivery man of working for a heartless, planet-ruining corporation.

The delivery man shrugged and said, 'I get a good rate of pay and a nice, warm van. It's the customers who are the problem.'

Saturday 20th January

Nick turned up at 8 am to collect Daisy for his first court-ordered visitation weekend. He was his usual hipster-twat self, wearing sunglasses, a distressed-leather jacket, black jeans and white Adidas. As a father of two, his dyed beard and teenage clothes look ridiculous.

'I didn't think you'd be here until at least eleven,' I said. 'You're usually hungover on Saturday mornings.'

'I'm doing dry January,' Nick explained, whipping off his sunglasses and attempting his signature blue-eyes and dark eyebrow flirt. 'I wake up at 6 am now with heart palpitations. And I'm experiencing restlessness, headaches, confusion and loss of appetite. But Mum will give me a thousand pounds if I do the whole of January.'

'It sounds like you're having withdrawal symptoms,' I said. 'How much were you drinking before you stopped?'

Nick admitted he drank one or two bottles of wine every night throughout December – which averages out at a staggering 70 units of alcohol a week.

'No wonder you're having withdrawals,' I said. 'You need to give your body a break.'

Nick looked at me fondly and said, 'It's nice you care. Sadie couldn't give a shit. She screamed at me for using all the headache tablets.'

I knew it would take ages to get Daisy ready, so offered Nick a cup of tea. He accepted, and we watched Daisy going up and down the stairs, 'packing' her little pink rucksack with random items like the TV remote and toilet roll.

'You don't need to pack our toilet roll,' I told Daisy. 'Daddy has toilet roll at his house.'

'Actually, it would be good to bring a roll or two,' said Nick. 'Just in case.'

'Just in case what?' I asked.

Nick explained that his mother usually brought over toilet roll and other household essentials. However, since Sadie made the facelift/Chanel No.5 comments, Helen has gone on strike. The Gables is now devoid of milk, toilet roll, mineral water, all-butter shortbread biscuits, cured meats, elderflower water, smoked salmon and cheese thins.

'That's appalling,' I said, meaning the fact Nick's mother did his shopping for him.

'Yeah, yeah, I know,' said Nick. 'I had to wipe my arse on a sock this morning.'

When Daisy was all packed up and ready (which largely involved unpacking... NO Daisy, you can't take the TV remote. Because I need it! And where did that ten-pound note come from?), I carried her to Nick's car.

'You're going to have a little sleepover at Daddy's,' I told her. 'I'll see you first thing tomorrow.'

Daisy cried and clung to me. 'Want Mummy. *Please*. Want to stay with Mummy.'

Was heart-breaking, but had to do the good Mum thing.

'It's OK Daisy,' I said. 'Daddy doesn't live far away. Just a little trip. He'll have lots of fun things at his house.'

Daisy relented when I said she could bring the TV remote.

With my lovely girl strapped into the car seat, I checked over Nick's Volvo and interrogated him about weekend plans, sleeping arrangements, etc.

Nick assured me he had an EU-approved car seat, properly fitted by a man at Halfords. He also showed me his car service certificates, which were in the glove box.

Waved a tearful goodbye to Daisy, then went inside to have a bit of a cry.

It felt awful, watching my little girl being driven away. I was sick to my stomach.

Kept reminding myself that Nick seems more responsible these days. I suppose, living with Sadie, someone has to be the grown-up.

Spent the morning fretting and worrying. What if Daisy doesn't like Nick's house? Will he remember to change her nappy? What if she gets scared and tries to run home?

While I was looking up GPS tracking devices and kiddie CCTV cameras, Brandi phoned.

'Can Callum and I come over?' Brandi asked. 'I've got to get out of the pub. Aunty Trina is driving me mad. She's boil-washed my Lycra dresses and made them Barbie-doll size.'

Said yes, as long as Callum behaves himself.

'I'm pregnant,' I said. 'It's not a good idea for me to be grabbing kids by the scruff of the neck in my condition.'

Five minutes later, Brandi turned up in her new pink Mini Cooper (who gave her finance for ANOTHER new car?) with fake plastic eyelashes on the headlights.

Callum was in the passenger seat, gripping a stick-on steering wheel and making Formula One noises. He'd drawn black, felt-tip on his eyebrows today, and looked like a badly made-up transsexual.

Brandi sported her usual full head of blonde hair extensions.

'Mum says we're living with you now,' Callum announced.

'You're just visiting,' I corrected.

'Oh.' Callum thought about that. 'A bit like a holiday from Aunty Trina?'

'I suppose so,' I said.

As I was finding violent toys for Callum to play with, John Boy sloped downstairs and offered everyone biscuits and orange squash.

'I love this place already,' said Callum. 'Which one is my bedroom?'

Missed a call from Alex, but haven't phoned him back.

I suppose we should sort things out. After all, the baby is only eight months away. But I'm just too tired right now.

Maybe we can work on our problems in the second trimester, when I get my energy back a bit.

Sunday 21st January

Woke up early this morning with mad cravings for Sprite and tangy cheese Doritos.

The shops were shut, so decided to make my own Doritos with corn flour, baking potatoes and grated cheese.

Ended up with a burnt mess of raw potato shreds and cheese.

Then the fire alarm went off.

John Boy woke in a panic. He rushed into the kitchen shouting, 'Get down. GET DOWN!', then attacked the pan with a can of squirty cream.

Within a minute, the cooker looked like a giant dessert.

Was very impressed by John Boy's quick reactions. He explained he'd learned to move quickly in Afghanistan.

'You had to be lightning fast out there,' said John Boy. 'Especially in the morning. If you weren't, all the fried eggs would be gone and you'd be left with muesli. Also, people could get killed.' He glanced down at his prosthetic leg and said, 'I still have nightmares about putting the lads in danger. They risked their lives getting me back on that tank. I'd give anything to be out there again, standing beside them.'

Realised that John Boy is a proper, brave war hero. And also a bit crazy. But probably the two go hand-in-hand.

Monday 22nd January

7 am

Althea just called. A free spot has opened up on some 'Womb Wisdom' pregnancy course she's doing, and Althea wondered if I wanted to participate.

The course is run by Althea's friend, Serenity, and is located somewhere between Great Oakley and London. It starts at lunchtime today, and Althea will be participating.

Asked Althea why she was doing a Womb Wisdom course, since she's not pregnant.

Althea said any woman, pregnant or otherwise, could connect with their child-bearing power through Serenity's feminist teachings.

'You'll discover your strong female spirit,' Althea enthused. 'Meet other empowered females. Stop pinning your hopes of happiness on a man.'

'What exactly happens on the course?' I asked.

Althea admitted there was a lot of moaning about men.

'But in an *empowered* way,' she assured me.

'It sounds all right,' I said, 'but what about Daisy? I can't get anyone to look after her at such short notice.'

Althea said I could bring Daisy along.

'Serenity welcomes children,' said Althea. 'She says they bring peaceful earth energy. Even Wolfgang.'

Have decided to go. The course sounds interesting and comes with a complementary Syrian buffet lunch.

Evening

Have just spent the day sitting around on Thai floor cushions with sad-faced, grey-haired pregnant women moaning about how men let them down.

None of the women seemed the least bit empowered.

The Syrian buffet was mostly gone by the time Althea and I arrived, with only a few dregs of cumin-sprinkled baba ganoush remaining.

Got home feeling much worse about my life, and impulsively phoned Alex.

Was so nice to hear a no-nonsense man's voice after all those women talking about their feelings.

Told Alex I missed him and hoped we could make things work. We've agreed to lunch tomorrow.

I asked Alex to choose the restaurant, wanting a strong man making the decisions for me.

Ironically, giving Alex control seemed to have a reverse psychology effect.

Instead of suggesting some fancy Michelin-star place with fragile glassware, Alex said, 'Where would you like to go, Juliette? I'm guessing you have rather specific tastes right now.'

I was a little bit too honest and said KFC.

Alex retracted his offer and suggested a Michelin-star place with fragile glassware.

We compromised on Nando's.

Tuesday 23rd January

Lunch with Alex.

Arrived at Nando's to find Alex waiting outside, looking displeased.

'They wouldn't let me reserve a table,' Alex complained. 'It's first-come, first-served. Like some sort of communist canteen. Where's Daisy?'

Explained that Mum had taken Daisy to the new drive-in dessert parlour. 'Dad will never go with Mum to places like that,' I said. 'She needs grandchildren as an excuse.'

Nando's was weirdly busy, so we ended up on a small table near the toilets. Things got worse when Alex realised it wasn't table service.

'No table service?' said Alex. 'Do we cook our own food too?'

I explained that we ordered and paid at the counter.

Alex didn't seem happy about that, even though it meant he could get back to work quicker.

After he had frowned at the menu for a while and decided on the 'least offensive option', he asked, in curt tones, about my new living arrangement with John Boy.

I said it was working out well.

'I'm happy someone is sharing the bills,' I said, 'and John Boy is happy to be away from Aunty Trina. You've got nothing to feel threatened about. John Boy is family.'

'I don't mind your family,' said Alex, adding with a little smile, 'in small doses.'

'You need to be OK with large doses,' I said. 'Especially when the baby comes along.'

'And what about my family?' said Alex.

'What about them?' I asked.

'You need large doses of *my* family too, Juliette. We're having a baby together.'

'I think Zach and Jemima are fantastic,' I offered. 'I've missed seeing your little sister. How is she?'

'She's boarding full-time now,' said Alex. 'So I'm not seeing much of her. It breaks my heart if I think too much about it. But don't change the subject. What about my mother?'

This was an unexpected turn in the conversation.

I mean, OK – my family aren't perfect. Mum's new party trick is burping the theme tune to *Game of Thrones*. But Alex's mother is absolutely nuts.

'I'm not sure it's possible to have a relationship with your mother,'

I said. 'She never remembers who I am.'

'So why should I have large doses of your family, if you won't make the effort with mine?' Alex asked.

It was a fair point.

The food arrived then.

Alex had butterfly chicken, macho peas, spiced beans, olives and green salad. He asked the waitress for cracked pepper, then made himself 'a light vinaigrette' with olive oil and extra hot chilli sauce.

I had half a chicken and chips.

We talked about the baby, the dating scan, parenthood and how different we both are.

'Perhaps I shouldn't have asked you to marry me so soon,' Alex admitted. 'But I felt it was the right thing to do.'

'That feels very hurtful,' I said.

Alex pointed out that I hadn't accepted his marriage proposal, which was equally hurtful.

'But it was so soon,' I said.

'Exactly,' said Alex.

Realised that we were both sort of in agreement.

We chatted about the future and the continued expansion of the Dalton leisure empire. Alex is overseeing some 'exciting acquisitions' this year – top of the list being a cruise ship business that would 'go under, if you'll excuse the pun' without a cash injection. Alex is taking a week-long cruise in March to 'test the waters, if you'll excuse the pun.'

'I was wondering if you'd like to come too,' he said. 'It would be a chance to spend some time together.' He gave a little smile and added, 'My mother has already invited herself along. She's not one to miss out on a holiday.'

'I can't take a week off in March,' I said. 'It's a busy month for the pub. And I have job applications and a daughter and a boiler that needs the occasional whack with a hammer. Anyway, your mother doesn't like me.'

'You mustn't take it personally,' said Alex. 'She doesn't like most people. And a Mediterranean cruise would be wonderful for Daisy. She can try real Italian fettuccini.'

'I'm not sure you understand two-year-olds,' I said. 'Daisy is primarily interested in bright colours and sugary foods. She doesn't care what day of the week it is, let alone whether her fettuccini is the real Italian version.'

'That's a shame,' said Alex. 'Real Italian fettuccini is an unforgettable experience. And I'd love Daisy to come along.'

'Why don't you come away with me and *my* family?' I said. 'Mum and Dad are going on a package holiday to Corfu in May, all local beer and spirits included. There's even a water slide.'

Alex had a coughing fit then and asked a passing waitress for a 'freshly laundered napkin'.

The waitress stared at him blankly. 'Oh. Like paper towels?' she said eventually. 'They're by the frozen yoghurt station. You have to get them yourself.'

Once Alex had got himself a handful of paper towels and refilled my Diet Coke, he said, 'If you really think going to Corfu with your parents will help our relationship, then I'll come.'

'It's OK,' I said. 'The package deal is already sold out. I can't see you on a cheap and cheerful Greek holiday, anyway. You'd complain about the glassware and lack of laundered napkins.'

'I can adapt to wherever I am,' said Alex. Then he called the waitress over and asked for 'any full-roasted Columbian coffee – I'm not fussy'.

We held hands and it felt nice, knowing that we both want to be together.

The difficult part will be working out how to do it.

Wednesday 24th January

Brandi has been kicked off her beauty course. She claims it's not her fault, insisting: 'Callum has been a right little shit this term. I've been putting parenting first.'

Callum protested his innocence, saying that his teacher has it in for him.

'Other kids ask questions and it's fine,' said Callum. 'But if I ask, I get in trouble. These freaky blond eyebrows don't help. They make me look evil when I'm not.'

Asked Callum what sort of questions he asks.

'Like, what does "buttocks" mean,' said Callum. 'Stuff like that.'

Apparently, this question had got him sent to the head's office.

'And the head wouldn't tell what buttocks meant either,' Callum added.

'It means your bum,' Mum announced, strolling into the kitchen to grab a handful of Cadbury's mini rolls.

Callum found this explanation hysterical. Now he keeps saying 'buttocks' and collapsing in peals of laughter.

Even Daisy is joining in.

'Buttocks! Buttocks!'

Aunty Trina has finally gone home. Apparently, her local church group were 'bereft' without her. She left this morning, promising to come back at Christmas with some even stronger bleach solutions for the stained kitchen counter near the kettle.

Thursday 25th January

Lunch at Althea's today. She served the usual watery 'Bean Bonanza' vegan curry, swimming with miscellaneous vegetables, but we didn't mind. Daisy and I had ham sandwiches and crisps on the train before we arrived.

After lunch, Althea told me she's on the hunt for a man and has tried out a few online dating sites.

'Wolfgang needs masculine influence now he's getting older,' said Althea. 'Someone reliable. The sort of person who'll notice if I've left the glue gun plugged in.'

I suggested Althea also add 'excellent upper-body strength' to her criteria. Holding Wolfgang down when he gets into one of his rages is no feat for a weakling.

Althea has put her profile on Tinder, but isn't bothering with Match.com because she objects to their slogan: 'Love your imperfections.'

'I mean, what imperfections?' said Althea, jamming camomile teabags into her rainbow-coloured teapot. 'Every human being is perfect.'

Admire Althea's confidence. She has such a strong sense of self-love.

I worry about my weight and single-mum status, but Althea sees her giant boobs and aggressive baby as advantageous. In her eyes, her body fat is natural and sexy, and Wolfgang is assertive and healthily challenging of the status quo.

Friday 26th January

John Boy sloped into the kitchen this morning with a black eye, cut jaw and broken front tooth. He went out last night with some squaddie friends, so I accused him of fighting.

'I didn't get into a fight,' said John Boy. 'I fell on a concrete dog.'

Apparently, some lads bet John Boy he couldn't lift an ornamental Rottweiler statue, located in the Goat and Boot pub garden.

John Boy could lift the statue. What he couldn't do was run around the garden with it. He ended up dropping the dog, falling on it and cracking his tooth in the process.

The black eye came from the pub landlady, whose treasured Rottweiler statue had been decapitated.

Karma, really.

The cracked tooth looks awful – like one of Brandi's boyfriends.

Keep telling John Boy to see the dentist, but he's too afraid. John Boy doesn't say afraid, of course. He says 'can't be bothered', but I know he's scared of dentists. I can't say I blame John Boy for his dentist phobia – he's got more fillings in his mouth than teeth.

Saturday 27th January

Have convinced John Boy to see a dentist. He's booked in for a temporary filling on Monday.

John Boy asked if I could come with him, because he thinks he might hit the dentist.

This is code for, 'I'm scared and need moral support'.

Agreed to go and hold his hand.

Afternoon

Keep googling stuff about baby size, weight etc.

Remember doing this when I was pregnant with Daisy.

It's nice knowing your baby is roughly the size of a grape (fruit, again), that it can hear music, etc.

However, early pregnancy is quite boring. The baby doesn't move around or anything, you just feel tired and rubbish, but don't *look* any different.

I like middle pregnancy, when you don't feel that bad, but everyone makes a fuss of you and people give up their seat on the bus.

Sunday 28th January

Feeling pretty good today.

Actually quite energised.

This is a welcome surprise, because I had no reprieve from the crappy first stage of pregnancy with Daisy.

I remember ticking off the first trimester, like a prison inmate.

Took advantage of feeling good to visit Laura and baby Bear in London.

Followed Mum's 'coping with kids on the train' advice and strapped Daisy into the Maclaren with a jumbo-sized chocolate chip cookie, then played the 'new shoes' episode of *Peppa Pig* over and over on my iPhone.

It was nice to catch up with Laura, but made me realise how far I fall short – both in motherhood and in life.

Laura has recently taken up baby yoga, which she loves.

'You lay your baby on the mat, then bend down to kiss them,' she explained. 'It's the perfect way to improve your stretch – who wouldn't go an extra few inches to kiss their child?'

Made a mental note never to attend mother-baby yoga. There's no way I want my motherly love rated on how bendy I am. I can't even touch my toes.

Told Laura how well I'm feeling today. She was pleased and reminded me to eat lots of iron-rich foods.

'You don't want a repeat of what happened during your last pregnancy,' said Laura. 'Remember the anaemia?'

Ugh. Remember pregnancy anaemia all too well.

Dr Slaughter put me on giant iron tablets that caused black stools and terrible wind. Even Dad, who has a poor sense of smell, wouldn't sit near me.

'Which foods are high in iron, but not disgusting?' I asked.

Laura recommended chicken liver parfait and caviar.

'They've delicious and not at all hard to get hold of,' Laura enthused. 'You can get good-quality caviar at Waitrose these days.'

Sometimes I feel Laura was born into the wrong family.

Admitted my diet has been awful since Christmas.

It seemed reasonable to eat crap when I was throwing up, but now the sickness has passed I have no excuse.

I think it's partly to do with the weather.

January is such a gloomy month.

Grey skies. Dark afternoons. And nothing to look forward to.

'But what about the baby?' said Laura. 'That's something to look forward to.'

'Are you joking?' I said. 'If I had my way, I'd gestate for five years. I have an uncertain relationship with the baby's father, a toddler running around and my boiler needs hitting with a hammer three times a day. Why on earth would I look forward to the baby coming out? It's total stress.'

Laura persevered with the good big-sister chat, asking me to focus on the positive.

'You must like *some* healthy foods,' she said. 'How about fruit?'

Admitted I haven't eaten anything green in a while. It's been processed food all the way.

I take my share of the blame, but also hold John Boy partly responsible. He's filled the salad drawer with fun-sized chocolate bars and the cupboard under the sink with five-litre orange-squash bottles.

I'd like to say I can resist temptation, but that would be a blatant lie.

I'm the opposite of self-controlled.

I am snack-controlled.

Monday 29th January

Took John Boy to the dentist this morning.

He was scared in the waiting room, but I managed to calm him down by reading to him from a stray *My Little Pony* comic from a wicker basket of children's books.

By the time we were called in, John Boy had stopped gibbering and was focused on Fluttershy and her rainy-day dilemma.

The dentist was a stunning South African lady with honey-coloured skin and swishy blonde hair. She gave us a beautiful, gleaming white smile and told a trembling John Boy: 'You're in safe hands. I've never lost a patient yet.'

John Boy's internal conflict was evident.

On one hand, he is compelled to convince any attractive woman he is a brave war hero. On the other hand, he was terrified.

To John Boy's credit, he did manage a joke about getting his leg blown off in Afghanistan, but his shaking hands and white face gave away his terror. He also gave a girlish whimper when the pretty dentist fired up her drill.

John Boy now has a temporary filling, which has to stay in place until they make the real one.

I assumed he had read the aftercare pamphlet, which advised against strongly coloured foods, but I was wrong. For dinner, he ordered a 'convalescent meal' of tandoori chicken, tarka dal and three heavily spiced samosas.

Now the filling has gone bright green.

John Boy actually looked better with no tooth at all.

Tuesday 30th January

Morning

John Boy's tooth is even greener this morning.

It's now the shade of a frozen pea.

John Boy isn't the slightest bit embarrassed, calling it his 'incredible hulk tooth' and chasing a squealing Daisy around with his shirt open.

Afternoon

Alex turned up unexpectedly, just after lunch. He pulled up in his shiny MG, tyres bumping over our shaggy, uncut grass.

John Boy couldn't stop laughing when he saw Alex's car.

'What's so funny?' I asked.

'His number plate says FEK,' said John Boy. 'Fekking hell Jonathan, we're out of Earl Grey.'

Invited Alex inside.

John Boy was in the kitchen, shoulders shaking with silent laughter.

'Hello, John Boy,' said Alex.

'All right,' John Boy managed. Then he squealed a hysterical, 'Sorry!' before running upstairs and bursting into loud laughter on the landing.

'What's so funny?' asked Alex.

'Your number plate,' I said. 'He thinks it looks like a swear word.'

'Very grown up,' said Alex. 'Such mature behaviour.'

'It's been good having him here,' I said. 'He keeps us stocked up on cereal and Monster Munch crisps.'

'How are you feeling?' Alex asked.

'Not bad at all,' I said. 'All the tiredness and sickness seems to have gone.'

'I wish you'd stop working,' said Alex.

'I like working,' I insisted. 'I have enjoyable conversations at the pub. It's nice seeing grown-ups after a day with Daisy.'

To be honest, 'enjoyable conversations' may be an overstatement. I like Polish Malik, but his turn-of-the century Italian literature and Russian history chats go right over my head. And Yorkie tells the same story over and over (about him winning a fight with someone twice his size).

Polish Malik says, 'Be quiet, Yorkie. Juliette is pregnant and tired.'

But the last time Malik said that, Yorkie launched into a story about the time he'd defended a pregnant woman, and consequently bested a man twice his size.

Wednesday 31st January

Shift at the pub last night.

Brandi looked after Daisy, which turned out to be a bad idea.

Daisy was still awake when I finished my shift, wired on hot chocolate and marshmallows, one eye twitching, watching *Game of Thrones*.

Clearly, the correct bedtime routine hadn't been followed.

'She hasn't fallen asleep yet,' said Brandi. 'So she can't be tired.'

But Daisy never just *falls* asleep.

Asked Brandi if she'd followed my 'sleepy time' instructions, which include:

+ Doing the funky chicken dance.

+ Administering 'one more cuddle', repeated five times.

+ Singing all three verses of 'Twinkle Twinkle Little Star'.

+ Telling a story about the crap food Mum gave us growing up (any will do).

+ Promising to tell another story tomorrow.

+ Overseeing 'a little try' on the toilet (I'm trying to start potty training. This was a terrible idea, as I'm way too tired. But now I have introduced the idea of weeing on the toilet before bed, Daisy demands this every night).

+ Answering the, 'Just one more thing' question – which varies each night between, 'Um…um… Where are we going tomorrow?' to 'Um…um … Will my new brother and sister be coming tomorrow?'

◆ And then dealing with variations of: 'Um…um … Have *secret*. Need to *whisper* it. I asked Father Christmas for *wings*.'

'No,' said Brandi. 'I didn't bother with any of that.'

Had to read Daisy three bedtime stories and do the Hokey Cokey before she fell asleep, thumb in mouth.

I'm getting worried about her thumb-sucking now. Her teeth are already crooked. Need to break the habit before her big teeth come in.

John Boy *still* sucks his thumb, which I assumed would have been a source of teasing in the army. But apparently, it wasn't.

'When you sleep in a dormful of men,' said John Boy, 'thumb-sucking is the least of your worries.'

Thursday 1st February

Alex turned up this evening, unannounced.

John Boy and I were sitting on the sofa eating Pringles, when there was a curt knock on the door.

'Don't answer it,' said John Boy. 'Only debt collectors knock like that.'

After assuring John Boy that my financial situation isn't *that* bad, I opened the door.

Was surprised to see Alex on the doorstep, and embarrassed to be wearing my unflattering Minnie Mouse pyjamas.

Invited Alex in for a cup of tea and some Pringles, but warned him I'd be going to bed soon – it was already seven o'clock.

Alex asked why John Boy's tooth was bright green.

'I was lifting a concrete dog,' said John Boy, pulling his shoulders back in that confrontational way men do.

Alex pulled his shoulders back too and said, 'That makes no sense whatsoever.'

I told the story.

'You should get that green tooth seen to,' Alex told John Boy.

'There's no rush,' said John Boy. 'I've been telling girls I'm a horror movie extra. I've got a few phone numbers out of it, and one shag behind the back of Wetherspoons.'

Alex pulled a disgusted face and said, 'Juliette, I brought something for you.' He handed over a luxurious holiday brochure. 'It's details about the cruise. I hoped you might change your mind and come along.'

'I really can't, Alex,' I said. 'My parents need me to work. No one else is trained to get rid of Yorkie at closing time.'

'I rang your father on the way over,' said Alex. 'He's happy for you to have the time off. Your sister has some time on her hands and can cover your shifts. Your father mentioned this 'Yorkie' character, and said he's frightened of your little sister, so there's no problem there. And your parents will look after Daisy.'

'They said they'd do that?' I asked.

'Your father said so.'

'For a whole week?'

'Yes.'

'But I'd feel so guilty,' I protested.

'Why?'

'Daisy could be traumatised.'

'Nonsense,' said Alex. 'The French aristocracy used to pack their children off to countryside nannies for the first three years of their lives. A week won't hurt Daisy.'

'Weren't the French aristocracy all executed?' I asked.

'Most of them, yes,' Alex conceded. 'But pre-revolution, they were a very happy, talented bunch.'

'It does look very relaxing,' I admitted, eyeing the glossy pictures of models eating lobster on a glittering sun deck. 'And I do need a break. I regretted not taking Mum up on the Corfu holiday offer.

Tell me more about the cruise – what are the dates?'

'Mid-March,' said Alex. 'Are you free for lunch tomorrow? We can talk over practicalities.'

'In Great Oakley?' I asked.

'London.'

'*When* will you be able to leave the city, Alex?' I asked. 'When I'm in labour? When the baby comes?'

Alex kissed me on the forehead and said, 'I'm working on having more free time. That's what this year is all about.'

Agreed to lunch, as long as Alex picked somewhere Daisy-friendly.

'I know the perfect place,' said Alex. 'Wonderful for families.'

'What's it called?' I asked.

'Catrina Dalton's place.'

'Your mother's house?' I said, in a slightly higher pitch than I meant to.

'Yes,' said Alex. 'It's about time you two got to know each other. Is something wrong?'

'Of course not!' I said, in an even higher pitch. Then I did a fake laugh to cover up my massive lie.

So we are meeting at Catrina Dalton's apartment tomorrow for Hungarian Goulash.

Alex claims Catrina's Goulash is 'restaurant quality', but Laura says different.

'Bring a handbag that can fit a Tupperware tub,' Laura advised. 'Then spoon the goulash into the tub when no one is looking. Just make sure you bring a handbag you don't like very much, because it will smell of cumin forever more. Catrina doesn't mess around with her spices.'

This is a typical ladylike Laura solution to an awkward situation.

Friday 2nd February

Lunch with Alex and Catrina Dalton today.

Could have been better.

Could have been worse.

Had a nightmare working out what to wear.

I stupidly googled Catrina Dalton, and discovered she was voted *Marie Claire's* best-dressed woman in 1984.

There are also multiple pictures of Catrina on Google images, circa 1980, with her signature blonde pleat and dazzling pearly teeth, wearing power business suits with gold-chain decoration and crushed-velvet ball-gowns.

The pictures sent me into a panic, and I ended up phoning Laura in stupid hormonal girl tears.

Laura had a courier service drive me over some ultra-stylish outfits, but of course they were all too tight and long. Fashionable women don't have boobs or generous bottoms. Also, they don't go out in winter – everything had three-quarter-length sleeves.

In the end, I realised it didn't really matter what I wore. Even if I could magic up the perfect outfit, I don't have the perfect body to put in it.

Decided on skinny jeans and a nice black jumper.

The driver picked us up at 11 am.

Daisy was excited to see the big, black car, shouting, 'Rex, Rex!'

Quite sweet how fond she is of Alex.

Felt increasingly nervous as we drove through London.

Catrina lives in West London, land of glossy teeth and hair. It's no place for children, or women who've had children.

We pulled up outside a sandy-bricked Georgian building, where a blue-lipped doorman stood by lollipop bay trees.

Alex waited on the pavement outside, hands stoically behind his back.

'Good trip?' he asked, opening our car door. 'Traffic not too bad?'

Daisy said, 'Smelly car.'

I laughed gaily.

Alex unstrapped Daisy and helped her out of the car. Then he said in a low voice, 'Just to let you know, my mother has had some surgery. She may not want to entertain for long.'

'Is she OK?' I asked, climbing out of the car. 'Should we do this another time?'

'It was just a cosmetic procedure,' Alex assured me. 'She's very keen to meet you, Juliette. There's no getting out of it.'

'She's already met me,' I said. 'Several times.

'Yes, but…not *properly*.' Alex picked up Daisy, then took my hand. 'She's never had you over for goulash.'

The doorman opened the door, tilting his top hat as he did so.

Alex gave the doorman a manly clap on the shoulder. 'Thanks Philip. How are things?'

'Very good, Mr Dalton,' said the doorman. 'Could you have another word with your mother? She's still calling me Johnathon.'

The lobby area had a 1930s feel, with cut-crystal vases of white flowers and old-fashioned wooden letter-holders. A big, sweeping marble staircase led to apartments on the first floor.

'How was the drive here, Juliette?' Alex asked. 'Not too unsettling?'

'No, I'm really fine now,' I said. 'The morning sickness has totally gone.'

Catrina Dalton appeared then, at the top of the staircase. She wore a white bandage around her hair, ears and chin, and tortoise-shell sunglasses. An odd sprout of blonde-grey hair poked out of the bandage, like a Maori warrior.

She was dressed in a red skirt suit with a black velvet collar and oversized buttons. The suit jacket was a little tight around the waist, straining against her older-lady-who-lunches-too-much middle.

'Alex. *Darling*. There you are,' Catrina called, whipping off her sunglasses.

Alex looked up. 'Anya. You remember Juliette.'

Catrina gave a jerky nod. 'Yes, the girl who is now having your child.'

I gave an awkward wave.

'Come upstairs,' said Catrina. 'The luncheon is ready.'

Catrina Dalton's apartment was much grander than the simple, stylish lobby. Burgundy and gold flocked wallpaper, a huge slab-marble dining table, chandeliers, swooping crushed satin curtains – it looked like a regency king had taken up residence.

The table was laid with gleaming cutlery and crisp, white napkins. Lumpy, brown stew and golden bread cobs sat in silver platters.

'I was very uncomfortable making the goulash,' said Catrina, gesturing with short, pink fingernails. 'But I know how you love my cooking, Alex.'

'You should have told me,' said Alex, pulling out seats for Daisy and me. 'I would have ordered from Giovanni's.'

'But you *love* my goulash,' said Catrina, green-gold eyes flashing. Then her mouth sagged. 'The surgery hasn't gone right this time, Alex.'

'You always say that.'

Catrina exploded with laughter. 'Oh yes! I've had so many procedures now. I'm like a ham on a carving board.'

A serving lady came in then, and presented Catrina with two pills on a white china plate.

'Thank you, Monique,' said Catrina, popping the pills and placing a hand on the lady's arm. 'Would you please serve for me? It's been difficult today.'

Monique served big ladles of goulash into white china bowls, then lifted bread rolls with a fork and spoon.

'I'm sorry to hear you're uncomfortable,' I told Catrina, smiling at the serving lady. 'If you need to rest at any point, I totally understand.'

Catrina gave a jolting nod. 'The worst of it is, they didn't take enough skin. I can still see lines.' She patted taut, white cheekbones.

'How's Jemima?' I asked. 'Alex tells me she's boarding full-time now. Does she enjoy it?'

'Oh, she loves it,' said Catrina. 'So many friends. They grow up quickly, these children. She'll be old enough to join my modelling agency soon, but I don't think she wants to. She's talking about being a scientist.'

'I miss seeing her in Great Oakley,' I said.

'She's getting too old for that little village,' said Catrina. 'Now listen – we must talk about this baby. How did it happen?'

Alex's head whipped around. 'Anya.'

'What?' Catrina feigned innocence. 'I can't ask?'

'We didn't plan the pregnancy,' I admitted. 'It just sort of happened.'

'An accident?' Catrina enquired. 'Is there really such a thing?'

'Zachary was an accident,' said Alex. 'You told him one Christmas, remember? I'm not sure he's ever got over it.'

'Things were different back then,' said Catrina, with a wave of diamond-covered fingers. 'Keeping babies away is so easy now. A woman can always decide.'

'Anya,' Alex barked.

'I didn't decide,' I said, my voice firm. 'Neither of us did.'

We ate in silence after that, silver spoons making polite clinks on porcelain.

Daisy said, 'Yuck food, Mummy.'

Tried to shush her, whilst enthusing about the overly spiced, buttery, lip-stinging goulash.

Then Alex said, 'I've asked Juliette to accompany us on the

cruise, Anya.'

Catrina became enthusiastic. 'Oh Alex. The cruise. I can't wait. You know, Carlos has *never* taken me away.'

'Juliette might be joining us too,' said Alex.

'It's a lovely idea,' I said. 'But it just doesn't seem practical. To leave Daisy for so long... I'd feel too guilty.'

Alex frowned. 'It's only a week, Juliette.'

'I left Alex for *months* at a time,' said Catrina. 'You mustn't stifle children.' Then she dropped her spoon dramatically and announced: 'No, it's no good. I'm afraid I need to lie down. Alex – help me to the bedroom.'

Alex helped her into the bedroom. Then he reappeared and said, 'My mother would like to speak to you.'

The spicy goulash danced unpleasantly in my stomach. 'In her bedroom?'

Alex raised an eyebrow. 'Don't look so terrified. They removed her false nails for the surgery.'

'She's going to say something horrible.'

'No. I've told her not to. You'll be fine. Go on – I'll be right here.'

'What does she want to talk about?'

'With my mother, you can never be certain.'

I put down my napkin. 'Daisy,' I said. 'Will you stay out here with Alex while Mummy gets verbally abused?'

Daisy nodded.

'Come with me, Daisy,' said Alex. 'We'll find the ice cream. Anya always keeps at least two tubs – chocolate and pecan gelato, and Sicilian lemon sorbet. Her guilty pleasure. We'll keep it our secret, OK?'

Daisy trotted off with Alex, while I headed into Catrina's room.

In the gloom of the bedroom, I could make out a glowing white bandage and glittering green-gold eyes.

Catrina sat up in bed, propped by several satin pillows.

'Take a seat my dear,' she said. 'Here. On the bed.'

It was just like Little Red Riding hood.

Catrina took my hand in her papery fingers and said, 'I'd like to buy you some clothes. Will you come shopping with me? Have you ever been shopping in Kensington?'

'No,' I said. 'I haven't. Thank you, that's really nice.'

'Now tell me.' Catrina pulled herself up, wincing as she did so. 'What's your faith? Your religion?'

'My dad is Christian,' I said. 'He reads out bible passages sometimes, but no one really listens.'

'Faith is so very important,' said Catrina. 'Alex and Zachary were brought up Catholic, of course. It seemed crazy to me that Harold would carry on these Irish traditions, but they're familiar to him.'

'I always thought I'd let my children decide their own religion,' I said.

'Oh you poor dear.' Catrina patted my hand. 'That is quite ridiculous. My family are Jewish, but do you think I had a choice? This baby will be a Dalton. It must be Catholic. And you must convert.' She patted my hand again. 'It will *help*.'

'I can't convert to Catholicism,' I said. 'I don't speak Latin or own any nice hats.'

'I will buy you a hat,' said Catrina, closing her eyes, head sinking back on the pouffy pillow. 'This is just the way things are. You can't make bacon out of a dog. I need to sleep now. Juliette? You must look after yourself. Women have to look after themselves. No one will do it for us.'

She opened her eyes then, and looked vulnerable and kind all at once.

'Yes,' I said. 'I'll do my best.'

When I got back to the table, Alex and Daisy were waiting.

'Your mother wants to take me shopping,' I said. 'And for me to become Catholic.'

Alex laughed. 'I should have guessed faith would rear its ugly head sooner or later. Did she tell you she used to be Jewish?'

'Yes.'

'Anya has never quite got over converting for a man who divorced her,' said Alex. 'Enjoy the shopping trip. She's very generous with my father's money. It's one of her best qualities.'

Saturday 3rd February

Nick was supposed to take Daisy today, but he has man flu.

'I'm not being a drama queen,' Nick insisted, sniffing loudly and doing a hammy cough into the phone. 'I'm very, very sick.'

'If you were really ill, you wouldn't be watching *The Sopranos*,' I said. 'I can hear it in the background. Parenting doesn't end just because you've got a runny nose.'

'Oh, come on, Julesy,' said Nick. 'I need a weekend to myself. Then I'll be fighting fit for next time.'

Agreed to let Nick convalesce, but only after telling him that when mothers are ill, they just get on with it. And then telling him that two more times.

Evening

John Boy came home this afternoon with lavish gifts: a large bottle of Moët for me and a crying, weeing Baby Annabelle doll for Daisy.

'I won big on a football bet,' John Boy explained. 'I want to share the love.'

John Boy had bought himself twenty-four limited-edition cans of Stella Artois and yet another pair of neon Nikes.

Thanked John Boy for his generosity, but Baby Annabelle is giving me post-traumatic stress re new-born babies. She cries randomly, like a real baby, and needs burping and cuddling to make her shut up.

Daisy isn't bothered by the crying. She simply carries baby Annabelle upstairs and returns without her. I suppose you could call this controlled crying, but it's also borderline neglect.

'She needs burping,' I fretted the second time Daisy abandoned the crying doll. 'You can't just leave her crying up there. How can you stand it?'

'She noisy, Mummy,' Daisy replied. 'Too noisy. I put in room.'

In the end, I went up to burp Baby Annabelle. Annabelle giggled coyly, fluttering her long eyelashes, then cried the moment I put her down.

Daisy has rescued me from a meltdown by wrapping Annabelle in a duvet and stuffing her in the boiler cupboard. But, as I explained to Daisy, you can't do that with real new-borns.

How on earth will I cope with two?

Evening

The supermarket shopping just arrived.

I'm such an idiot, forgetting to tick no substitutions AGAIN.

They sent me black hair dye (instead of blonde) and liver and beef dog food (instead of a steak and kidney pie).

Sunday 4th February

Feel awful this morning. Not sick, but just really, really tired and headachy.

I don't know if it's the pregnancy or winter blues.

The house is a terrible mess. My skin has gone horrible. I'm craving chocolate and coffee. All I want to do is lounge around watching movies.

Brandi and Callum came over after lunch. Suggested a nice, quiet Disney film, but Callum made vomiting gestures, so we compromised on *Jurassic Park*.

It was a bad choice, because Daisy was traumatised.

I thought *Jurassic Park* was reasonably child-friendly, but at least half the film comprises kids screaming. Also, someone gets eaten on the toilet halfway through.

John Boy, being a 'proper' horror fan, was bored and fell asleep sucking his thumb.

Brandi and I took pictures of John Boy's thumb-sucking and posted them on Facebook.

Over 300 likes so far.

Monday 5th February

Catrina Dalton's assistant just phoned. She asked when I was free for a shopping trip with Mrs Dalton.

Have arranged to go this weekend. Dad will take Daisy.

I'm quite excited. Clothes shopping with the best-dressed woman of 1984!

Maybe I'll be stylish, for once in my life.

Tuesday 6th February

Think I have flu. Being pregnant and ill is AWFUL.

Haven't felt this bad since Althea and I drank a whole bottle of limoncello, then experimentally fried an egg in baby oil and ate it.

It's HORRIBLE being ill when you have a child. How did people cope when they lived in caves? And how on EARTH will I cope with the new baby?

Am back at Mum and Dad's house being looked after.

Asked Mum if she'd be kind enough to go shopping and buy me Heinz tomato soup, Lemsip Extra Strength and a can of Cherry Coke.

Mum agreed, but came back with Cadbury's Heroes, custard creams and a large pork pie.

Politely asked if Mum had remembered the tomato soup, medicine and caffeinated drink.

Mum told me not to be so bloody fussy.

Hauled myself to the shop for the necessary convalescent provisions. Returned and heated the soup, only to have Mum drink my Cherry Coke when my back was turned.

Evening

Nana Joan joined us for a takeaway curry tea. She'd just had her blonde hair extensions redone and flicked them angrily as we helped her up the stairs into Mum and Dad's kitchen.

We thought Nana was cross about her ridiculous new extensions, which were almost waist length and made her look like a wrinkly old Barbie doll that had melted and spread in the oven. But actually, Nana was cross because Mum forgot to put her football bet on – the same bet John Boy won.

Mum shouted about gambling being a waste of money and a bad example for grandchildren and great grandchildren.

Nana shouted back that she would have won £173.

Mum apologised and put the kettle on.

We ended up playing gin rummy with Nana Joan, so she could win some money back.

Nana Joan is almost unbeatable at gin rummy. Card playing gets very competitive at her old people's home and Nana has a championship title to hold onto.

Nana shared a few championship secrets with me: an accelerated learning 'memory palace' technique to access her neural pathways more speedily, and Pro Plus caffeine tablets for concentration.

Wednesday 7th February

Made it to the Co-op today for more soup and Cherry Coke.

The Co-op's Visa card machine was broken, so had to get money from the hole-in-the wall cashpoint outside.

In my confused, flu-ridden state, I entered my pin incorrectly three times and the cash machine sucked my card into its baying mouth.

It will take five days to receive a replacement card.

Five days!

The bank only has to print a bit of plastic.

It takes less time to fit a kitchen. Well, according to Ikea anyway.

So I am now pregnant, ill and without means to pay for anything.

AND I still don't have any tomato soup or Cherry Coke.

Afternoon

Laura just visited with baby Bear in tow. She wanted to see how I was feeling, and also boost my immune-system with some homemade herbal tea.

It was kind of Laura to come, but to be honest the visit left me feeling stressed out.

Laura was constantly rocking, jiggling, feeding and soothing baby Bear – reminding me that babies are a *lot* of work.

How will I do all that rocking and feeding with a toddler running around?

And what if I get ill? How will I cope?

Alex says he'll support me, but realistically this will be financial support. Whether we're together or not, I can't imagine him being on the scene very much.

The best I can hope is to be a beautiful prisoner in some London apartment, with a stranger on call to buy me Cherry Coke.

Told Laura about shopping with Catrina this weekend.

Possibly, I'll be too ill to go. I hope so, anyway – I'm having last-minute nerves about parading my unstylish face around stylish shops.

'Shopping with Catrina will be fun,' said Laura. 'She'll get you some lovely things. She's generous, if nothing else. And she's your baby's grandmother. You should spend some time together.'

'Do *you* spend time with her?' I asked.

'I can manage her in small doses,' said Laura. 'I've learned a few tricks from Zach. Like always meeting in restaurants, so you never have to eat her goulash.'

Thursday 8th February

Had a bleed this morning.

Majorly worried.

Phoned the hospital. They told me lots of women bleed during their pregnancies and go on to have healthy babies.

However, it could also be a sign of miscarriage.

The tired-sounding midwife asked me to come and get checked over.

Drove straight to the hospital, calling Alex at every red traffic light.

He didn't answer.

Waited in the maternity ward, amid the screams of birthing women.

Daisy asked if the women were being eaten by dinosaurs.

Alex called me back while we were waiting. He felt gratifyingly guilty for missing my earlier calls, and said he'd come immediately.

Told Alex I'd probably have had the scan by the time he arrived, but he said, 'In an NHS hospital? I doubt it.'

He was right.

Alex turned up an hour later, and I still hadn't been called in for the scan.

Finally, a midwife came to hook me up to the ultrasound. She was one of those no-nonsense midwives, telling me off for wearing a complicated wraparound cardigan and shouting, 'Just sit still!' while she squeezed the cold stuff onto my stomach.

Finally, she put the swishing plastic thing on my tummy and said, 'You're fine. I can hear the heartbeat.'

Burst into tears.

Alex said, 'Thank goodness,' his jaw clenched extra tight.

'Keep an eye on things,' said the midwife, glancing at the wall clock. 'Come back if the bleeding starts again. Off you go then.'

'What should I do now?' I asked.

'Just carry on as normal,' said the midwife. 'Lots of women have bleeds. Some bleed throughout the whole pregnancy.'

'She's going on a shopping trip with my mother tomorrow,' Alex interjected. 'Should she cancel? My mother can be tiring.'

'Oh, no reason to do anything differently,' said the midwife. 'It all looks fine.'

When we left, Alex suggested (again) that I see his private maternity specialist, Dr Rupert Snape – just to be on the safe side.

I was left in a tricky moral position.

I don't agree with private medicine. Everyone should get decent, free healthcare, and I wholeheartedly support the NHS. However, I really *did* want another scan, just in case, and wanted to know more about *why* I had the bleed.

Decided I couldn't fix the under-resourced NHS overnight, so accepted Alex's offer.

When it comes to your children, morals go out the window.

Outside the hospital, Alex and I stood for ages by the little duck pond, looking into each other's eyes.

'I'm so relieved,' he kept saying. 'So relieved.'

It was the first time I realised how much this baby meant to him.

Friday 9th February

Shopping with Catrina today.

We met at Sloane Square tube station.

Catrina was late, complaining about parking and 'arseholes'.

Despite the cold weather, she had no coat. She wore tight white trousers, a black suit jacket with a red carnation in the buttonhole and carried a giant Gucci bucket bag over her arm.

The plastic surgery bandage was gone, replaced with a sleek, blonde-grey pleat, but Catrina's skin looked uncomfortably taut. She kissed me elaborately on both cheeks, leaving traces of perfume.

'It's been so long since I went on a girls' shopping trip,' Catrina gushed. Then she linked arms with me and talked about the deterioration of Sloane Square.

'All these tourists, darling. It wasn't like this before. You must be careful. We should stay close together.'

The shop assistants all knew Catrina.

'Some of these places would have closed down without me,' she joked. 'I tell you, they are happy as a monkey about its tail when I visit.'

One white-blonde store assistant pulled Catrina into a cheek-kissing hug, declaring: 'I'm telling you, I love this woman.'

Catrina gushed, 'Zank you, zank you.'

'Just don't slap me today,' the shop assistant laughed.

'Oh no, darling. Not today.' Catrina led me to a rail of navy and white striped dresses. 'A Breton stripe would be fun. Don't you think?'

'They're lovely dresses,' I said. 'But they're too fitted. I'm going to be as big as a cow soon.'

Catrina blinked. 'Surely you're not *planning* to put on weight?'

'It's sort of unavoidable,' I said. 'Because I'm pregnant.'

Catrina gave a gay little laugh. 'Of *course* you are. I'd forgotten.' She waved the assistant over. 'We need maternity clothes. A dreadful time for fashion. I burned all mine once the babies came. You know, when I first came to London, I had no idea how to dress. I used to make my own clothes. Can you imagine?'

After holding various maternity outfits over my body, Catrina and the assistant shooed me into the dressing room.

The outfit I liked most was a black-and-white striped top teamed with black suit-jacket and maternity trousers. It was very smart. The sort of thing I'd usually wear to a job interview.

Catrina and the shop assistant gushed when I came out of the fitting room.

'Beautiful. *Beautiful.*'

'Those clothes will grow with you,' said the assistant, tugging at hems. 'The fabric will last and last – you could wear this outfit *after* the pregnancy.'

'Trust me, darling,' Catrina laughed. 'You will not want to wear any old maternity clothes once the baby comes out.'

After a few more shops, Catrina suggested a cocktail.

'It's only eleven o'clock,' I said.

'Exactly,' said Catrina, checking her diamond-encrusted Rolex. 'We're late.'

We drove to the Mayfair Dalton in Catrina's white Mercedes.

Catrina ordered us both Martinis (I reinstructed the waiter – asking for a Diet Coke), drank hers within five minutes, then veered wildly from topic to topic, covering restaurants in Paris, the legal profession, Spanish men, house prices in Kensington and Alex's father.

Quite a bit of the time, I wasn't sure what she was talking about. Her slight drunkenness, Hungarian accent and random conversation points made things confusing.

'So Alex will want you in London when the baby comes,' she said, swerving topics again. 'Playing the good wife.'

'He keeps asking me to move to London,' I said, relieved to participate in the conversation. 'But it's not right for Daisy. I like Great Oakley. I like being near my family.'

Catrina laughed long and loud, showing several gold fillings.

'How funny! Alex won't want to be a little country mouse. So you'll live apart, then? A lot of people do these days, I suppose.'

'I'm hoping Alex will move back to Great Oakley. To the family estate.'

'Don't count on it, darling,' said Catrina. 'I counted on a lot with Alex's father. You know, he didn't even share a bedroom with me. Imagine that! He'd visit *my* bedroom, finish his business, then leave. And you know, I became Catholic for him. My parents were proud Jews. They suffered so much during World War II, but never gave up their way of life. For me to abandon my upbringing, my beliefs…it was a great sacrifice. Harold never understood. *Never.*'

After another hour and two more Martinis for Catrina, a waiter said, 'Ms Dalton. We have a car ready to take you home.'

'For God's *sake*,' said Catrina. 'I have my own car.'

'But Ms Dalton,' the waiter whispered, 'If you're stopped under the influence again, you could face a custodial sentence.'

'I wasn't even *drunk* that time,' Catrina shouted. 'Only one Martini and a little Champagne. That policeman was making a name for himself.'

'We'll have a staff member drive your car back,' said the waiter. Then he took Catrina's arm and helped her stagger outside.

I sat for a moment, not quite sure what to do. After a while, I picked up my shopping bags and headed home.

On the train back, I phoned Alex.

'How was it?' he asked.

'It was fine. But your mother had three cocktails before lunch.'

Silence.

Then Alex said, 'Where?'

'The Mayfair Dalton.'

'I'll talk to the staff there. They should know not to give her more than two Martinis.'

Alex asked if I had time for a quick lunch with him, but I was already on the train home.

I didn't say it out loud, but I'd had enough of Daltons for one day.

Saturday 10th February

Nick's visitation day.

He picked up Daisy at 9 am in his Volvo.

I still find it an odd juxtaposition – a forty-something bearded hipster at the wheel of such a sensible car.

I was wearing my new, smart maternity outfit, and Nick said, 'Why are you dressed like the Duchess of Cambridge? You don't suit all that stuff, Julesy. That life isn't you.'

'Well *you* don't suit that Volvo,' I fired back. 'You look like you've carjacked an elderly German couple.'

Nick said that Volvos were 'ironic cool for dads in the know'.

He's such a pretentious dickhead.

Sunday 11th February

It rained all day today.

SOOO bored.

Daisy and I have been stuck inside watching *In the Night Garden*.

Do the Haahoos ever do anything? What *is* their purpose, except going to sleep?

Alex rang after lunch. He's got us an appointment with his private maternity specialist on Wednesday.

After he had given me the date and time, he demanded to know what all the noise was in the background.

I explained that John Boy and Daisy were pretending to be Formula One cars.

'And you won't live in London because you say it's too noisy,' said Alex.

I could feel his raised eyebrow fifty miles away.

Monday 12th February

Just phoned the bank to find out why my new card hasn't arrived.

Went through loads of security.

Tried to give my surname and postcode using the phonetic alphabet (A for Alpha, B for Beta), but don't really know the phonetic alphabet and inserted random words: 'Hotel, biscuit three, one, telly, unicorn.'

The bank told me my new card hadn't been printed yet.

'But I could have fitted a kitchen by now!' I exclaimed.

The call handler asked what kitchens had to do with bankcards.

Tuesday 13th February

Althea has blown her pension pot on art.

She's just come back from a Buddhist retreat with Wolfgang and is trying to live in the moment.

I was shocked – not about Althea buying art, but about her having a pension.

'Oh yeah,' she said. 'When I was working at the Tate Modern they signed me up for one. Wolfgang's Dad thinks I should hang onto it, but life is about living, not overthinking the future. I could die tomorrow and Wolfgang would never get to enjoy that graffiti portrait of David Bowie.'

Wednesday 14th February

Valentine's Day

Saw Alex's maternity specialist today.

Can't stop crying.

Dr Snape couldn't find a heartbeat.

Alex and I walked into the consultation a happy couple, excited (if a little nervous) about the future, just 'playing it safe' and 'checking up' on things.

We walked out like zombies.

Alex raged about the NHS scan not picking it up, but Dr Rupert Snape said the baby must have been fine during the previous scan, because heart-rate monitors don't lie. He couldn't tell me why the baby had 'failed to thrive' since then, but assured us that the previous midwife did all the right things.

'Many women do bleed in early pregnancy,' he confirmed. 'It needn't be a cause for alarm.'

Dr Snape says I'll have a period in the next few days or weeks and 'pass' the baby.

If I don't, I should come back in for a forced evacuation.

It was hard to take anything in.

I'm still in shock.

Outside the clinic, Alex held me for the longest time.

I wanted to cry, but I couldn't.

Alex convinced me that Daisy should stay with Mum and Dad for the rest of the day – just while I get my head around the news. Then he drove me home, led me up to my bedroom and suggested a little rest.

Feel numb and weird.

Part of me thinks the maternity specialist could be wrong.

I still *feel* pregnant.

Had missed calls from Althea, Laura and Brandi, all wanting to know how the consultation went.

Mum and Dad haven't called – I suppose Alex must have told them what happened.

Alex stayed the whole afternoon, right by my side, frowning and staring out the window.

When the light began to fade, neither of us turned on the light.

'How are *you* feeling?' I asked him, at one point.

'Devastated,' said Alex.

'Well, there's no reason to marry me now,' I said. 'You got off scot-free.'

'Juliette, that's not funny,' said Alex.

And I shut up, because he was right.

John Boy came back just before tea and shouted up the stairs, 'Julesy? Do you and Daisy want half a doner kebab? I couldn't finish it.'

Alex cantered downstairs and said, 'John. If you wouldn't mind keeping your voice down. Juliette isn't feeling well.'

'Has she got diarrhoea?' I heard John Boy ask.

'No,' Alex snapped. 'She hasn't got diarrhoea.'

'If she ate the frankfurters I left in the fridge ... Jules, DID YOU EAT ONE OF THOSE FRANKFURTERS?'

'She doesn't have diarrhoea,' Alex barked. Then he jogged back upstairs and informed me he was going to the village deli to buy nourishing foods.

When Alex left, John Boy knocked softly on my door.

'Julesy?' he asked. 'Everything all right?'

I shook my head and started crying.

John Boy sat on the bed. 'Is it something to do with the baby?' He acts stupid sometimes, but John Boy can be very perceptive.

I nodded.

John Boy gave me a nice, brotherly hug, then fetched a stack of *Walking Dead* comics and a cup of sugary tea.

After he had closed the curtains, he phoned Mum and Dad.

'Jules has had a bit of an upset,' he whispered. 'She needs peace and quiet. It might be best if Daisy stays with you for the night.'

I heard Mum screech something down the phone, and then John Boy reply that people in shock needed quiet voices and no bright colours.

When Alex came back, John Boy was attempting to soothe me by playing lullabies through his tinny phone speaker.

Alex snapped, 'Turn that noise off. Juliette needs to rest.'

'Shush,' said John Boy. 'When someone is in shock, you mustn't startle them.'

'Please *leave* Juliette's bedroom,' Alex demanded. '*I'm* looking after her. This is nothing to do with *you*.'

At that point, I lost my temper.

'Alex, don't start bossing him around. He's trying to help.'

'Fine,' said Alex. 'I'll go then, shall I? If you have all the help you need.'

'Yes. Fine. Go. You always do.'

'You really want me to go?'

'Yes. Actually I do.'

And he went.

Thursday 15th February

The tears came today.

I should have rested more. I drank too much at Christmas. I ate all that yellow food.

What if Dr Rupert Snape got it wrong?

Googled variants of 'wrong diagnosis miscarriage'. But when I went to the toilet, more blood came out.

Came downstairs to find John Boy and Brandi talking in hushed voices at the breakfast bar.

'What are you doing here?' I asked Brandi. 'Where's Callum?'

'He's with Mum and Dad,' said Brandi. 'I came over to see how you're doing. I'm so sorry Jules.'

Brandi had a miscarriage four years ago – a few years after Callum was born. It sort of worked out for the best, because her boyfriend went to prison soon afterwards.

'I just feel so guilty,' I said. 'I drank all that Prosecco on Christmas day.'

'You can't blame yourself,' said Brandi. 'Miscarriages are really common.'

But I do blame myself.

Who else am I going to blame?

Afternoon

Just picked Daisy up from the pub.

Mum and Dad offered to drop her off, but I needed to get some fresh air.

'The lord giveth and the lord taketh away,' said Dad.

'I've put two tequila bottles in the shopping basket under Daisy's pram,' Mum whispered. 'Get drunk and have a good cry.' Then she told me about her own miscarriage – the one she had before Brandi was born.

'They're very common, love,' she said. 'One in four pregnancies.'

On the way home, Daisy started chattering about her new brother or sister.

How do you explain miscarriage to a two-year-old?

I said there had been a problem and the baby wouldn't be coming after all.

Daisy asked if it was because of 'sodding Royal Mail'.

I wish Mum wouldn't swear so much – two-year-olds pick up everything.

Friday 16th February

More bleeding today – the last of everything, I think.

Apologised to the toilet, like a lunatic.

So, so sad.

Daisy seems oblivious. She's her usual, happy two-year-old self, chattering away, asking why I'm spending so long in the toilet, and if I'm doing 'a big poo'.

Laura came for an unexpected visit after lunch, which was nice.

'I'm sorry,' said Laura, giving me a lovely big sister hug. Then she told me that she'd had a miscarriage before she met Zach.

'Why didn't you tell me?' I asked.

'I felt OK about it,' said Laura. 'I wasn't ready to have a baby. The timing was wrong.'

Wondered if there is anyone I know who *hasn't* had a miscarriage.

Phoned Althea. She said yes – she'd had a miscarriage at university. She and her boyfriend had a spiritual ceremony in the park and buried the little Ewok Babygro she'd bought.

'Why didn't you *tell* me?' I asked.

'It wasn't a big deal,' said Althea. 'It's nature, isn't it? I don't tell you every time I do a shit. Anyway, people get really awkward when you talk about miscarriage. It's the last taboo. Maybe you should post something on Facebook. Shake up the establishment a bit.'

Meant to have an early night, but ended up lying awake in bed, Googling 'reasons for miscarriage.'

Just before I fell asleep, John Boy knocked on the door. He held a snarling, scratching Sambuca in his arms.

'I found him meowing at the back door,' said John Boy, swerving to avoid claws. 'What should I do with him? Carry him back to the pub?'

Sambuca leapt out of John Boy's arms and jumped onto my bed. Then he curled up and fell asleep on my lap.

He's still sleeping there now.

It's annoying, because I really need the toilet.

Writing my diary is difficult too. Any sudden movements cause Sambuca to scratch and spit.

It's like holding a pan of sausages in your lap.

Have three missed calls from Alex.

Haven't phoned him back.

Saturday 17th February

Agreed that Nick could have Daisy this weekend, due to my highly emotional state.

Nick has just left, promising Daisy all sorts of crafts and baking.

I hope Daisy doesn't become used to Nick's try-hard parenting and expect me to lay on activities.

Very hormonal today.

I think it's something to do with my body readjusting – that's what all the websites say.

All I know is I feel fat, needy and a bit depressed.

Cracked and phoned Alex, because I needed to share the sadness in my soul.

Alex arrived on my doorstep an hour later with a huge bunch of water lilies.

We hugged.

I think Alex is feeling depressed too.

'For the first time in my life, I don't want to work,' he said.

I couldn't really empathise, since I never want to work.

'You know that cruise ship holiday you were talking about,' I said. 'Is it still going ahead?'

Alex said yes – theoretically. Subject to some satellite phone arrangements.

'I'd like to go,' I said. 'Have a proper break.'

Alex said he'd make the arrangements immediately. The next cruise leaves in mid-March, and he's going to try and get us both on board – 'assuming there are first-class suites available.'

Told Alex I didn't care about first-class suites.

'But I do,' he said.

Sunday 18th February

Nick phoned at 9 am. He wanted me to come and pick up Daisy.

'Why can't you drop her off?' I asked.

Nick said Helen has taken his car. Her own car is being professionally cleaned, following a Horatio vomiting incident.

'Why did you let Helen take your car?' I asked.

Nick admitted the Volvo didn't technically belong to him, because Helen had bought it.

I should have known.

When I came to pick Daisy up, Nick answered his front door looking rested and happy.

Daisy didn't come running out like she normally would – she was busy making glitter unicorn greetings cards for Santa Claus and Upsy Daisy.

Apparently, Nick and Daisy, 'the dynamic duo', had a fabulous time doing mud painting in the garden, popping popcorn and watching movies in the 'snug'.

Bloody part-time parents.

Nick accused me of being grumpy and hungover.

'Actually Nick, I'm not hungover,' I snapped. 'I've had a miscarriage.'

Nick looked momentarily shocked, then said, 'Sadie had a miscarriage a few months after Horry was born. I mean, we weren't planning on having another baby, but it was still really sad.'

'Why didn't you mention it?' I asked.

'People don't talk about it, do they?'

Monday 19th February

Althea came over today and demanded I leave the house.

'You look pale and English and your pyjamas are starting to smell,' she declared. Which is a bold statement from Althea, who generally doesn't mind bodily odours.

Decided Althea was right.

Showered. Put on my nice, new maternity clothes and accompanied Althea and Wolfgang to London.

Althea suggested we 'hang out' at Wolfgang's favourite playgroup, just down the road from Bethnal Green station.

It seemed like a lovely idea, but once again the big-city playgroup was like an exclusive VIP nightclub, with a 'one in, one out' policy.

Initially we were refused entry, but Althea kicked off, shouting about Wolfgang's dad being in a famous punk band that liked setting fire to things. Then she grabbed my arm and said, 'She's with me.'

It reminded me of all those festivals and gigs we used to go to, when Althea got me into the VIP areas. She always had the best technique: straightforward aggression.

The playgroup was nice – a spotless gymnasium with sprung floors and no broken toys.

'So how are you feeling?' Althea asked, over fair-trade tea and fruit flapjacks.

Said I was sad and probably still hormonal. Although hormones are hard to judge, because losing a baby is just really, really depressing anyway.

'*Why* did it happen?' I said. 'I'm a good person. I think of others. I always recycle.'

'Life can be random,' said Althea. 'Everything belongs to nature, at the end of the day. The universe's great cosmic cycle means we'll all be born again. A cloud doesn't die. It simply transforms.'

But I've never really believed Althea's reincarnation theories. They're full of logic holes. Even she can't remember what the snake eating its tail is supposed to mean.

Told Althea I'm considering antidepressants, but she shouted me down, saying they were a 'shit buzz'.

She speaks from experience, because the doctor prescribed her Prozac after David Bowie died.

'They don't do *anything*,' Althea complained. 'I even tried banging three at once. Fuck all happened. Anyway – you can't medicate grief. It doesn't work that way.'

She's probably right.

There's no quick fix.

It's like that *Going on a Bear Hunt* book.

You can't go over it. You can't go under it. You have to go through it.

Tuesday 20th February

I think the pregnancy hormones are still leaving my body, because I'm STILL feeling tired and low.

Daisy keeps asking me why I'm crying.

Told her I'm sad because her little brother or sister isn't coming.

'Why?' she asked.

Told her that the baby wasn't very well, so couldn't be born.

'Why?' Daisy asked again.

Realised that instead of asking intelligent, philosophical questions, Daisy was just being irritating.

This is yet another developmental milestone.

The 'Why?' question.

WISH I could stop crying.

Daisy is trying to be helpful. She pushes toilet roll into my eyes and says, 'There, there babes. Dry your tears.' But actually, the rough toilet paper is a real eye irritant.

Phoned Mum to talk about Daisy seeing me so sad, and possible psychological implications thereof.

'What if I'm fucking her up for life by crying all the time?' I said.

Mum pointed out that two-year-olds are self-centred, and therefore oblivious to parental unhappiness.

'All Daisy wants is attention,' said Mum. 'Happy attention, sad attention, it's all the same.'

Daisy has been round Mum and Dad's quite a bit this last week. Feel guilty about that too, because Daisy gets a sausage roll and some sort of chocolate product every visit.

Told Mum about the cruise holiday with Alex, and she went uncharacteristically silent.

'Oh, that's going ahead, is it?' she said, eventually. 'I thought it was up in the air.'

'What's the matter?' I asked. 'Can't you look after Daisy?'

'Oh yes, we can do that,' said Mum. 'It's just I had a surprise for you.'

'What sort of surprise?' I asked.

'You remember that Teletext holiday I booked back in January?' said Mum. 'I knew you'd regret saying no, so I booked you on with us. I told a little white lie – it wasn't fully booked. I was going to surprise you the next time you moaned about needing a break. If you don't want to come, we'll understand. But just so you know, the tickets are non-refundable.'

'Why wouldn't I want to come?' I asked. 'I'm desperate for a break. Two breaks are better than one. Thanks so much, Mum.'

'So you're off on two holidays,' said Mum. 'You lucky sod.'

She's right.

I am a lucky sod. Time to stop moping now.

Evening

Alex is texting me meaningful lines from famous books.

It's very unlike him.

Sometimes, he even adds heart emojis.

He also sent a Harrods asparagus and serrano ham quiche by courier in time for tea, with a note:

A bit of comfort food for supper. Much love, Alex xx

It was a lovely thought, but we have different ideas about comfort food.

Put the quiche in the fridge for lunch tomorrow and ordered Domino's pizza.

Sambuca is still here. He sleeps on my bed, and no amount of cajoling or smoked salmon bribery can move him.

Laura says Sambuca is God's way of showing me love, but Sambuca is too violent to be a message from God.

He's more likely to be from the other one.

The fire and brimstone fellow.

Wednesday 21st February

Althea came round last night with a bottle of homemade blackberry vodka.

We had a drink and a chat, and I got it all out – the guilt, the sadness, the anger.

'I think Alex is depressed too,' I said. 'He sent me a quiche.'

'Men express their emotions in different ways,' said Althea sagely.

Didn't realise I felt angry, until Althea made me do emotional role-playing. She told me to imagine she was God, and asked me to cry, wail and rage at her.

Althea also knitted an orange aardvark to represent my unborn child, and we buried it together in the garden. She was right – I did feel a certain closure. I don't know if it was the odd burial of knitted hippy items, or getting to shout and wail, but I'm more at peace today.

After we buried the woolly aardvark in the garden, Althea made sure I got up the stairs OK.

She didn't need to.

I really was fine. Not drunk at all.

It's just that last step was a bit slippery.

Thursday 22nd February

This morning, John Boy tried to fix our toilet seat that won't stay up.

Listening to him do DIY was like hearing an emotionally charged radio drama.

Disaster: 'Oh FUCKING hell! How does that... NO! NO! NO!'

Redemption: 'Ah HA! *That's* how it goes in. Cheeky bastard.'

Conflict: 'GET IN YOU BAD BUGGER!'

Unbridled anger: 'YOU STUPID BLOODY TOILET SEAT. YOU STUPID BLOODY THING!'

Dramatic tension: *World-weary sigh.*

Redemption: 'I've only gone and bloody done it!'

The toilet seat is a *little* better. It now falls down *half* the time, so it's a game of Russian roulette, wondering if it's going to close on you or not.

I suppose John Boy's right – it has brought a bit of excitement to an otherwise mundane activity.

Afternoon

Catrina Dalton has sent me a scarf and a tiny leather folding thing of uncertain use, both boxed and wrapped in logo-embossed tissue paper.

The gifts came with a little hand-written note saying, 'Sorry for your loss. I have been through this and it is hard. We will have fun on the cruise. Catrina xxx'

Very thoughtful and kind.

Although bad news about the cruise – I didn't realise Catrina was still coming. Should have specified to Alex that I wanted just the two of us, but I suppose Catrina was already booked in.

Phoned Catrina to say thank you.

Catrina barked, 'Who is this?'

I told her my name, and she said, 'Juliette who? I don't know a Juliette. Juliette *Binoche*? You don't sound French.'

I said, 'Alex's FRIEND. Juliette who came to LUNCH at your APARTMENT. Remember? You made GOULASH and we went SHOPPING.'

'Oh!' Catrina exclaimed. 'Oh yes. Juliette.'

'I JUST CALLED TO THANK YOU FOR THE PRESENT,' I shouted.

'What present?'

'THE SCARF. AND THE...LEATHER...ITEM.'

'The Paco Rabanne coin purse,' said Catrina. 'It's nothing, my dear. I'm just sorry for what you're going through. I've been there myself. Miscarriage... It's a very sad thing. Devastating. You question yourself as a woman.'

'Thank you,' I said, feeling tearful again. Bloody crying. I'm so bored of it now – it's been endless.

'Harold was very callous when I miscarried,' Catrina continued. 'He blamed the cocktails. Can you imagine? Women all over the world *smoke* and eat rubbish. You know, I do so love to smoke, but I didn't touch a cigarette when I was pregnant, not one. And I ate wonderful, nourishing food – smoked salmon, caviar, goulash. Wear the scarf, won't you?'

Promised I would.

Hung up and cried.

Daisy said, 'Mummy sad. Again. Why?'

Said I was still sad about the baby. Told her that grief takes a long time. That it comes in waves. That I may never feel totally OK about losing the baby, but the sadness is passing.

Daisy said, 'Why?'

Asked her to stop bloody saying, 'Why'.

Friday 23rd February

In my grief, I've been neglecting my motherly duties.

Obviously, I make sure Daisy has the basics, but I've let a lot slip. Clothes I wouldn't have dreamed of letting Daisy wear outside the house, like her favourite pyjamas teamed with patent leather shoes, have become totally acceptable. And her ponytail is now always wonky, with shark's fins of hair sticking up because I don't have the energy to brush everything neat and tidy.

The house is an absolute mess – especially the front garden.

Aside from the weeds, there are two car seats on the lawn now, because John Boy bought an old Land Rover from Yorkie last week. Yorkie sold him the car for £100, because the annual insurance, tax and petrol cost ten times what the car is worth.

John Boy sees the car as a project, and is replacing the old, battered stained seats. He managed stage one (pulling the seats out), without realising that the new red-leather seats are coming from China and will take six weeks to arrive.

Some ladies from the Catholic Church came to visit last week, and I could tell they viewed the unkempt garden and discarded car parts as room for improvement. Still – they were good Christians and didn't judge me, asking instead if I wanted to visit their church.

Said I didn't have a faith as yet, because I could never make up my mind.

The ladies gave me a nice leaflet and a mini bible and told me about love and Jesus.

Asked if Jesus knew why I'd lost my baby.

The women looked embarrassed and didn't know what to say. It's true about miscarriage – it is one of the last taboos.

Saturday 24th February

Althea just phoned.

She's making a mermaid fancy-dress costume, but is struggling to find big enough seashells.

'I need more clay,' said Althea. 'An extra five pounds at least – enough to make twelve-inch shells. Do you have any?'

'I don't have any clay,' I said. 'Why would you think I had clay?'

'For Daisy to mess around with,' said Althea. 'Every house with kids should have clay.'

Cried.

Told Althea that, not only do I not have clay, but I'm also slipping in other motherly duties.

'I gave Daisy Frosties for breakfast and lunch,' I blubbed.

Althea shouted at me about over-striving for perfectionism. Then she offered to bring over some tubs of paleo cereal.

Thanked her, but declined. It would be a waste of dehydrated beetroot and sprouted seeds. Daisy is way too fussy.

Am finding it hard to give Daisy a balanced diet right now. Partly, this is due to my own current unhealthy habits. I can't very well be scoffing chocolate bars, then telling Daisy to eat a balanced meal.

This morning, Daisy caught me hiding behind the fridge door, stuffing a wagon wheel into my mouth.

'What's that Mummy?' Daisy asked.

Told her it was something unhealthy and that sometimes mummies ate things they shouldn't.

Daisy threw a perfectly reasonable tantrum because I wouldn't share the Wagon Wheel. But honestly, it would be terrible to give her chocolate at 7 am.

Sunday 25th February

Mum and Dad went to the garden centre this morning.

They came back with a present for me – a little apple tree.

'The branches are bare now,' said Dad. 'But when spring comes, they'll be covered in glorious, pink blossom.'

We pulled up weeds, mowed the lawns – front and back – and planted the tree right outside the kitchen patio doors. Then Mum helped me tidy the house.

We dusted, hoovered and threw out clutter, including Daisy's stash of Happy Meal and Kinder Surprise toys.

Once the house and garden were tidy, we made cheese salad sandwiches and a big pot of tea. Then we sat in the kitchen, looking at the apple tree.

'We choose a pink blossoming tree,' said Mum, putting her hand over mine. 'Because I think the baby would have been a girl. And anyway, they don't do blue blossom trees.'

This evening, when I went to bed, Sambuca wasn't there.

Phoned to check he was back at the pub.

Mum confirmed that, 'The little bastard is here, scratching the cereal boxes to bits.'

I suppose Sambuca knew it was time to leave.

Finally starting to feel better.

Monday 26th February

Decided to buy carpet for upstairs today.

The downstairs and staircase were carpeted last year, but I ran out of money to do the landing and bedrooms.

It's an expense, but the insulation will help lower our gas bill. The rushes of air up my pyjama legs late at night confirm the bare bedroom floorboards let in a lot of cold air.

The draughts, combined with the creaky floorboards, also create a haunted-house atmosphere, which generates stress and anxiety – both of which are bad for women in vulnerable emotional states. Especially now John Boy has caught onto my paranoia and makes 'woooo' noises when I walk along the landing.

Took Daisy to the huge shopping 'village' outside of town to browse new carpets.

It's the best place to shop for flooring, because there are so many carpet places there: Carpet Right, All for Floors, Allied Carpets, Carpets for Less, the Carpet People, Cost-co Carpets and Carpets R Us.

After a lengthy browse, I selected a special offer Saxon twist carpet remnant.

It was a heavy roll, so the carpet shop manager bullied an assistant into carrying it to the car for us.

Unfortunately, I couldn't remember where I'd parked.

We walked around the huge car park for twenty minutes, while the carpet assistant muttered about unrealistic workplace expectations and the fact his coffee was going cold.

Daisy found our car in the end.

She recognised the bird poo on the bumper.

Evening

Alex just phoned.

His assistant is booking the cruise and needs to know how many suitcases I'll be bringing.

'One,' I said. 'Obviously.'

'I don't see why it should be obvious,' said Alex. 'My mother is bringing five suitcases.'

The nearer we get to the cruise departure date, the more uneasy I feel about being stuck on a boat for a week with Catrina Dalton. But she did send me that nice scarf.

Maybe it will be OK.

Tuesday 27th February

Wolfgang's birthday party today at Althea's house.

The theme this year was 'Revolution!'

I didn't have the energy to do proper fancy dress, so just put Daisy in a red Minnie Mouse party outfit. Hoped Althea would ignore the Disney iconography and focus on the revolutionary red colour.

She didn't.

'Minnie Mouse is a symbol of the capitalist West,' Althea bellowed. 'Disney is everything this party is against.'

It's OK for Althea – *she* has a little *boy*. Trying to keep girls away from Walt Disney is like opening a packet of M&Ms and only having one – impossible.

Wolfgang was dressed as Che Guevara and looked very fetching in his beret and army fatigues.

Althea looked good too, in an imposing kind of way. She was dressed as Joan of Arc, boasting hand-welded plate armour and a six-foot pikestaff.

The pikestaff caused a few arguments, because Wolfgang kept trying to grab it.

While Althea was blowtorching the birthday candles, Wolfgang finally managed to get both hands on the pikestaff, causing a major scuffle.

'NO, Wolfgang,' Althea bellowed, trying to prize his muscular fingers free. 'Mummy's weapon. You've got a machine gun.'

To try and distract him, I gave Wolfgang his birthday present: a wooden shape-matching set approved by the Early Years learning programme.

Wolfgang let go of the pikestaff, grabbed the Early Years shape-matching set and snapped it in half.

'He's a bit aggro about that Early Years learning stuff right now,' Althea explained. 'They're trying to pigeonhole him at nursery, with all their Early Years charts and tick boxes. They say Wolfgang is behind in his literacy, but if anything, he's ahead of other children. What other kid his age knows all the words to 'Life on Mars'?'

A few of Althea's London mum friends were at the party, and one of them was breastfeeding a new-born. I wanted to smile at her and tell her how lovely her little girl was. But instead, I snuck into the toilet for a bit of a cry while Daisy was confused by vegan Smarties.

Felt better for the cry. It wasn't like the crying before – the really sad crying.

Starting to feel OK.

Wednesday 28th February

Stopped by the pub this morning to give Dad back his garden shears.

Mum offered me a bag of prawn crackers to take home, left over from last night's Chinese takeaway.

I asked her why prawn crackers in particular, since there was half a beef chow mien in the fridge (which I quite fancied for lunch).

'You're always banging on about healthy eating,' said Mum. 'So I thought you'd want the fish.'

'Prawn crackers aren't fish,' I said. 'They're fish-flavoured carbohydrates.'

'I thought prawn crackers were healthy,' said Mum.

Told her they most certainly weren't, but took the bag anyway, plus the chow mien.

Am appalled that Mum, with her type-two diabetes, doesn't know that prawn crackers are not a type of fish.

She's supposed to be back on her diet now, so goodness knows why she's ordering Chinese food. Probably she thinks that's healthy too.

Thursday 1st March

St David's Day

Raining today.

Took Daisy to a local playgroup called Montessori Tiny Treasures.

It was run by an imposing grey-haired lady called Dotty Clobber, who had very strict ideas about how children should play.

The play session was run in Dotty's Gothic-style house, in a dark sitting room with the curtains drawn, because Dotty is allergic to sunlight.

There were stone gargoyles and a box of various, half-used sun cream bottles on the front porch.

Children had to select toys for 'independent play' from a shelf of wicker baskets, then put them carefully back for the next child to play with.

The other mums were wary of Dotty, eyeing her nervously before they touched anything.

The children were the same.

At one point, a child touched the wrong thing and Dotty laid an imposing hand on his little shoulder.

'We don't do that here,' said Dotty, in a low, menacing voice.

The little boy dropped the toy and retreated to rock gently back and forth in the corner.

I was so busy trying to understand what Daisy could and couldn't touch that we forgot about having fun.

Was a relief to get out in the rain again.

Friday 2nd March

Decided to have a spring clean today and get rid of more clutter.

I was never brilliant at minimalist living, but now Daisy has come along I am getting buried under stuff.

Got ruthless and threw out a load of broken/unsuitable toys, while John Boy distracted Daisy with his new flashing trainers.

Was sort of hoping Alex might call today, but he hasn't.

The cruise is two weeks away, and I feel most couples would be on the phone every night, chattering excitedly about the countries they're going to visit. But I suppose this is common-place to Alex. He's always jetting off to different countries. And I'm not really sure you could call us a couple, anyway.

Saturday 3rd March

Nick just phoned.

Sadie has left him. Apparently, she had a meltdown over a lack of sourdough bread at the Co-op, packed a bag and stormed off to London. She has since sent Nick a text message detailing everything she hates about living in Great Oakley – top of the list being Nick. She has also sent a picture of a sourdough bread bakery on Brick Lane.

'Where was Horatio when all this happened?' I asked.

'At Mum's house,' said Nick. 'Having a sleepover. Sadie and I needed a night off.'

Nick does seem to be in genuine anguish, but I think most of it is ego-related. After all, he's wanted to split up with Sadie for ages.

Nick asked if I could chaperone Daisy for her visit today, because he had Horatio and couldn't cope with two children.

We agreed to meet at Tiny Tumbles, the out-of-town soft-play.

Nick was actually early for a change, drinking Styrofoam coffee when we arrived. Horatio was with Nick, sleeping in one of those off-roader prams with a dummy in his mouth.

After I'd settled Daisy in the ball pool, I accepted Nick's 'Do you want some crap coffee?' offer.

He gave me a long, angry speech about things being 'over' with Sadie and how he'd never let 'that lying, two-faced cow' back into his life. He begged me to get back with him (again), insisting we were happy together.

Then Sadie appeared.

It was a terrible shock, seeing her looming over the table.

She looked OK actually – she's lost most of the baby weight and was dressed in leather jeans and a bright-red coat. Her hair was cut into a new, shorter style – a brown bob with blonde tips framing her jaw. It suited her, but her big, round, moon face was decidedly more lined and careworn than in our friendship days.

'So *this* is who you're with?' Sadie accused, her voice low. '*Now* are you going to tell me there's nothing going on?'

Nick stood up. 'How did you know I was here?'

'Your mother told me,' Sadie spat. 'Why are you with *her*?'

'I have a name, Sadie,' I said. 'Juliette. Remember? Your ex-best friend? Mother of Nick's *first* child.'

At this moment, a clown with a giant, fake head and spotted bow-tie, ambled over to our table waving big, foam hands.

'Hi! I'm Tiny Tumbles. Ready for the Tiny Tumbles show?'

Sadie shouted, 'I don't want the fucking Tiny Tumbles show. I want to know if my fiancé has been screwing around.'

Nick shuffled guiltily on his seat, his eyes imploring me not to tell Sadie what he'd just said about me making him happy.

Sadie's lips thinned. Then she turned on her heel and walked out.

The clown said, 'Tiny Tumbles likes *happy* families. Not *sad* families.' And looked at *me* like I was some sort of floozy!

'Don't judge *me*,' I said. 'That girl slept with *my* fiancé.'

Tiny Tumbles said, 'It's the children I feel sorry for,' then ambled off to the Silly Pavilion.

Shouted at Nick for bringing drama into my life, then waddled into the ball pool to get Daisy.

'You're leaving?' said Nick. 'But I paid an extra fifty pence for unlimited coffee.'

Ignored him and dug around the plastic balls.

Finally found Daisy buried in the deep end with a new friend called Maggie.

Daisy gave an outraged scream when I told her it was home time. 'Want MAGGIE! MAGGIE MY BEST FRIEND!'

It took the whole car journey home to calm her down.

Bloody hell. Nick and all his drama.

I wish I'd thought more carefully about who to have kids with.

Men should come with warning signs.

Sunday 4th March

John Boy's Land Rover renovation project is really coming along. He's put the old seats back in (a temporary measure, while he waits for red leather seats from China), glued metal studs around both bumpers and added a horn that plays seven notes from the A-Team theme.

John Boy and Callum have been bombing around the fields today, hooting the horn and playing Sepultura at full volume.

Callum is in an especially good mood, because his eyebrows have grown back, and he has, in his mind, reassumed his position as 'school love machine'.

Told John Boy he was setting Callum a very bad example – teaching dangerous driving when there is already a high chance Callum will become a dangerous driver.

Monday 5th March

Alex came over this evening, just as I was serving up tea.

I was treating Daisy to wholemeal fish fingers, sweet potato chips and peas – a nice, healthy meal to offset all the rubbish I've been giving her lately.

'You must have had a tiring day,' said Alex, 'to be feeding Daisy that oven-ready rubbish.'

After a knee-jerk, 'Fuck off!' I said, 'They're *wholemeal* fish fingers. And *sweet potato* chips.'

'They're packaged nonsense,' Alex countered.

'Well what would *you* feed her then?' I challenged.

'Home-made spinach pasta with fresh pesto. Toasted kale chips with sea salt. Fresh organic seasonable vegetables.'

I explained that as a single parent I have limited time and money. 'Getting healthy food into children is hard,' I said. '*You* try it.'

Alex said he certainly would.

'When?' I asked.

'For such an important endeavour, I will give Daisy two hours of my time tomorrow,' said Alex. 'Daisy, prepare yourself for some delicious, healthy food.'

Didn't mean to snort with derision and mutter, '*She won't eat it*'. It just sort of came out.

Daisy is delighted that Alex is coming to see us again. She loves him so much. I suppose it's not surprising – he's stable, sensible and really cares about her. These are all things I'm told children like.

Tuesday 6th March

Alex arrived at lunchtime today with a sheaf of child-friendly healthy recipes designed by his marketing team. He also brought five bags of shopping from the Harrods food hall.

Alex had a simple but effective technique for healthy-eating success. He called it 'the numbers game' and it involved cooking something, offering it to Daisy, then moving right on to preparing the next thing. He made detailed notes about what was palatable to Daisy, what wasn't and what could be tried again in a reworked format.

Daisy has now tried:
+ Fresh egg pasta with homemade pesto
+ Bone-marrow broth
+ Courgette fritters with parmesan
+ Homemade vegetable lasagne
+ Homemade baba ganoush with vegetable crudités
+ Seabass with parsley butter and asparagus spears
+ Eggs Florentine
+ Organic peanut butter on celery sticks
+ Caviar, smoked salmon and cream cheese blinis
+Roasted vegetable chips with peri-peri dressing
+Homemade chicken dhansak with wild rice
+Homemade spelt breadsticks with olive oil and balsamic dipping sauce

Of the twelve dishes, Daisy liked five and loved three.

She also enjoyed the snacks, including the very simple to prepare peanut butter on celery (which she called 'peanutter on lelly').

After creating a final menu plan, Alex washed and dried up, rearranged my cupboards into a more efficient order and took out the recycling.

I didn't realise he was so domesticated, but apparently, they're big on self-sufficiency at Windsor College.

'But I can't prepare time-consuming meals for her three times a day, seven days a week,' I insisted.

Alex called this 'pessimistic'.

'You only have to find three meals she likes,' he said. 'Breakfast, lunch and supper. Then cook large batches and freeze them.'

'It doesn't work like that with children,' I said. 'Just because she likes something one day, doesn't mean she'll like it the next.'

Alex said he'd brainstorm with kitchen staff at the Mayfair Dalton and consider ways to bring greater variety into Daisy's diet without losing efficiency.

Asked Alex about the cruise (just a week away now – bon voyage!), but he was in too much of a hurry to 'chit chat'.

His assistant will email me over the final menu plan when it's ready.

Wednesday 7th March

Alex's menu plan arrived.

Grudgingly, I admit it's quite good.

I mean, some of the things I can make without too much effort. The homemade carrot pasta is right out, of course, but three-cheese Welsh rarebit is worth a try.

Have started thinking about clothes for the cruise next week. It's all so exciting. A whole week on an adult's cruise holiday! What on earth am I going to wear? And what will I do with myself, when I'm not running around after a child?

Hope I don't think about the miscarriage too much. I haven't wallowed in self-pity for a while now, but every so often I have an unexpected cry.

Assessing potential holiday attire is tricky right now, because Daisy has just discovered a new game – wearing lots of clothes (mine and hers) all at once.

This morning, Daisy came downstairs in a motley assortment of fancy dress clothing, multiple pairs of socks, my floaty summer dress, my kaftan thing and my 'Choose Love' t-shirt.

When I helped Daisy get changed, I found out she was also wearing four pairs of my pants and a Minnie Mouse swimming costume.

Thursday 8th March

Alex came over this evening for a 'quick supper'.

He brought two-dozen quails eggs and asked where I kept the celery salt.

Asked what celery salt was.

Alex was appalled.

'It's one of the cupboard staples no kitchen should be without,' he said. Then he listed other staples I was lacking, such as chorizo sausage, Dijon mustard, pesto and paprika. He also remarked on my lack of kitchenware.

'You don't even have a cheese knife,' said Alex. 'Or an earthenware roasting brick. And no dicing mandarin.'

'What would I use paprika for?' I asked.

Alex listed ten dishes that would benefit from a sprinkle of paprika, including chilli con carne, beans on toast and popcorn.

Felt annoyed that he's expecting such gourmet standards of me.

'You think beans on toast with paprika is gourmet?' said Alex. 'Maybe there's no helping you.'

Thought Alex might want to discuss the cruise (six days now!), but he didn't even mention it until I brought it up.

'Aren't you excited?' I asked. 'The clear, sparkling waters of the Mediterranean. Ancient architecture and sensational food in the bustling city of Rome. Tapas and cava on the sun-drenched streets of Barcelona.'

Alex gave me one of his half smiles and said, 'Someone's been reading the cruise brochure.'

Admittedly, I've glanced at it recently.

After all, it's right there on my bedside table.

Alex said he was keen to spend time with me, but the cruise itself was a busman's holiday, since he works in the travel business.

'Europe isn't new for me,' he said. 'It's coming home.'

Friday 9th March

John Boy was in a good mood today because he won the pub darts tournament last night. He'd never played darts before, but Yorkie was too drunk to see straight, so John Boy ended up taking his place to stop anyone else getting hurt.

John Boy got two triple twenties in a row, then a bullseye to finish.

'It's all that rifle training,' said John Boy. 'It's made me a crack shot. And I was good at the numbers too.'

Apparently, John Boy could work out the darts calculations in his head, while other, sober players were scribbling numbers on beer mats.

Asked John Boy why he didn't pass his maths GCSE. He said he never sat it.

'My teachers put me with all the thick kids, 'cause I was the joker,' said John Boy. 'I drew one little cartoon about my teacher's bad breath, and bang. They packed me off to the special needs class.'

I'd forgotten they used to do that in the 1980s – label all the naughty kids as having learning difficulties.

Suggested John Boy consider retaking his exams, but he doesn't see the point.

'I'm happy enough,' he said. 'I like working at the pub. I just wish Gwen would take me back.'

I didn't realise John Boy still thought about Gwen.

It's so easy to get caught up in your own issues, and forget that other people are going through heartbreak and loss too.

Poor John Boy.

Saturday 10th March

Mum has decided to try out another diet.

This will almost certainly lead to rows.

Mum gets very agitated when anything gets between her and food – a prime example being the time she was banned from the local fish and chip shop.

She didn't want to wait while Mr Sainty, the chip shop owner, got more frozen fish from out the back, so she went behind the counter and shovelled out her own chips into a polystyrene tray.

When Mr Sainty returned with a bucket of cod he was furious and immediately told Mum she was barred.

Mum was unrepentant, telling him his fryer needed a good clean.

Sunday 11th March
Mothering Sunday

Goodbye little unborn baby.

Mummy loves you very much.

Monday 12th March

Starting to feel *really* nervous about leaving Daisy to go on this cruise.

A week is a long time for a two-year-old.

Have told Daisy about the holiday, but I don't think she really understands. She keeps laughing about the 'funny mummy sleeping on a boat' joke.

'I really *will* be sleeping on a boat,' I say.

But this just makes her laugh harder.

Mum says I'm worrying too much. 'Daisy will hardly know you're gone,' she said. 'Your Dad has a week of wholesome fun planned. And I'll take her for unwholesome ice cream and pizza and all sorts. She'll have a lovely time, and so will you.'

Mum has fond memories of a P&O cruise she took around the Canary Islands, before she met Dad.

'It was meal after meal,' she reminisced. 'Breakfast. Elevenses. Lunch. Afternoon tea. Dinner. And then a midnight barbeque.'

Asked which countries the ship visited.

Mum couldn't remember.

'I didn't get off the boat much,' she said. 'If you did, you risked missing a meal.'

Dad will drive me to Southampton tomorrow, ready for the 11 am boarding. He wants to leave at six in the morning, so we'll arrive by nine (two hours before we're allowed on the boat) because Dad gets panicky about timekeeping.

I've tried to talk Dad into leaving later, but he won't be persuaded. He's bringing a flask of tea and a pack of cards in readiness for a long wait.

Tuesday 13th March

The drive to the ferry port was even quicker than expected.

Dad and I arrived at 8.30 am for the 11 am boarding. This gave us two and a half hours to stare at the magnificent cruise ship waiting in the port, its many windows and portholes glinting in the morning sun.

I told Dad about the restaurants on board, various swimming pools, leisure facilities etc. Dad asked if I'd checked lifeboat capacity or printed out a map of evacuation points.

'Of course not,' I said. 'This is five-star luxury. They'll have excellent safety procedures.'

Dad pointed out that the Titanic was five-star luxury.

'You won't care how many restaurants are on-board if you're

sinking,' he said.

Dad can be so negative sometimes.

At 9 am, Mum phoned.

'There's a car here for you, Jules,' she said. 'A limousine. Ready to take you to the ferry port.'

Didn't realise the trip included road transport.

Asked Mum to apologise to the limo driver and tell him we were at Southampton already. Mum said she'd already given him a cup of tea and a bacon sandwich.

Dad and I waited in the car, drinking plastic-tasting tea and playing cards on the glove compartment lid.

Finally, the check-in and boarding gates opened.

Am now aboard the Golden Wind – a gleaming, glossy cruise ship boasting eight fine-dining restaurants, a choice of swimming pools, a spa, a shopping street and a wellness/relaxation centre.

There's a state-of-the-art medical bay, which must be very reassuring for the many elderly people on board.

I am staying in a luxurious ocean-view suite with its own balcony and all sorts of exciting hotel room extras, like a trouser press and fold-out ironing board.

I also have a personal butler – a handsome, muscular twenty-something Senegalese man named Emmanuel.

Emmanuel has gleaming white teeth and black skin, studies classical literature, writes poetry in his spare time and speaks four different languages. He offered me a glass of Champagne (politely correcting me when I picked up the wrong glass), then hung all my clothes in the walk-in wardrobe and laid out my toiletries symmetrically on shelves above the sink.

I waited on the sea-view balcony for Alex, sipping Champagne and having a thoroughly nice time.

But Alex didn't come.

Emmanuel refilled my Champagne glass, brought me a plate

of toasted ciabatta fingers, and then swept up the crumbs whilst humming the *Marriage of Figaro*.

But still no Alex. Tried to call him, but no answer.

I even tried calling Catrina, but she didn't answer either.

'Emmanuel,' I asked. 'When will the other guests arrive?'

'Other guests?' Emmanuel asked, seeming confused. 'You are the only guest in this suite, Madam. Are you referring to the adjoining suite?'

'There's an adjoining suite?'

'Oh yes, Madam. For your family member, Ms Dalton.'

'What about Alex Dalton?' I asked.

Emmanuel said he didn't think a Mr Dalton was staying at this end of the ship, but he'd check.

As he phoned guest services, we heard the urgent, hysterical voice of Catrina Dalton outside the suite, demanding a Martini and a sedative.

'I know you have good sedatives on board,' Catrina shouted. 'We're on international waters. They relax the laws. I won't need a prescription.'

Opened the door to find Catrina fanning her face frantically with a cocktail menu. A porter was behind her, pushing a huge golden trolley of suitcases.

'Catrina,' I said. 'Are you OK? What on earth happened?'

'Oh Juliette.' Catrina's eyes were panicked and frightened. 'It's the most terrible news. There's been a storm on St Barts. Alex is stranded.'

'Is he OK?' I asked.

Catrina nodded. 'Yes, yes. He's fine. But the airport is closed. He can't get back today. The ship will leave without him. What am I going to do? Who will take care of me?'

At this point, Emmanuel stepped out of the suite and said, 'I will take care of you, Madam. I'm the butler for the north suites and it is my pleasure to help you in any way I can.'

'You're my butler?' Catrina asked. 'Oh thank goodness.' She clasped Emmanuel's strong hands. 'I need a vodka Martini. This is an emergency.'

'I'll fetch one from the cocktail lounge,' said Emmanuel.

'But then I'll be alone,' said Catrina, eyes panicked. 'I hate to be alone.'

'Perhaps a glass of Champagne then,' said Emmanuel. 'I have a bottle on ice in the butler's pantry. I can unpack your luggage and read you some poetry.'

'I need something stronger than Champagne,' Catrina decided. 'You must go to the cocktail lounge, but be very quick.'

'I'll stay in the suite with you,' I offered.

Catrina turned sad eyes in my direction, 'Would you? I so hate to be alone.'

'Of course,' I said. 'It would be my pleasure.'

It wasn't really a pleasure, because Catrina demanded the suite curtains be drawn to 'calm her nerves', then gabbled on about how awful it was that Alex hadn't sent someone in his stead.

When Emmanuel brought Catrina her Martini, he also had news about Alex.

'Mr Dalton has arranged a helicopter to take him to Barcelona,' Emmanuelle explained. 'So he'll board at the next port. We'll take care of you in the meantime.'

After three Martinis, Catrina decided to lie down and rest. I took the opportunity to explore the many facilities aboard the Golden Wind.

Emmanuel asked if I wanted a guided tour ('The ship can be a little overwhelming, Madam!'), but I politely declined, saying he should stay with Catrina.

He then furnished me with a huge, pull-out map and pointed out the favourite restaurants and relaxation spots.

'The sunset from the top deck is breath-taking,' he told me. 'A wonderful place to write poetry, if you are so inclined.'

Thanked him for the advice, then went for a stroll.

Decided to do a lap of the ship, but my legs ached at the halfway point so stopped for an Irish crème coffee on one of the many sun decks and watched the cold shores of England melt into the distance.

Catrina was in good spirits on my return. Emmanuel had found her some strong pharmaceuticals, and she was living it up – mixing cocktails with opiate-based painkillers.

'You will take me to dinner, won't you Juliette?' Catrina asked. 'We need to take care of each other. Women shouldn't eat alone. Collect me at 8 pm. I need to rest now. Trauma is very, very tiring.'

Then she put on huge, Bose noise-reducing headphones and asked Emmanuel to bring her 'any vodka-based cocktail – surprise me.'

Late evening

Dinner with Catrina.

We settled on a Japanese restaurant, because Catrina wanted 'clean' food, whatever that means. I think she regretted the choice when she saw the limited alcohol menu – only Asahi beer or warm saké.

I embraced the new experience, ordering warm saké served in a little wooden box thing with Japanese writing on it. It was disgusting.

I was less adventurous after that and ordered stir-fried noodles and a nice bottle of beer.

Catrina ate octopus, eel and some other miscellaneous raw fish. She was an erratic companion, heaping praise on the waiters one minute, going wild-eyed and swearing about the 'appalling St Barts crisis control' the next.

By Catrina's third wooden cup of saké, she had moved on to a familiar topic – Alex's father, Harold.

It's crazy – they were divorced twenty years ago. Talk about holding a grudge.

Does it really matter now that Harold gave his third wife exactly the same diamond tennis bracelet he bought her? Or that he still has the same carpets in his house that they bought together twenty years ago?

Wednesday 14th March

The ship docked at Barcelona this morning, and Alex came on board.

It should be cause for celebration, but actually Alex and I aren't speaking.

Bloody Alex.

We're not staying in the same suite, or anywhere near each other!

In some odd gesture of chivalry towards a woman he knocked up last year, Alex is staying at the OTHER END of the boat. In ship terms, this is approximately a mile away.

He can't understand what I'm upset about, because he made sure Catrina and I got the balconied staterooms at the front of the ship – which are apparently better. But it's not about who has the best view. We're supposed to be on this cruise together.

Arrived in Barcelona in the early hours of the morning, but Alex didn't come on board straight away because the cruise ship had to set up its landing vessels. However, Emmanuel passed on a message saying that Mr Alex Dalton would meet us in Barcelona for lunch, then board the ship.

Emmanuel then told me that Alex would be staying at the other end of the boat.

I was furious.

Sensing my annoyance, Emmanuel said, 'When Mr Dalton

boards after lunch, I'll be happy to arrange a golf cart to take you to him.'

After an angry breakfast of poached eggs with hollandaise sauce, freshly squeezed orange juice, a fruit basket, croissants, strawberry jam and a stack of pancakes (well you have to try everything, don't you?), Catrina and I boarded the little ferry boat to Barcelona port. 'If you're not back by 3 pm, we will *leave* without you,' the PA system announced, over and over again.

It was very stressful.

When Catrina and I disembarked, Alex was waiting by the gangway. He helped us both off and asked how we were finding life at sea.

Catrina kissed Alex elaborately on both cheeks, then hopped in a taxi – she was meeting Carlos at Passeig de Gracia for upmarket shopping.

When Catrina left, Alex embraced me like we were in an old-fashioned black and white movie, looking deeply into my eyes. He didn't seem to realise I was annoyed with him, instead asking if the rich food on board had disagreed with me.

'I don't have indigestion,' I snapped. 'I'm upset you're booked into a different suite. *And* one at the other end of the ship.'

Alex frowned. '*You're* upset? How gloriously self-centred of you. You do realise I've been dealing with the devastation of a tropical storm and been stranded for two days without a trouser press?'

Felt bad then, but was too proud to say so.

We glared at each other.

Then Alex said, 'Look, can we just put grievances to one side? This is a beautiful city, and a beautiful morning.'

'You mean pretend I'm not annoyed, when really I am?'

'Exactly.'

'I think that's called dysfunction, isn't it?' I said.

'It's called respecting the occasion.'

But I'm not from a family that keeps things in. When I get annoyed, I tell everyone.

'Fine,' I said. 'We'll do it your way. I'll pretend everything's OK.'

It was a tense morning.

We stopped at a little paella restaurant (one of Alex's favourites) near Barcelona Cathedral and ate a silent lunch. Then we visited Barcelona Cathedral, and I gave Alex one-word answers to his tedious questions about history.

Back on the cruise ship, I huffed off to my suite and played Uno with Emmanuel.

Wish Alex was here to enjoy the sunset with me, but I'm too proud to ask him.

Thursday 15th March

Day at sea, supposedly enjoying the luxurious boat.

The reality was Alex and I sitting at opposite ends of a big swimming pool, sipping fresh orange juice, while Catrina had a loud satellite phone argument with her boyfriend, Carlos.

Catrina was angry with Carlos for not meeting her in Barcelona. I can't say I blame her – he lives in the city and was only a short walk from their meeting spot. At least, if Catrina's shrieks were to be believed.

Catrina didn't seem to notice the tension between Alex and me. Apparently, in the Dalton family it's perfectly normal for a couple to sit so far apart.

At lunch (after a terse discussion about which restaurant to choose, and angrily agreeing on Californian fusion), Alex bumped into some old university friends playing quoits on the top deck.

After the usual 'what a small world' banality, Alex asked the friends to join us for lunch.

Was even angrier then, because I was forced to be cordial and pull out a few smiles.

Sat like a well-behaved first lady at Alex's side, smiling politely and swallowing my fury.

To be fair, I couldn't really join in the conversation anyway, because I've never hit a partridge, grouse or pheasant with my Land Rover, all Champagne tastes the same to me and although I'm sure the royal family are 'charming', I've never met any of them in person.

By the time dessert came, the men were having a lengthy and confusing caviar debate. It got quite heated at one point, with one man standing and shouting about Iranian caviar being 'superb', and how dare you!'

Friday 16th March

Really sad and homesick today.

The ship's mobile phone service isn't working, so had to swallow my pride and borrow Alex's chunky satellite phone to call Daisy.

Mum picked up.

Cried when I heard her voice.

Mum asked what I was making so much fuss about, since I was in the lap of luxury.

Said I missed Daisy and the pub and normal people.

Mum said Daisy couldn't speak to me now, because she was up to her elbows in homemade playdough.

'Your dad has stirred up his usual bloody economical 3 lbs of salty flour and oil for Daisy's enjoyment,' Mum explained. 'Daisy has to play with it quickly before it turns rock hard.'

Cried some more.

Mum relented, and lured Daisy away from the playdough by laying a trail of Smarties along the landing.

'Mummy?' said Daisy, when she got to the phone.

Was so lovely to hear her voice.

'Gorgeous girl!' I said. 'Do you miss me?'

'No, Mummy,' said Daisy.

'I'm a long way away, Daisy,' I probed.

'I know, Mummy,' said Daisy. 'On a ship. With a *bed*.'

'I love you so much, Daisy,' I said.

Daisy didn't reply, so I prompted, 'Do you love me?'

Daisy said, 'Yes.' But I'm not sure there was much depth to the sentiment, because she added, 'And I love you and red Smarties.'

Mum came back on the phone after that and asked about the cruise.

I said it was luxurious, but lonely. Told her about Alex and the suite situation, and that Catrina is either drunk or unconscious most of the time.

'I miss Daisy so much,' I blubbed.

'Stop wallowing, love,' said Mum. 'Most mothers would love a couple of days off and a luxury cruise. Count your blessings.'

I suppose that's the thing when you've had kids.

You're tired when you're with them, guilty when you're not.

Saturday 17th March

Docked in Cannes today.

Catrina was delighted and put on a white trouser suit and lots of gold jewellery in preparation for Rue d'Antibes shopping.

'I am a little phobic of *French* French people,' Catrina declared. 'But Cannes is an international city. No one here is *French* French. They have good manners and clean bathrooms.' Then she regaled me with stories of yacht luncheons and fabulous times with Mick Jagger.

On the shuttle ferry to shore, Alex and I still weren't talking. Then Alex spoke fluent French to the gangway attendant, and I momentarily forgot I was angry with him.

'You speak French?' I asked.

'Oui,' Alex replied, with a wry smile. Then he told me that, as a boy, he'd briefly attended a French prep school on St Barts – the island he'd recently been stranded on.

'I learned to speak French quickly there,' Alex explained. 'Because the boys beat the living daylights out of anyone who didn't.'

'You were always such clever boys,' said Catrina, with a fond smile.

Sunday 18th March

Final port today.

Rome.

Can't believe time has passed so quickly.

Am taking Mum's advice and trying to appreciate this trip and have a nice time.

Life is too short to be grumpy with Alex, so have softened a little. I'm sure he had good, if misguided, reasons for booking his suite so far away.

We dock in Rome at midday, and I've accepted Alex's kind offer to take me for an Italian lunch.

Catrina isn't doing so well, so will probably stay on board. She had a panic attack this morning when the breakfast buffet ran out of smoked salmon, and was taken to the luxurious medical bay to calm down.

I think the staff there are quite used to glamorous, elderly attention-seekers. They knew just what to do, wrapping Catrina in a blue cashmere blanket and offering a small Italian sherry in a crystal glass 'for the stress'. Then they popped her in a wheelchair and rolled her out on deck to watch Rome appearing on the horizon.

She seemed happy enough when Alex and I came to check on her. The staff had left the sherry bottle on a little fold-out table by her wheelchair.

'I should rest here,' Catrina told us, refilling her sherry glass. 'I've seen Rome a hundred times. There's nothing new for me. All the olive oil and tiny little glasses of wine. It's as exciting as a kiss to a dead person. I'll let the medical staff take care of me.'

Personally, I'm looking forward to Rome. I've never been there before, and am expecting sun-baked streets, pinky-yellow buildings and endless flavours of whipped gelato.

Alex wants to take me for a 'real' Italian pizza when we dock. He patronisingly asked if I'd ever had pizza from a wood-burning oven before. Explained, in stern tones, that *of course* I had.

At Pizza Express.

Evening

Lovely day.

Rome was beautiful, and Alex was the perfect gentleman – protecting me from the mopeds that routinely shot out of alleyways.

We both threw coins in the Trevi Fountain, so tradition says we'll be back again one day.

Then we had lunch.

Had to concede Alex was right about the pizza – it was 'vastly superior' to my numerous Pizza Express experiences.

Ate chocolate gelato for dessert. Then pistachio gelato, as we passed the Vatican. Tried strawberry gelato by the Colosseum, and finally Ferrero Rocher flavour by the Trevi Fountain.

All very good.

On the way back to the ship, we passed a beautiful Italian boutique.

Alex asked if I wanted to choose a dress for dinner. Got embarrassed and mumbled no thank you, I'm fine.

Alex cut through this with a curt, 'Stop being so British.'

Relented, and tried on a stunning silver dress that flowed like water. Alex said he'd buy it for me, but I refused when I saw the price tag.

Five hundred and fifty euros!

You could buy twenty dresses for that at Top Shop.

Evening

Alex bought me the dress.

I think he must have sent Emmanuel out for it while we were having afternoon cocktails.

I *wondered* why Alex was so insistent I go back to my room and 'change for dinner'. In fact, it almost started an argument, because I thought my white summer dress and wedge shoes were perfectly fine.

Eventually, Alex persuaded me to 'at least get some warm clothing'. So I went back to the cabin, and there on the bed was the silver dress and a dripping real-diamond necklace.

Felt very taken care of and special.

While I was in the suite, I phoned home to check on Daisy.

Mum answered.

'Can I talk to Daisy?' I asked.

'Not right now,' said Mum. 'She's downstairs working in the pub.'

'Working in the pub?' I said. 'How is she working in the pub?'

'Oh, just wiping a few tables and putting the snacks out,' said Mum. 'Many hands make light work.'

Mum pushed aside my complaints of child exploitation, saying that Daisy was well paid.

'How is she being paid?' I demanded.

'She can have any flavour of crisps she wants,' said Mum.

Eventually persuaded Mum to go downstairs and get Daisy.

After much complaining, and huffing and puffing down the stairs, Mum put Daisy on.

'Mummy shit!' said Daisy.

Was momentarily confused. Then realised she meant, 'ship'.

'Yes, Mummy on ship,' I said. 'Home tomorrow.'

'Good Mummy. Miss Mummy.'

'I miss you too!' I said, delighted by the unprompted show of sentiment.

'And I miss Callum,' Daisy continued. 'He at school now. And I miss red rabbit shoes.'

Late evening

Lovely night.

Catrina went to bed early with a migraine and a bottle of Dom Perignon, so Alex and I had dinner alone.

It was magical.

I wore the silver dress, and Alex said I looked, 'unbelievably beautiful'. He suggested a seafood restaurant for our final night, so we had lobster and Champagne and watched the sun set over Rome.

An orchestra played while we ate (it made me think a little of the Titanic sinking, but I tried to put that out of my mind), so Alex and I listened to beautiful music and talked about nothing in particular.

The VERY best part of the evening was the late-night bridge game.

I thrashed every elderly person on the ship AND ultra-competitive Alex.

Glad I had those sessions with Nana Joan. Her memory palace technique really paid off.

Alex didn't come back to the suite with me. I suppose it would have been a bit strange, with his mother snoring next door. Or possibly he was bitter about being thrashed at cards. But it *was* our last night. Was sort of hoping for some kind of romantic action.

I guess, after all that miscarriage stuff, there's no hurry.

Monday 19th March

Flight home today.

Travelled first class, which was an experience.

I wish someone had told me everyone dresses up to travel first class. It was like a private members' club, with everyone in suits and other modes of formal dress.

My comfy travel sweats were very out of place.

Alex suggested 'the ladies' (Catrina and I) sit together, while he caught up on business. Was annoyed about that, but couldn't very well say so with Catrina right behind me.

Luckily, Catrina took a sleeping pill, pulled on a Burberry eye-mask and conked out in the seat beside me, so I got to enjoy the luxurious first-class experience without her paranoid ramblings about plane crashes.

I've become rather fond of Catrina on this trip. Yes, she's a little crazy, but so are my family. And she actually complimented my curly hair today, saying I looked like 'a young Jane Fonda, from when perms were popular'.

Afternoon

Home!

Ran into Mum and Dad's living room, arms outstretched for Daisy to run into.

Daisy eyed me warily. Then she said, 'Messy hair, Mummy. I get brush.'

It's true what Dad says. Kids live in the moment.

Evening

Just rang Alex to reminisce about the cruise.

He said, 'I don't want to speak to you.' Then he hung up.

Phoned him back, but he didn't answer.

Have sent texts, asking what's wrong, but he hasn't replied.

What on earth is going on?

Have a sickly feeling in my stomach.

Tuesday 20th March

Have texted and called Alex so many times now.

He won't answer.

Even rang Catrina Dalton, but she didn't answer.

Phoned Laura to ask if Zach knows anything, but he doesn't. Laura said she'd find out what she could, but advised me to keep busy in the meantime.

'Don't drive yourself crazy asking questions only Alex can answer,' Laura advised. 'I'm sure he'll be in touch soon. Just be patient. It's probably a simple misunderstanding.'

Decided to spring clean the cottage to take my mind off things, but it turned out to be impossible with Daisy trailing behind me, messing everything up.

In the end, I cracked and asked John Boy the questions only Alex can answer.

'What's going on? Why is Alex doing this? Why isn't he taking my calls? What could I have done?'

John Boy wasn't much help, saying Alex was beyond his male understanding.

'Usually blokes say what they mean,' he reasoned. 'But this is what girls do – go off in huffs and expect you to figure it out. And I don't understand girls.'

Wednesday 21st March

Shift at the pub last night.

Asked anyone who would listen about Alex, but the regulars soon got sick of me painting a hundred different scenarios.

In the end, I got so desperate that I talked to Yorkie. This was a silly thing to do, because everyone knows Yorkie stops making sense at eight o'clock.

Yorkie asked if I wanted Alex's kneecaps broken.

'No,' I said. 'I just want answers.'

'If I break his knee caps, he'll give me answers,' Yorkie reasoned.

It was the most sense he'd made all evening.

Thursday 22nd March

Still nothing from Alex.

Quite angry now. He could at least have the decency to tell me what's going on. It's torturous, being shut out like this.

Am trying to take my mind off things by enjoying time with Daisy. She's such a funny little thing. Callum has taught her a new song:

Old Macdonald had a bum, ee ai ee ai ooh.

And from that bum he did a poo, ee ai ee ai ooh.

To be fair, it's a fairly sophisticated lyrical construction for Callum, who usually sticks to straightforward swearing in his songs – the Callum classic 'bugger bugger poo poo' being one such example.

Friday 23rd March

Tried to talk to John Boy about Alex today.

John Boy refused at first, saying he was fed up with me 'banging on about that posh twat'. But he reluctantly agreed when I offered him chocolate marshmallow biscuits and a four-sugar cup of tea.

By John Boy's third chocolate marshmallow biscuit, he had an idea: 'Why don't you turn up somewhere you know Alex will be? Then he'll have to give you answers.'

'We move in pretty different social circles,' I said. 'We're not likely to bump into each other.'

'So how did you meet in the first place?' John Boy asked.

'In the woods as kids,' I said. 'But I doubt Alex hangs out in the woods any more. Unless he's weirder than I thought.'

Then I remembered something.

'Alex goes to Westminster Cathedral with his mother,' I said. 'Quite often, I think. Certainly for major services.'

'There you go then,' said John Boy. 'Just hang around outside one Sunday and wait to bump into him.'

'I'd feel like I was stalking him,' I said. 'There's no excuse for me hanging around Westminster Cathedral. I've got atheist written all over me.'

'What else can you do, if he's not returning your calls?' said John Boy. 'If heaven is worth fighting for, you've got to fight, fight, fight for this love.'

Have decided to follow John Boy and Cheryl Cole's advice and become a psycho stalker.

But not *this* Sunday.

Need to work up the courage, which could take a few weeks. And maybe Alex will have phoned by then.

Afternoon

Visited Althea in London this afternoon.

Wolfgang was having a full-on tantrum when we arrived. The tantrum was so bad that Althea had shut Wolfgang in his bedroom – something she rarely does, because it often means replacing the bedroom door.

Asked what the tantrum was about.

'He's upset because I recycled the horrible sexist Action Man his dad gave him,' said Althea. 'But attachment is the root of all suffering. Life is change. I told him to meditate and get over it.'

From upstairs I heard an ungodly howl, followed by a thump, ring! Thump ring!

Althea said Wolfgang was pounding his Buddhist prayer bowl against the wall.

We talked about Alex, but Althea was dismissive, telling me to let go and move on.

'You don't need that hot and cold shit,' she said. 'Kick him to the curb and find a nice, vegan man.'

But I really do want to find out what's going on.

Surely this is all some simple misunderstanding.

Saturday 24th March

Dropped Daisy off at Nick's house today for his visitation.

'You will make sure she gets a healthy lunch, won't you?' I asked. 'She's been at Mum and Dad's house a lot, so she's eaten loads of crap.'

Nick said he had a homemade asparagus quiche in the oven.

Backtracked then, knowing Daisy doesn't eat stuff like that. 'I mean, you can bend the healthy eating rule a bit,' I said. 'If she's really hungry. Don't let her get really hungry.'

Nick told me to stop being 'so controlling'.

I tentatively asked if Sadie had moved back in since the Tiny Tumbles episode. Nick said no – he doesn't know where she is but suspects she's staying with her mother in Southampton.

That's around 200 miles away.

Which is excellent.

Sunday 25th March

Horrible day.

SADIE was at Nick's house when I picked up Daisy.

I could hear her banshee screeching, 'WHERE THE FUCK IS MY VIVIEN WESTWOOD FEDORA!' as I walked up the garden path.

Felt sick to my stomach.

Pounded on the stained-glass door and banshee screeched back,

'DAISY! DAISY! MUMMY'S HERE! NICK, BRING ME MY DAUGHTER THIS INSTANT!'

Nick opened the door, looking flustered.

'Sadie came back last night,' he said, in a terse whisper. 'Don't blame me. I'm a victim in all this.'

'Why didn't you tell me?' I shouted. 'I would have come and picked up Daisy.'

'I didn't want to wake Daisy up,' Nick wheedled. 'And we've had fun this morning, the dynamic duo. We made pancakes. Sadie only got up half an hour ago.'

'I don't want Sadie's craziness around Daisy,' I bellowed, storming into the house and lifting a bewildered Daisy from the breakfast bar. 'Where's her coat? And why is she only wearing one shoe?'

Spent an awkward five minutes waiting, while Nick hunted for Daisy's other red rabbit shoe. He finally found it, soaking wet, under a flowerpot in the garden.

'Think about Daisy,' I said. 'She shouldn't be around this craziness.'

'You can talk,' said Nick. 'Have you been round your parents' house lately?'

'My parents love Daisy,' I said. 'Sadie doesn't love anyone but herself.'

Nick got all puffed up then. '*Legally*, I can have anyone I want here. So don't make a big fuss, yeah? We don't want to end up back in court.'

Monday 26th March

Spoke to Laura re Sadie being at Nick's house and the legal side of things.

It's true.

Nick can have over whoever he wants while Daisy is there, as long as they haven't been convicted of a sexual or violent offence.

Laura hadn't heard anything about Alex. Zach was 'completely in the dark', and Catrina Dalton doesn't know anything either.

Phoned Mum on the way home and told her how upset I felt – both about the Sadie situation and the continued radio silence from Alex.

Mum asked if I wanted to come round for a glass of wine.

Thought this was an odd comment, because Mum usually offers me Guinness, or a shot of whatever random liquor isn't selling well at the pub.

It turns out Mum has joined a wine club. She's bought herself a huge balloon glass that fits a whole bottle of wine and is having twelve 'carefully selected vintages' delivered to the pub every month.

Warned Mum about diabetes and excessive alcohol, but she's convinced red wine is some sort of health drink – citing Dr Slaughter as a reference.

It is typical of Mum to pick and choose Dr Slaughter's words of wisdom. He's told her to reduce salt and sugar, eat more vegetables and switch to decaffeinated coffee – none of which she's done. But the dubious alcohol advice she chooses to take on board.

I've never met a doctor who doesn't drink, yet they're the ones who commission all the 'a glass of wine is good' studies.

Tuesday 27th March

Daisy had a nightmare last night and came into my room. She was a ghostly, shadowy figure at the end of my bed, breathing like Darth Vader.

Nearly screamed the house down, but managed to hold it together and only shrieked: 'Jesus fucking Christ, what is THAT!'

John Boy came hopping into the room with no shirt on, wielding his metal leg as a weapon.

'It's OK,' I told him. 'It's just Daisy.'

John Boy hopped back to his room. Ten seconds later I heard snoring.

Quite impressive how John Boy can go from 'ready to fight' to 'fast asleep' within ten seconds. I suppose it's all his army experiences.

Asked Daisy about her bad dream. She said that Daddy's girlfriend hit her with a giant bean.

Panicked.

Quizzed Daisy about Daddy's house.

Daisy told me again about the 'yuck pie' (the quiche), strange-tasting green ice cream (possibly pistachio flavour?) and watching the *Lion King*. Then she talked about Daddy's girlfriend screaming and covered up her ears.

'Want to sleep in your bed,' Daisy sobbed. 'Ever and ever.'

Have a horrible knot in my stomach today.

I can't let Daisy stay with Nick again – not if Sadie could be there. And I know this is going to cause a massive drama.

Phoned Alex.

Predictably, he didn't answer, so I sent another humiliating text asking what I'd done wrong.

He hasn't replied.

If I think about Alex too much, it drives me a little bit crazy. It's the not *knowing* and not being able to know. Surely he realises this is torture?

Wednesday 28th March

Phoned Nick to talk about the Sadie situation.

Tried to remember our counselling sessions, and refrained from describing Sadie as 'mental', 'bat-shit crazy' or 'a banshee'.

Said Daisy had a nightmare about Sadie, and it was very important not to have the wrong people around when Daisy came over.

Nick got all formal and said he'd spoken to his solicitor, who confirmed there was no legal reason why Sadie couldn't be around.

Lost my temper then and shouted, 'But Nick, Sadie is bat-shit crazy. She's a bloody banshee. Daisy's been having *nightmares* about her mentalness.'

'Don't give me more problems, Jules,' Nick whispered. 'It's bad enough managing Sadie. She's got nowhere to go now she and her mum have fallen out. If I kick her out at weekends, she'll go crazy.'

That's the whole trouble with Nick – deep down he's a coward.

'Man up, Nick,' I snapped. 'And think about your daughter, for once in your life.'

Thursday 29th March

Feeling a bit overwhelmed today.

Don't know what I'm going to do about the Nick/Sadie situation.

On the positive side, I do have another holiday to look forward to – sunny Corfu in May. It'll be fun going away with the family, and quite a change from the luxurious, formal cruise ship. They'll be waterslides and a slushie machine for Mum, and a kids' club for Daisy and Callum.

Told Daisy about our sunshine break.

'We're going to Greece,' I enthused. 'Lots of exciting feta cheese and syrupy pastries. There'll be a big swimming pool and a waterslide.'

Daisy was very excited about swimming with Nana. 'Geronimo!' she shouted, imitating Mum whooshing down a waterslide.

Was a little hurt, because I'm fun in the swimming pool too, albeit a little more focused on water safety and technique.

Daisy now has a new game called 'holidays'. The game involves filling her Dora the Explorer suitcase with things like toilet roll, towels, my shoes, an ornamental cactus and the chicken breast I bought for tea. She has also packed the central heating controller somewhere, and now doesn't know where it is.

Explained the seriousness of this to Daisy, but she didn't understand because she doesn't feel the cold.

'Not chilly, Mummy,' said Daisy. 'LOVELY sunshine.' But the thermostat says it's only 12 degrees in the house.

If I were an employer, I would be taken to task for breaking health and safety regulations.

Friday 30th March
Good Friday

Can't believe it's Good Friday already.

Haven't bought Easter eggs, let alone arranged child-friendly Easter activities.

Headed into town to load up on chocolate and ended up in Poundland with a basketful of Easter egg misshape bargains.

Daisy had Christmas money from Nana Joan, so I let her go mad in the toy aisle, stocking up on plastic crap. She chose a water pistol that won't shoot water, a twenty-piece tool set (three screwdrivers have already snapped) and a kite that broke off its flimsy cotton thread and flew away. The only thing that hasn't broken is a fluffy bunny she's named 'Curry'.

Althea would say that Daisy has learned a lesson about possessions and attachment. But I fear the opposite is true.

Daisy was so traumatised by the lost kite that she has become extremely attached to the broken water pistol and Curry the rabbit (who has now lost an ear).

At tea time, Daisy sat Curry on her knee and asked John Boy philosophical questions about how missing body parts might affect a rabbit.

Saturday 31st March

Daisy is cranky as anything today – partly because Curry the rabbit lost his other ear, but also because her back molars are coming through.

With all the horrors of baby teething behind us, I'd forgotten there were more teeth to come.

Althea confirmed that molar growth can create mood swings in children. She speaks from experience, because all Wolfgang's teeth have come through now. He still has one giant front tooth that dominates his mouth, but a collection of pointed fangs have now joined it.

Admitted I'd called and texted Alex again. Althea was very kind, saying, 'You're only human, Julesy. Of course you want answers. But haven't you got all the answers you need? I mean, do you really want to be with someone who acts this way? Cuts you out of their life without explanation?'

Told her she didn't know Alex like I do. 'He gets crazy jealous because of his messed-up childhood and can flick his feelings off like a switch,' I explained.

'That sounds like battered-wife bullshit to me,' said Althea. 'Find yourself a nice, sane man who shops organic and doesn't drive a wanker sports car. Look, do you want to come over mine and do some art-textile therapy? Wolfy and I are making modern Easter sculptures. I've got a load of wrought iron and a new welding set-up in the shed.'

Politely declined. I haven't done art textiles since school, when I was emotionally abused during my GCSE project.

I made a space rocket with chicken wire and papier-mâché, then painted it light red. The rocket looked exactly like a giant penis, with my name stuck at the base.

I had to stand for assessment, while pupils *and* teachers laughed at my sculpture.

My art teacher, Mrs Winterbottom, let me down that day. She brought in three other staff members to point and snigger.

Sunday 1st April
Easter Sunday

Plucked up the courage to stalk Alex.

Needless to say, it didn't end well.

Laura told me that Alex and Catrina were attending the Westminster Cathedral Easter Service, so I left Daisy for a chocolate fest with Mum and took the train to London.

The plan was just to find out *why* Alex has gone all cold. I know Althea is right – Alex shouldn't have cut me off without explanation. But I reasoned if we could just *talk* to each other, I can at least move forward.

After hellish rail-replacement bank holiday train service, I arrived in London and hung around outside the cathedral like a Victorian orphan waiting for scraps.

When the service finished and the crowds poured out, I thought Alex wasn't there at first. But then I saw him, dressed in a fitted, black suit, his skin gleaming. Catrina was beside him, done up like a Christmas turkey in a peacock blue coat, matching pillar-box hat and white gloves.

On Alex's other side was a pretty, blonde girl, who wore a bright red coat and a star-struck smile.

As I watched, Alex took the girl's arm to help her down the steps. She looked shy and delighted.

My heart dropped to my stomach.

Had a sort of out-of-body experience and marched up to Alex screaming things.

Alex glared at me, then said, 'Have you quite finished?'

'What did I do to deserve this?' I shouted. 'After everything we've been through this year. To just cut me out with no explanation.'

'I don't owe you any explanation,' said Alex. 'It's you who owes *me* an explanation.' Then he stalked away.

Catrina followed Alex, smiling and waving at no one in particular, but the blonde girl stayed where she was.

'You're Juliette, aren't you?' she said, offering a kind smile. 'I'm Bethany. Alex has told me about you.'

'What has he told you?' I said. 'What's going on? We went on a cruise together. Everything was fine, and now he's just cut me out.'

The girl's eyes turned sad. 'Look, I think you have to move forward. Alex and I…it's going well. We're both excited about the future. Take care, OK?'

As the girl walked away, I stood in my shell of a body, feeling my aching, broken heart.

Got home to find Daisy and Callum both on a massive sugar high, tearing around the pub, hitting each other with Easter egg baskets.

Mum had let them eat a whole Easter egg each, plus three slices of 'unicorn' cake (Betty Crocker frosted chocolate cake covered with a 'rainbow' of M&Ms).

Wanted to cuddle Daisy but had to catch her first – which took some doing.

Felt reassured knowing that Daisy will always love me.

She has to.

It's sort of the law.

I think Daisy realised I was emotionally vulnerable, because she asked if she could eat her Smarties Easter egg from Nana Joan, and order Dominoes for tea.

Agreed to both things.

Went to bed after tea and cried myself to sleep.

Monday 2nd April

'WHY?' I keep asking, over and over again. 'The cruise was great. Why did he just ditch me like that? Why is he seeing HER? WHY?'

No one can give me any answers, and everyone is sick of my questions. I got so desperate, I even phoned Nick to ask why a man would go all cold and start seeing someone else.

'Probably a sex thing,' Nick replied, which made me feel a hundred times worse.

The school Easter holidays start today, and Callum is off for TWO weeks.

Understand now why parents complain about school holidays being so long.

Just want to wallow in heartbreak at the pub, but Callum is shooting round like a chipmunk.

Mum says I should look at the positives.

'What positives?' I asked.

'Well,' Mum reasoned, 'telling Callum off is distracting you from your love-life drama.'

Tuesday 3rd April

Nick phoned late last night with a drunk confession.

To cut a long story short, I need to kill Sadie.

'I have to get something off my chest, Julesy,' Nick told me, words slurred. 'It's to do with wanker Dalton. I did something stupid.'

Went quiet then, because Nick is always doing something stupid. For him to be phoning to admit something...well, it must be major.

'I told Sadie about your miscarriage,' said Nick.

I'd forgotten what a girly gossip Nick can be.

'It's all right,' I said. 'I don't mind people knowing. What's this got to do with Alex?'

'Sadie thought it was my baby,' said Nick. 'She thinks I got you pregnant.'

'Why?' I asked.

'She put two and two together and made one hundred,' said Nick. 'Because I mentioned your miscarriage, Sadie got jealous and thought it must be my child.'

Nick went on to tell me that Sadie had shared news of our 'affair' with a theatre friend, who was close to the Dalton family.

'So I reckon that's why posh twat Dalton doesn't want to know you any more,' said Nick. 'It's going to come out sooner or later, so I thought I'd better do damage limitation. Before you rip my bollocks off.'

Suddenly, everything clicked into place.

So *that's* why Alex stopped talking to me. He thinks I got pregnant by Nick. What an *arsehole*. How could he believe that?

Would ordinarily be annoyed with Nick for sharing my news, but to be fair, he couldn't have guessed that Sadie would twist things in her mind.

I'M furious now – with Alex, more than anyone else.

How could Alex believe third-hand gossip without talking to me? And then move on to someone else so quickly?

Sadie has done me a favour. She's helped me see who Alex REALLY is.

Thank goodness I didn't end up having a baby with him.

Forget him and his jealousy and his bloody weird family.

What an arsehole.

Wednesday 4th April

Lay awake last night, furious with Alex and everything he's put me through.

To believe I'd get pregnant by Nick, and then pass Alex off as the father! And then to cut me out, without saying a word, and hook up with some blonde Sloane Square husband-hunter type. To put me through that *torture*. How dare he!

Phoned Althea at 1 am, complaining that I had fury insomnia.

Althea is good to phone late at night, because she has no set sleep cycle.

'Acid burns the vessel,' said Althea. 'You've got to let that shit go, Jules. Karma will do the work.'

When I explained that Alex had believed a third-hand vicious rumour and got himself a new girlfriend, Althea said, 'Fucking hell. What a massive cunt. Forget karma. Go and shit on his doorstep, the big, posh twat.'

Appreciated the support.

Phoned Laura. She said she'd tell Alex how the rumour started the next time he came over to see Zach.

'I wouldn't bother,' I said. 'I don't even care any more. If he could believe something like that, I'm better off without him.'

Went round Mum and Dad's this morning for a bit of family love.

Unfortunately, Mum and Dad aren't speaking to each other.

They've had a row about After Eight mints.

Dad bought three boxes from Tesco at £1 each (a 70% saving), ready for Christmas. He was very pleased with his economic purchase, until he discovered Mum had eaten all three boxes.

Mum was unrepentant.

'He's lived with me for thirty years,' she said. 'He should know by now that if he brings chocolates into the house I'll eat them.'

Dad, who was listening from the study, shouted back: 'Three whole boxes, Shirley! In as many days. You're supposed to be on a diet.'

'Oh for Christ's sake Bob, they're only wafer-thin mints,' Mum shouted back.

Then she put on the Rolling Stones at full volume.

Dad retaliated by playing his Best of Cambridge Folk Festival CD.

Thursday 5th April

Brandi is seeing a Kurt Cobain lookalike called Richie Pitt. She must be serious about him, because she's let him meet Callum.

Asked Callum what Richie was like.

Callum shrugged. 'He's not like Mum's usual boyfriends. He's got a job.'

Sometimes, Callum startles me with his mature observations. Other times, I wonder how he'll ever survive childhood when he burns himself *every morning* on Brandi's hair straighteners.

Apparently, Richie took Brandi and Callum to a gaming café yesterday.

'You'd think gaming would be fun, but it wasn't a great choice for a child,' Callum informed me. 'There were no kids' meals or colouring books or anything, and all the games were really complicated. But I *did* get to roll a seven-sided dice, so I think maybe Richie's all right. If he gets a decent haircut.'

Callum proceeded to critique Richie's style, starting with his floppy, blonde chin-length hair and ending with his scruffy trainers.

'If you wear white trainers, you have to keep them clean,' Callum declared. 'Otherwise you end up looking scruffy. He's an adult. He should *know* that.'

Friday 6th April

Visit from health visitor, Pam Fairy, today.

She came to do Daisy's two-year health check.

Daisy is two and a half now – another indicator of our NHS in crisis.

I'd completely forgotten about the appointment, and was shouting, 'DAISY! Will you *stop* saying bollocks,' as I opened the front door.

I was expecting the Amazon delivery man, so seeing Pam was a shock.

Rapidly shushed Daisy, who was shouting, 'ollocks, ollocks' in the background.

Pam wore a woolly cardigan over her huge bust and smiled kindly at the state of the house.

'You don't need to tidy up on my account,' she said, sitting her bulky bottom on a kitchen stool. 'I've seen plenty of messy houses.' But I still did a rapid tidy, throwing slippery *Walking Dead* comics, singing toys and inappropriate DVDs aside.

Everyone knows health visitors are looking for neglect.

Made Pam a cup of tea, while she got out her shiny, white baby scales.

'Sorry the visit is half a year late,' said Pam, pressing the button on her scales. 'But resources are stretched tight at the minute. If I want so much as a Jaffa Cake, it comes out of my own pocket.'

Offered Pam one of John Boy's chocolate digestives, and she seemed grateful.

Then Brandi and Callum turned up unexpectedly.

Told Brandi the health visitor was here, and she'd have to come back later.

'But I promised Callum he could see his cousin,' said Brandi. 'He'll be ever so disappointed.'

Relented, with the proviso that Callum would be exceptionally well-behaved.

Introduced my sister and nephew to Pam Fairy, then offered Callum a chocolate biscuit.

'Those biscuits are *bollocks* for kids, Aunty Julesy,' said Callum. 'Don't you have any Barney Bears or party rings?'

I tried to pretend Callum hadn't said 'bollocks', and asked: 'What's the magic word?'

Callum looked at me blankly. 'Abracadabra?'

Asked Pam a lot of anxious mum questions, like:

✦ Why is Daisy's nose running *all* the time? Is it because I didn't breastfeed?

  ✦ Is it normal that she wakes up at 6 am?

  ✦ How can I stop her swearing?

  ✦ Pam gave the usual vague, non-committal responses like, 'it's just a phase', and 'she'll grow out of it' and 'every child is different'.

Had a lot of other questions, but Pam kept checking her watch.

In the end, I was glad she left early.

Callum had just spelled out 'COCK' with the Junior Scrabble set.

Saturday 7th April

It was supposed to be Nick's weekend with Daisy, but I'm refusing visitation until the Sadie issue is resolved. That ugly, paranoid rumour she spread was the last straw – I'm not having my daughter around a jealous maniac who makes unfounded accusations.

I know it's sort of illegal, but I have to protect my child. If Sadie is paranoid enough to think Nick knocked me up again AND go round telling people, what else is she capable of?

Mum has suggested we all go to the seaside tomorrow, since I'll have Daisy first thing and the pub is closed for maintenance.

Have agreed to come with the proviso that Mum wears her swimming costume on the beach ONLY, and not strolling along the promenade.

Afternoon

Alex called.

Didn't answer.

Then Alex called again and again and again, until I finally picked up and shouted, 'What?'

After a long, awkward silence, Alex said, 'I just wanted you to know. The girl you saw outside the church. Her name is Bethany and she's a family friend. She also works in my marketing department.'

Felt sick, hearing her name.

'I have nothing to say to you,' I said. Then I changed my mind, and proceeded to tell Alex, at length, how much pain he'd caused me and how disgusting it was that he'd believed that rumour.

'I don't believe it now,' said Alex. 'Does that help? Your sister was good enough to tell me how the rumour started.'

'But you believed it originally,' I said. 'How *could* you? As if I'd *do* something like that.'

'Jealousy,' said Alex. 'I was blinded by it. I want you to know I'm seeing a cognitive behavioural therapist. Bethany suggested it. A lot of things have come up – some betrayals from childhood that are colouring my perceptions. The therapist thinks I've buried a lot of trauma.'

'This isn't about projection,' I said. 'It's about respect.'

'I respect you, Juliette,' said Alex. 'But trauma and logic don't always co-exist. I'm working on it. I don't know what else to say. It probably is for the best that we're not in a relationship while I deal with all this.'

I laughed. 'You call what we had a relationship? A few car trips to London and sporadic sexual intercourse? We didn't even share a suite on the cruise.'

'I was trying to be respectful. We'd not long lost our baby.' Alex's voice broke then. 'Listen, I'm sorry I believed the rumour. But you haven't helped things. Letting Nick Spencer come over whenever he feels like it.'

'Don't start blaming me for this,' I said. 'Nick is Daisy's father. I can't keep him away.'

'You were letting him come around whenever he wanted. No planned visits. It was disrespectful. He knew that. Look – what are you doing tomorrow?'

'Mum has arranged a trip to the seaside,' I said. 'I don't really want to go, but she's insisting on a family day out.'

'The seaside?' said Alex. 'Christ – is that what the great British public do at the weekend these days?'

'What's wrong with the seaside?' I asked.

'Insufferable seaside art and tatty beach toys that fall apart in seconds. I'll never forget Jemima, in floods of tears over a snapped spade.'

'Don't you have any hotels by the seaside?' I asked.

'Of course not,' Alex replied. 'Not the British seaside. My hotels are high-end. Listen – Juliette. I've made a terrible mess of things. I understand that. You may never forgive me, but can I at least see Daisy? I don't want her thinking I've forgotten her, just because you and I aren't getting along. Can I join you on this trip tomorrow? We're both grown-ups, aren't we?'

'You just said you hated the seaside,' I pointed out.

'I can have my PA source some decent spades. Make the best of it.'

In the end, I relented – for Daisy's sake.

Alex and I have no future, but I know Daisy misses him. She often pretends to be a driver and takes her teddies to London in a fancy black car. And she won't shut up about all those 'yummy scrummy' meals Alex made her.

It's annoying, because there's no way I'm making my own pesto.

Evening

Shift at the pub tonight.

Daisy and I had tea with Mum and Dad.

We spent the whole meal guessing what Alex will wear to the

beach.

'He can't wear leather shoes,' said Mum. 'But I can't imagine him in anything else.'

We are all perplexed.

Sunday 8th April

Alex wore a polo shirt, long white shorts and deck shoes. Leather ones. He met us at the train station, hands in pockets, swinging a bag of spades.

'Hello, Juliette,' said Alex, putting a delighted Daisy on his shoulders and shaking hands with my parents. 'Good morning, Mr and Mrs Duffy.'

Mum said, 'Don't expect a bloody fanfare from me after you believed that *shit* about my daughter.'

Alex replied tactfully, 'Let me help you get those things on the train. I've upgraded you to first-class.' He manoeuvred the pram and Mum's giant beach bag into the first-class carriage, then lowered Daisy onto a comfy leather chair.

Mum was delighted with the luxurious accommodation and extra-large seats.

'You get a proper amount of bum room here,' she enthused. 'And look. Free biscuits.'

Dad was treacherous to his egalitarian 'one class for all' ideals, enjoying tea in a china cup and 'none of this polystyrene nonsense'.

When we dismounted the train, Dad took big lungfuls of 'clean, sea air' and told us, yet again, about his boyhood visits to Scottish beaches, and the 'bracing frost' on the sand at this time of year.

Mum moaned about the five-minute walk to the promenade.

As we looked for a good sandy spot to rest our things, Dad tutted about all the shops selling plastic rubbish and colourful sugared rock and lollies.

'We never had any of this in my day,' said Dad. 'Look at all this toot. Inflatable unicorns! It's consumerism gone mad.'

Mum said, 'Oh don't be such a bloody killjoy, Bob,' then proceeded to buy an inflatable unicorn, four cans of Vanilla coke and two giant swirly lollies.

When we finally found a good spot, Dad hammered in the windbreaker, set up chairs and laid out a tartan picnic cloth. He informed Mum, in his sternest voice, that she was *not* to open the picnic box until he'd got everything laid out.

'He's always been like this,' Mum informed Alex. 'You can't have so much as a sticky bun until he's got everything just so. I don't pay any attention.' Then she opened the picnic box.

'What's happened here?' said Mum, a panicked note in her voice. 'The sausage rolls are gone. There's no sausage rolls. Bob, there are no sausage rolls!'

We all looked inside the picnic box and found Mum was right. The sausage rolls and other picnic items had been replaced with Curry the rabbit, plastic gem stones, some hardback books, a bible and several large rocks. The only food item left was a single bag of Walker's prawn cocktail crisps.

I immediately suspected Daisy.

'Daisy,' I asked. 'Where's all the food?'

Daisy explained she'd put the picnic food in Mum and Dad's bed to keep warm.

I didn't have the heart to tell Daisy off. She meant well.

Luckily the chip shop was open, so we brought five polystyrene trays of chips and Mum finally calmed down.

After lunch, Mum gave Daisy a giant swirly lollipop (very possibly grown in the merry old land of Oz). This was against my advice and resulted in a huge sugar-induced tantrum.

Daisy because irrationally furious with a little boy in a yellow t-shirt.

'NO, boy. DON'T like yellow. Take it OFF.'

Daisy screamed and screamed at the impertinence of the yellow t-shirt, making angry gouges in the sand with her chubby little fingers.

I tried to cuddle her, but she thrashed and wiggled and scratched my face, shouting obscurely, 'WANT Cuddle! CUDDLE!'

'Daisy,' I said. 'I'm already giving you a cuddle.'

This triggered a meltdown of mega proportions. Red-faced rage, hitting, scratching, biting, helpless crying.

'Juliette, can I be useful?' Alex asked.

'No, I'm fine!' I lied, feeling the burn of vibrant red scratches.

'Shove some crisps in her face,' said Mum. 'That always did the trick when you were little.'

The crisps worked, but the scratches on my face needed first aid.

Luckily, Dad had brought his St John's Ambulance kit, and was able to administer TCP.

Nice day in the end.

Everyone was pleased Alex bought those extra spades, because all the ones Mum bought snapped.

While we were sitting on the sand, drinking cans of Vanilla Coke and eating crisps, Alex said: 'We never did things like this in our family.'

'You lived in the Bahamas,' I said. 'You've had your fair share of beaches.'

'Not with my parents,' said Alex. 'And my grandparents lived in Hungary and West Virginia. We hardly ever saw them.' He threw a stone at the water. 'But I can't change who I am or where I came from. Any more than I can fix those broken spades.'

Daisy came running up then. She'd dug a hole she was especially proud of and wanted to show it off.

Unfortunately, the yellow t-shirt boy had dug a rival hole beside Daisy's.

It was twice as big, with a perimeter of pretty shells around it.

I don't think the boy meant to be competitive – he was just an artistic little fellow, humming quietly to himself as he made slight alterations to the shell design.

Daisy gritted her little teeth, clenched her fists and shook with rage. Then she pushed the boy into his hole.

The little boy started crying.

I shouted at Daisy, then apologised profusely to the little boy.

The little boy's dad came running over, looking furious. I thought he was going to tell Daisy off, but instead he shouted at his son, calling him 'a pathetic little cry baby'.

It was horrible.

'He's not pathetic,' I said. 'My little girl pushed him.'

'You're a skinny weed,' the man sneered at his son. 'Get a hold of yourself, or I'll give you something to cry about.'

'Leave him alone,' I said. 'He didn't do anything.'

'Who asked you, you silly cow?' the man replied.

Mum leapt to her feet, but Alex was already beside me. He put an arm around my shoulder, pointed a threatening finger at the man and said, 'Apologise immediately.'

The man gave a reluctant sorry.

Alex talked in a low, authoritarian voice about bullying children and the long-term impact of verbal abuse.

The dad broke, talking about his own chaotic upbringing.

'I know I'm not doing things the right way,' he sobbed. 'But I've never *seen* the right way.' In the end, he agreed to phone a free counselling service that Alex recommended.

On the train home, I told Alex how impressed I was that he told the man off.

'You found *that* impressive?' Alex asked. 'My company turns over millions of pounds every year.'

'Yes, but it takes courage to stand up to people like that.'

'It wasn't courageous,' said Alex. 'There was nothing to be afraid of. Trying to win you back – now that would be courageous.'

Monday 9th April

Phoned Laura to talk about the beach trip.

It feels nice that Alex still cares about me and Daisy.

'But he won't change,' I lamented. 'He said so himself. And now he's seeing this other girl. How can I get over him dating someone else?'

When Laura didn't take the bait, I said, 'Have you heard anything about this girl he's seeing?'

Laura said no.

'But she met his *mother*,' I said. 'Things must be pretty serious.'

'Not necessarily,' said Laura. 'The Daltons aren't like a normal family. It's all lunch dates and power games. Harold Dalton has rewritten his will at least twenty times.'

Tuesday 10th April

Visited Nana Joan today.

She's at war with a fellow care-home resident – a busty Nigerian lady called Carmen Akawolo.

Nana is furious because Carmen has been given special permission to make banana puff puffs in the care home kitchen.

Nana is especially annoyed, because a new resident she has her eye on (a man called Tony Champion, who keeps horses and has two new metal knees) is a fan of the banana puff puffs and gets up early to enjoy the first batch.

'I'm telling you, she can only push me so far,' said Nana. 'Any more disrespect, and I'll smash in those perfect white teeth of hers.'

I made Nana some calming camomile tea, and we got chatting

about *Game of Thrones*.

'That Sansa Stark,' Nana tutted, shaking her head. 'What that girl's been through. It's a crime.'

Nana has reached the age where she talks about fictional people like they're real.

After I'd made her some toast on her portable gas stove, we looked at mobility scooter websites.

Nana doesn't really need a mobility scooter – she could just as easily catch the bus. But there's a real 'keeping up with the Jones' at her old people's home. When one old person gets a fancy reclining chair with massage function, suddenly they all 'need' one.

The scooter Nana wants is called Easy Rider and comes in a choice of over fifty cushion fabrics.

Nana wanted smiley emoji fabric, but we agreed that wipe-clean faux leather was more practical, although a little bit 'sex dungeon' with the gleaming silver wheel rims Nana favours.

Asked her why she liked the Easy Rider model, with its heavy motor and huge wheels. Wouldn't she prefer the small, compact design of the 'Driving Miss Daisy' scooter?

Nana replied ominously that she wanted power to ram if necessary.

Bumped into Carmen Akowolo on the way out. She was smiling her lovely smile and offering banana puff puffs around the communal lounge.

Carmen patted Daisy on the head, called her 'a little darling' and pressed two buns into Daisy's fingers – one for now, one for the journey home.

Daisy shared one of the banana puff puffs with me.

It was delicious.

I didn't tell Nana.

Wednesday 11th April

John Boy is helping out in the pub kitchen while the chef is away.

Wasn't sure if this was sensible, having seen John Boy's reliance on packet noodles, but it turns out he made breakfast in the army.

The pub menu has been changed temporarily. It now only offers one meal: sausage, fried eggs, baked beans and bacon. John Boy may extend his range tomorrow and offer toast as a side order. He's enjoying being in the kitchen and considering getting a hygiene certificate/basic catering qualification.

It seems like a positive step.

John Boy didn't do well in his GCSEs. He wasn't entered for maths or English, but was allowed to sit subjects that schools don't really respect, like woodwork and art. He got a C in art, but failed everything else.

As John Boy puts it, 'You could spell FUC with my results.'

Thursday 12th April

Am considering local nurseries for Daisy.

She'll get free funding when she's three years old – which isn't so far away – and it will be good for her to be around other children.

Daisy loves Callum and Wolfgang to bits, but I'd like to broaden her horizons. Perhaps find some friends who don't swear as much or tease her for enjoying Disney movies.

Wolfgang has already started nursery, so phoned Althea for advice.

Althea likes nurseries as a concept (a surprise – I thought she'd find it all too establishment), but doesn't like Wolfgang's current childcare set-up.

Reading between the lines, Wolfgang is the problem, not the nursery. Staff are struggling to handle him, and he's responded to discipline by doing dirty protests in the cosy corner.

Friday 13th April

Nick's day with Daisy tomorrow.

Texted to say he is welcome to see her at our house.

Nick hasn't replied yet.

Typical.

Afternoon

Nick rang, demanding to see Daisy at his house, even though Sadie is home.

'Well we're at an empath,' I said. 'Because I'm not leaving Daisy in a house with a mental case.'

'Do you mean an impasse?' Nick said.

Grudgingly admitted that yes, I did mean an impasse.

'Why can't you see Daisy at my house?' I asked.

'I can't do that,' said Nick. 'Sadie will go mental. I like my testicles where they are.'

'Well Daisy can't come round to yours,' I said.

'This is illegal,' said Nick.

'So was not paying maintenance,' I countered.

'Two wrongs don't make a right,' Nick replied. 'Look, I know Sadie's mental, but she wouldn't hurt a child.'

'She's insane,' I said. 'She said all that crazy stuff about me being pregnant with your baby.'

'So that's what this is about,' said Nick, in an infuriating Columbo voice. 'You're trying to get your own back because I talked about your miscarriage.'

'Not at *all*,' I snapped. 'Daisy had nightmares last time she was round at yours. There's no way I'm putting her through the stress of you and Sadie shouting and arguing.'

'Daisy thought *that* was an argument?' said Nick. 'That was Sadie mildly irritated. When Sadie argues, things get broken.'

As if that was supposed to make me feel any better.

Nick refused to come round to mine and refused to ask Sadie to leave.

So we really are at an empath. I mean, an impasse.

Saturday 14th April

Althea is going to Legoland tomorrow and has offered me a free adult ticket worth £30, plus a 'kids go free' voucher.

The adult ticket was originally for Wolfgang's dad, but he backed out at the last minute when Althea refused to put reins on Wolfgang.

I've accepted the free tickets, much to Daisy's delight and excitement, and offered to drive us all down there tomorrow (Althea doesn't want to ride her moped and sidecar on the M25).

Have moved my pub shift around, so I can sleep over at Althea's tonight in preparation for a 7 am set-off.

Need to chivvy Althea in the getting-ready stakes, because otherwise we'll end up leaving at midday. It's all very well believing time is a man-made construct, but Legoland has set closing hours and I intend to get maximum value from my free tickets.

Got a few angry text messages from Nick this morning, but am ignoring them.

Althea thinks there'll be consequences.

She's probably right. Nick is a sneaky, vengeful sort. But what else can I do?

Mum also thinks I'm doing the wrong thing. She says that Sadie's shouting isn't the end of the world, and I'll turn Daisy into a wimp if I'm not careful.

'Your dad and I argue every day,' said Mum. 'And you turned out just fine.'

'I didn't turn out just fine,' I said. 'I'm separated from the feckless father of my first child. I got pregnant by someone totally cold and aloof. Now aforementioned feckless dickhead is living with my horrible ex-best friend and creating a toxic environment for my child. I don't see my life as "just fine". I see it as "massive room for improvement".'

Felt like a real failure then, and cried.

Mum told me to go have a brandy.

Didn't have any brandy, so had a shot of John Boy's Malibu (he's made me swear not to tell anyone he drinks this).

Mum was right.

Alcohol did make me feel better.

Sunday 15th April

Legoland.

Was aiming for a 7 am set-off, but realistically that was never going to happen.

Wolfgang needed a cooked vegetarian breakfast (three eggs, five Linda McCartney vegetarian sausages, fried halloumi, mushrooms, tomatoes and a thick slice of fried rye bread) before we could leave, and Daisy had the usual meltdown about wearing clothes.

The car journey wasn't too bad – we only suffered minor damage to the car interior. But we didn't get to Legoland until lunchtime.

After eating our picnic, the kids fought over which rides to go on first.

Wolfgang wanted something thrilling, and Daisy wanted something pink.

Althea had to bellow 'Oi!' to bring the children to order. Then she told them she would make the decision.

After ten minutes of turning the map around and around, Althea finally settled on the Duplo play area, because it had 'awesome Lego sculptures'.

We set off.

Stupid to let Althea map-read. I should know by now she takes a very creative approach to navigation.

We ended up in the super-pink girly 'Lego Friends' zone and couldn't find our way out.

As we wandered around searching for the exit, a trio of dancing girls appeared, singing, 'Best Friends Forever' in fake American accents.

Wolfgang liked the song and added his growly voice to the musical mix.

However, Althea put her foot down, claiming if we didn't escape she'd need a 'shot of insulin'.

Eventually, we found our way to the Duplo play area.

As soon as we arrived, Daisy demanded the toilet.

Told her to go in her nappy.

Daisy said, 'No nappy. Baby nappy.'

After weeks of failed potty training, she certainly picks her moments to be continent.

Turned the map around and around, looking for a toilet.

Eventually found one, back in the Lego Friends zone.

Told Daisy the toilet was too far away.

Daisy took in a sharp intake of breath, poised for a mega-tantrum.

'Just take her in the bushes over there,' said Althea. 'No one will see.'

It seemed like a sensible suggestion.

Took Daisy into the shrubbery for a wee, but she announced she also needed a poo.

'No Daisy!' I said. 'Not here. Hold it in. NOT HERE!'

Daisy ignored me and pooed on the grass.

Then I heard a heart-stopping 'Choo choo!'

The Duplo train thundered through the undergrowth, its carriages filled with smiling families.

There was nowhere to hide.

Daisy was a defecating tourist attraction, and I her paralysed enabler, as carriage after carriage drove by.

Some people gasped, others covered their children's eyes.

'Althea!' I shouted. 'Althea, I need wet wipes and a carrier bag!'

Daisy waved and shouted excitedly, 'Train! Train! I do poo!'

A few kind souls waved back.

After many carriages of shame, Althea pushed through the shrubs with a packet of wet wipes and a carrier bag.

'What are you all looking at?' Althea shouted at the remaining carriages. 'It's a perfectly natural function. You all do it.'

Needed a large dose of sugar after that, so we headed to Papa Moles for many ice creams and doughnuts.

I think a few families from the train may have recognised us, but were kind enough not to mention it.

All in all, I'm not sure the free Legoland tickets were worth the trauma.

Monday 16th April

SUCH sore feet today. Theme parks are a real marathon.

Thankfully, found my Christmas present from Nana Joan – gel-filled ultra-comfort foot insoles.

Nana was right. They are like walking on a cloud.

Afternoon

Just bumped into Helen today at the Co-op supermarket.

I was bouncing around the aisles, enjoying my gel-filled insoles, when Helen's big witch nose and black helmet of shiny, bobbed hair appeared from behind the discounted Cadbury's creme eggs.

'Juliette,' said Helen. 'Nick says you're refusing to bring Daisy to the Gables. I hope you realise that's against the court order.'

'Helen,' I said, 'you really should mind your own business.'

'It's a sin to deprive a loving father of his child,' Helen continued, examining a bag of rocket salad. 'And a very spiteful way to behave. I thought more of you.'

'Daisy had nightmares the last time she visited Nick's house,' I said. 'It's your son you should be talking to – not me.'

'Oh, you're being very dramatic,' said Helen, with a wave of her leather driving glove.

Couldn't think of any decent reply to that, so settled for a simple, 'Fuck off, Helen.'

Tried to walk away with dignity.

Unfortunately, in my haste, one ultra-comfort gel-filled innersole leapt free from my sandal.

I realised, as I turned to see the insole lying on the supermarket floor, that it was exactly the same size and shape as a sanitary towel.

Impulsively shouted, 'It's not a sanitary towel!' as I shoved the insole into my handbag.

Wish I hadn't said that.

Tuesday 17th April

Was in such a flap yesterday after the Helen supermarket ambush that I left two bags of shopping in the car.

Only remembered this morning, when Daisy asked where her new toothbrush was.

Dashed out to retrieve the shopping, and found various frozen and refrigerated items melted, misshaped and spoiled in the car boot.

I struggled to open Daisy's new toothbrush too, because it was in one of those plastic welded cardboard packets. I tried ripping, biting with my teeth and snipping with nail clippers, but the packet wouldn't budge. The tough plastic even pushed the kitchen scissors out of alignment.

In the end, I had to use the ten-inch combat knife John Boy gave me as a moving-in present.

John Boy was right – a big knife does have its uses.

Wednesday 18th April

Mum invited me over for 'nutritious homemade soup' today.

This is all part of her supposedly healthier diet.

The soup wasn't all that nutritious, since Mum added butter, garlic croutons and grated cheddar, but I suppose it's good she's moving in a healthier direction. Her lunch is usually a 1970s buffet affair, comprising sausage rolls, pork pies, crisps and biscuits.

Told Mum about bumping into Helen at the supermarket.

'That old tart,' said Mum. 'She's got a nerve, criticising you when *she's* responsible for that pathetic little shit of a son. If I'd have seen her, I would have chased her around the supermarket aisles.'

Said I'd told Helen to fuck off.

Mum congratulated me.

Sometimes, I think the women in our family should be less angry (with the exception of Laura, who is extremely reasonable), but as Mum says, anger runs through the Duffy women like the caramel syrup core in Ben and Jerry's Karamel Sutra ice cream.

Thursday 19th April

Brandi brought her new boyfriend to the pub today.

Callum's right – he really isn't her usual type.

Richie is skinny as a rake, with pale, grey-tinged skin and unkempt blonde hair. He couldn't look anyone in the eye and spent most of the visit playing some war strategy game on his mobile phone.

Mum ignored his shyness and went into interrogation mode:

'Where do you live? What do you do for a living? Do you have kids yet?'

She covered Richie's lifestyle, family and sexual preferences. Then she found a weakness – Richie is a year younger than Brandi.

'What are you doing with someone older?' Mum probed. 'Can't you find anyone your own age?'

Brandi said, 'He's very mature for his age.'

'He's no good for you then,' Mum joked. 'If he's mature.'

'I *am* mature,' Brandi insisted.

It's hilarious that Brandi thinks she's mature. She still kicks off if someone else gets the free plastic toy in the Sugar Puffs packet.

When Richie and Brandi left, Mum said, 'Well he was a big, long streak of piss.'

For once, we were all in agreement.

Friday 20th April

John Boy was a bit down today. He's had way more sugary tea than usual – seven cups so far.

Asked why he was sad, and he said, "Cause I don't have a girlfriend.'

I suppose he's still pining over Gwen, but really they were never well-matched. Gwen was very well-to-do. John Boy is a gentleman at heart, but he is also a bit of a football hooligan.

Saturday 21st April

Ugh.

Have some kind of stomach bug today – almost certainly brought on by John Boy's attempt at dinner last night.

John Boy's getting better at expanding his range and has progressed beyond full English breakfasts. But I don't think he's quite competent enough to make his own gravy yet.

My apple tree has blossomed into fluffy, fragrant pink flowers. I looked at it today and thought of the baby Alex and I lost. It made me think that the baby isn't lost after all, but waiting for the right time to come out. Just like the blossoms, it will come when the time is right. It just won't have Alex for a father.

Sunday 22nd April

Callum has been put in the special needs class at school. They don't call it special needs any more – they call it extra support. But it's basically the same thing.

Brandi is going to talk to Callum's teacher tomorrow. She is furious, so I can't see the talk going well. In my experience, teachers don't like parents shouting at them.

Monday 23rd April St Georges Day

Callum has been taken out of the special needs class, following Brandi's visit.

I asked Brandi how she got Callum moved, and she said she'd promised to spend a lot of extra time reading with him at home.

But I'm not sure *Closer* and *Heat* magazines count as good reading material.

Tuesday 24th April

Shift at the pub tonight, so had tea with Mum, Dad, Brandi and Callum.

Mum greeted us at the door with jam doughnuts and bad news. Callum has head lice.

Went upstairs, and found everyone sitting around like monkeys, inspecting each other's hair.

Felt immediately itchy, but Mum only found grey hairs and dandruff on me.

Brandi doesn't have nits either. Nothing could survive all that peroxide she uses.

Wednesday 25th April

My head is very itchy today.

Am paranoid that I've caught Callum's nits. He's had three treatments of Hedrin, but I read somewhere that head lice are scarily hard to kill these days.

Checked Daisy's hair, but I don't think there's any way lice could make a home. It's really just fluff.

Asked Mum to check my hair again, and she got all nostalgic about childhood parasites.

'This takes me back,' said Mum, tugging at my hair with the Nitty Gritty comb. 'You never would sit still. Sit STILL Julesy!'

Then she went on about the nightmare of head lice when you have three girls at home.

'And the treatment was bloody awful in those days,' said Mum. 'None of this 'gentle non-odour' business. It used to take the skin off your hands and made your eyes water.'

Mum's a bit irritable today because she broke her diet last night.

The brewery came by with a load of new beers to sample, and she decided it would be 'unprofessional' not to give them a whirl. Then there was a darts tournament in the pub, so she laid out the usual platters of hot chips and sausages along the bar.

The five sample pints from the brewery weakened her resolve, and she ate two platters of chips and an unspecified amount of sausages.

To her credit, Mum had a bowl of porridge with skimmed

milk this morning.

The trouble is, whenever she eats low fat stuff, she has twice as much.

Thursday 26th April

Had another go at potty-training Daisy this afternoon, before my pub shift.

Mum gave me a good tip – take Daisy's clothes off and potty-train her in the garden.

Daisy did the tiniest little bit of wee in the potty, which resulted in me whooping and cheering and giving Daisy princess stickers.

I think we're finally getting somewhere.

Friday 27th April

ARG!

I have head lice!

Have been scratching all day.

Demanded Mum check my hair again, and she found three eggs.

Went to the chemist and browsed the many nit lotions and potions on sale.

Things have changed since I was a kid.

We were given nasty-smelling chemical stuff, but now everything claims to be 'pesticide- and odour-free'.

I remember going to bed with choking, toxic nit lotion that burned my scalp and ears.

Bought a bottle of Herbal Healing, which uses natural tea-tree oil and is kind to skin.

Kids today don't know how lucky they have it.

Dad was sceptical about the Herbal Healing treatment.

'It says it works in fifteen minutes,' he said. 'I can't see anything working in that time. When we were kids, they used to shave our heads and paint them with violet-coloured chemicals. We lined up at school for hymn practice looking like a row of Bryant and May matchsticks.'

Saturday 28th April

Nick's weekend with Daisy.

Suggested a compromise – meeting in a park, or other neutral ground.

Nick refused, calling me manipulative.

'Why should I have to dance to your tune?' he said. 'It's *my* visitation weekend.'

'This isn't about me wanting to have my own way,' I said. 'I just want what's best for Daisy.'

'Why are you making my life even more difficult?' Nick complained. 'Living with Sadie is hard enough. Oh god, I think she's listening.'

There was an ominous pause, and what sounded like a plate being smashed.

Then Nick said he had to go.

Felt a little bit sorry for him then.

Just a little bit.

Sunday 29th April

Daisy has learned to hustle, and she's not even three.

Last night she called out, 'Mummy. Where rabbit? Rabbit gone. MUMMY.'

I investigated the empty cot and found her striped rabbit hidden under the pillow.

'Daisy,' I said. 'Did you hide this?'

'Yes. Hide it,' she announced proudly. 'Then you come.'

Today, Daisy hid striped rabbit before bedtime and refused to divulge its location, believing if rabbit was lost, she wouldn't have to go to bed.

'If we can't find rabbit, you'll have to sleep without her,' I said.

Daisy suddenly remembered rabbit had been 'put away' by 'someone' in the oven.

Monday 30th April

Tried again to potty-train Daisy after lunch.

This resulted in wee all over the floor.

Praised Daisy for doing slightly less wee on the floor than last time.

Felt frustrated, but had to keep it inside. The books all caution you about getting upset, but surely Daisy should be able to use a toilet by now?

Wolfgang has been continent for weeks, and even cleans the toilet himself. He also makes his own breakfast – a 'mix up' of Althea's spelt and paleo breakfast cereals, combined with soy and almond milk.

Phoned Althea for advice re potty training.

Althea said Wolfgang was just physically advanced. Except in the respect of getting breakfast, which Althea put down to 'just greed'.

'Listen – don't worry about all that 'doing stuff at a certain age' bullshit,' said Althea. 'Kids never signed up for those medical charts. They're ready when they're ready.'

On the subject of age-related milestones, I'm also worried about Daisy's drinking habits.

According to baby-expert-and-Nazi, Gina Ford, Daisy should no longer drink milk from a bottle. Over the age of one, it should be a sippy cup.

Daisy is nearly three now. That's years of neglect.

Gina wasn't specific about what could happen to a baby who 'overused' bottles, but I fear bad things.

At one point, I bought three different types of sippy cup: the classic Tommee Tippee, a futuristic Advil 'no spill' with lime-green handle and pink Minnie Mouse cup that spills everywhere.

Daisy hated all of them.

'You'll probably find baby's milk consumption goes right down once a sippy cup is introduced,' Gina writes.

The reality: 'Baby will throw sippy cup in your face and scream, bottle, bottle! A month later, you will find dangerous black mould inside the unwashable sippy cup and wonder if perhaps baby knew best after all.'

Tuesday 1st May

The bloody nit stuff hasn't worked.

I'm still itching like crazy, and Mum found three more eggs.

Looked on Mumsnet and found mile-long threads from women who'd had reoccurring head lice for months – even years.

There was a picture of a sad, shaggy-haired mum who'd avoided the hairdressers for two years due to head-lice embarrassment.

Marched into Great Oakley chemist and demanded the strongest stuff they had.

The teenage girl behind the till didn't seem to have any specialist knowledge about medicine, but read the packaging out loud at frustratingly slow speed.

'Kind to…hair and…skin. Part the hair…apply section by… section with comb…included and –'

'I don't want kind to hair,' I said. 'I want chemicals. Strong chemicals.'

The girl picked up another packet. 'Organic...treatment for... head lice made with...'

'Not organic!' I shouted. 'I want something STRONG.'

Ended up buying something that claimed to kill head lice, scabies, 'crab mites' (whatever they are) and pubic lice. It said: CAUTION! NOT FOR ASTHMA SUFFERERS.

Felt assured there must be some strong stuff in there.

Went home, doused myself in chemicals and inhaled the sweet smell of lung-burning toxins.

Really need to get these head lice dealt with, because the Corfu trip is only a few weeks away.

Feel very lucky that I'm having two holidays this year. And grateful, for once, that Mum ignored my instructions.

Sometimes Mum does know best. Except about Guinness being good for pregnant women – she really isn't right about that.

Wednesday 2nd May

Took Nana to a funeral today. It was for an old friend and fellow care-home resident, Ducky Newton, who apparently made us cakes when we were younger.

Couldn't remember 'Ducky's famous seed cake', but she sounded like a lovely woman.

Nana wore a tight, low-cut black dress, and had 'livened up the boring colour' by spraying silver glitter over her cleavage.

Nana also wore heavy concealer over a black eye, because she'd been fighting with Carmen Akawolo.

Nana and Carmen are both so similar – fiery old ladies with huge bosoms and no-nonsense attitudes.

Carmen is twice Nana's size, but Nana evens the score with blind fury.

Carmen was at the funeral, wearing a sleek black dress with frills around the hips.

She and Nana eyed each other fiercely.

I kept a firm clutch on Nana's arm, fearing trouble and several lost hair extensions.

At the wake, I had a quiet word with Carmen's nephew, apologising for the fight and saying I hoped there were no hard feelings.

We had a nice chat, the two of us, about how funny old people can be.

'They're supposed to be wiser than us!' the nephew laughed.

I laughed too.

In my family, old age is no guarantee of wisdom.

Thursday 3rd May

Callum is in trouble for fighting. To be fair, it doesn't sound like his fault. Another kid pulled his trousers down.

'And they're making a big fuss about the mid-term Corfu trip,' Callum complained. 'They're so jealous, those teachers. I keep telling them education doesn't start and finish in the classroom.'

It's good that Callum takes Dad's little sayings on board.

Friday 4th May

Corfu only a week away!

Mum keeps singing, 'We're all off to sunny Spain, Arriba Espana!', even though we're going to Greece.

Will be lovely to get some sunshine and splash around with Daisy in a swimming pool.

Bit of a sun tan, a nice rest and shitloads of ice cream and beer.

Arriba Corfu!

Saturday 5th May

Visited Laura today.

'Alex was here this morning,' she told me. 'Did you know he was visiting?'

This threw me a bit.

'No,' I said. 'Why should I know what Alex does or where he goes?'

'I thought you two might be in that 'friend zone' again,' she said. 'The one you both go to, because neither of you can let the other one go.'

'We're not friends,' I said. 'I have nothing to say to him and couldn't care less what he's doing.'

Then I asked why Alex had visited Laura's home.

'He came to see Zach about suit fittings,' Laura told me.

'Why did they need to talk about suit fittings?' I asked.

'Zach and I are having a special lunch,' said Laura. 'I wanted to talk to you about it, actually. Are you free at the end of May?'

Told her yes – I'll be back from Corfu by then.

'Good,' said Laura. 'So Mum and Dad will be free too?'

'Yes,' I said. 'Why are you having a special lunch?'

'Zach and I are having a little ceremony,' said Laura. 'To say a few words about the future.'

'Laura,' I said. 'Is this a *wedding?*'

'Oh I wouldn't call it that,' said Laura. 'Just signing a piece of paper. But it's no big deal.'

'Is it a marriage paper?' I asked.

Laura admitted that yes – she and Zach would be signing marriage papers.

Whooped and cheered and gave her a big hug. So happy for her.

Can't believe a member of my family is marrying a Dalton.

Sunday 6th May

Phoned Alex this morning.

He picked up on the first ring, which was gratifying.

'Juliette,' he said. 'It's good to hear from you.'

Told Alex I wanted to get in touch before Laura's wedding, to make sure we were on the same page.

'I don't see why we wouldn't be on the same page about the wedding,' Alex replied. 'It's life we disagree on.'

There was silence, then Alex said, 'You know, we signed the deal with Starlight Cruises this week. It reminded me of our trip together.'

'And our separate cabins,' I said. 'You weirdo.'

'I feel sad we couldn't make it work,' said Alex.

'Me too,' I said. 'Sometimes.'

Alex said, 'Only sometimes?'

'Yes,' I said. 'Only sometimes.'

Asked Alex if he was looking forward to the wedding.

'I'm looking forward to seeing you,' he said. 'But there are other people I'd rather not see. My father being one of them.'

Monday 7th May

Laura just called.

She's stressed about the wedding that isn't a wedding.

Catrina is starting to interfere and wants Zach to have a big 'society' do with old family friend Burt Bacharach performing at the reception.

Laura wanted to talk to me, because she needs someone to 'keep her feet on the ground'.

I was the right person for this, because I have no idea what a society wedding is. Feel my 'why doesn't Catrina mind her own business?' comments were very grounded.

Tuesday 8th May

Daisy's language is really coming along, but there are still a few things she can't pronounce – no matter how many times I correct her.

Daisy says, 'Harry Popper' instead of 'Harry Potter', 'Shovel up' instead of 'Shove up' and 'Meatabix' instead of 'Weetabix'. She also says, 'Oh quakers!' when she's surprised. Where on earth did she get that from?

Have started thinking about what I'll need for Corfu.

You have to pay extra for hold luggage, so I'm packing everything in my little hand-luggage bag. I always wear the same thing every day on beach holidays anyway (denim shorts, my nice, flattering kaftan top and a swimming costume underneath), so I've decided to cut out the unnecessary packing and only bring the aforementioned everyday outfit, plus changes of underwear and travel toiletries.

Althea is impressed with my minimalist ethos.

'Good on you, Jules,' she said. 'Let go of attachment to all that materialistic crap. It's the path to enlightenment.'

I didn't tell her that the holiday will involve unlimited food and alcohol, which almost certainly isn't the path to enlightenment.

Wednesday 9th May

Have cracked and decided to pay extra for a hold bag.

There are SO many things Daisy won't sleep without now – there's no way I can fit them all in my cabin bag and Daisy's tiny Dora the Explorer suitcase. Also, Daisy wants various items of bulky fancy dress, including a Snow White outfit with full taffeta underskirt.

When I arrived at the pub for my shift, there was a lot of packing going on there too.

In Callum's case, this mainly meant unpacking, because he'd loaded up his camouflage bag with plastic knives, real knives, BB guns and gunpowder pellets.

Midnight

Just finished my pub shift.

Sleeping at Mum and Dad's tonight, because we all have to be up at 3 am for the airport shuttle and 7 am flight.

The anti-social flights were only £17 each way, which is cheaper than the train to London. Well worth missing a few hours' sleep for. And, like Mum says, we can always drink our way through the tiredness when we reach the other end.

Thursday 10th May

The super-early flight to Corfu caused a lot of arguments.

I'd forgotten how bad my family gets when we're tired.

Lack of sleep seems to exaggerate everyone's worst characteristics.

Mum was grumpy, snapping about the lack of full English breakfast on the flight, and going on and on about the men at security taking her multipack of Walkers crisps.

Dad was beyond anxious, shouting at everyone for dallying in the duty-free hall, demanding we get to the check-in gate an hour before take-off and having a minor panic attack when he saw the gate had *already been called.*

John Boy was still drunk from the night before and got lost in duty free.

I was OK.

After having a baby, tiredness doesn't affect you in the same way. You get tough, like an SAS soldier. There were accusations that I was irritable, but that's because everyone else was being so annoying.

Mum snuck some hard-boiled eggs through security, and insisted on peeling them extremely LOUDLY, *and* dropping bits of shell and egg really *near* my feet.

Callum's headphones made tinny, irritating sounds.

John Boy was snoring on *purpose*.

Daisy fell asleep with one leg dangling off the chair *also* on purpose, so I couldn't get out to go to the toilet.

Dad kept asking the air stewardess to repeat herself, then squinting when she gave her answer. He did this on *purpose*, because he knows it irritates me.

In the end, I accepted Mum's suggestion of a breakfast bloody Mary.

Everything became less irritating after that.

Landed in Corfu at 10 am, Greek time.

Got to the resort by 11 am.

By 12 pm, we'd all had a shot of Ouzo (it's a local tradition), a few pints of Greek lager (well, you've got to try the native blend) and a Malibu cocktail (we're on holiday!).

Mum and Nana made a scene by encouraging each other to down drinks at the bar, before Nana literally fell off her bar stool and had to be carried to a sun lounger for a little lie-down.

I think it's fair to say all the adults were tipsy when the lunchtime buffet opened. However, the restaurant manager needn't have been such a spoilsport. I mean, yes – we were singing. But we're on *holiday*.

The buffet was fabulous, and included barbequed lamb, huge bricks of feta cheese, freshly baked bread, roasted Mediterranean vegetables, double-cooked chips, a load of yellow kids' food for Daisy and Callum and a variety of honey-soaked Greek desserts.

We all enjoyed filling up, except Dad who ate a moderate meal of soup and bread, followed by a piece of fruit and a nice cup of tea, claiming there was no need to be excessive.

Fun afternoon by the pool, trying out the various different cocktails and playing an interesting German game called Rummikub, which is a sort of plastic-tile version of rummy. Nana Joan won every game, of course.

Callum and Daisy had a nice time at the Clowns Kid's Club, playing Duck Duck Goose for three hours.

Tucked up now on nice, clean white sheets.

Daisy is sleeping in the travel cot.

All is good in the world.

Very contented.

Althea's right.

Who needs a man?

Friday 11th May

Trip into Corfu town this morning.

Mum wanted to shop for tourist tat, and Dad fancied seeing the old Roman ruins.

The weather, although a lot warmer than England, was a little overcast and windy, so I wrapped Daisy up in her warm cardigan and little flowery flared jeans.

Mum, on the other hand, had no respect for the weather. She has only two levels of holiday dress – semi-nudity or semi-nudity with a sparkly shawl around her shoulders. For the town trip she chose semi-nudity: a short, see-through chiffon kaftan with no shawl.

As we walked beside the dock, the ocean wind treated fisherman to a view of Mum's wobbling bottom. The well-dressed Greek city dwellers, in slim-fitting suits and tailored shirts, clipped neatly past us, trying not to stare as chiffon was whipped here, there and everywhere.

We made it back to the hotel in time for lunch, then sat by the swimming pool playing Uno, drinking beer and inventing cocktails.

Mum came up with the best cocktail – rum, swirled with raspberry and strawberry slushy into a pleasing, colourful whirlwind.

None of us fancied the cold swimming pool (the only people swimming were teenagers, and they weren't really swimming – they were daring each other to jump into the freezing water, before shrieking and leaping out again), but we were perfectly happy drinking and watching the kids run around.

'And just think, we could do this all over again,' said Dad. 'In the wilds of nature.'

We all stared at him blankly, until he reminded us about the camping trip he wants to organise.

'None of us want to go on a bloody camping trip, Bob,' said Mum. 'All that hard work, setting up tents and barbeques, and for what? Less comfort than you get back home.'

'You can't beat waking up in a grassy field and cooking on open fires,' said Dad. 'Give me that over all this excess any day of the week.'

We all sipped our giant slushy and rum cocktails and ignored him.

Saturday 12th May

Think I've put on weight.

The thing with buffet food is you just have to try everything, and on all-inclusive holidays there's a lot to try. This morning, the buffet included: fried eggs, scrambled eggs, poached eggs, omelette, little sausages, bacon, fried potatoes, various cheeses, hams and pickles, kippers – and then the sweet stuff: real, thick Greek yoghurt with golden honey, pancakes, waffles, fresh bread, croissants, Danish pastries, pains au chocolat, cinnamon buns, chocolate cereals and breakfast cookies (both raisin and chocolate chip).

It's all very enjoyable, but it's not good to have a three-course breakfast (pancakes and toast to start, full English for the main, and dessert pastries, biscuits and coffee to finish) every day.

Dad suggested a short walk along the beach this morning, to 'work off all that heavy food', but Mum refused to go, saying that diabetics shouldn't walk too far.

'On the contrary, Shirley,' said Dad. 'Exercise is proven to be very beneficial to diabetics. You should walk at least an hour every day. Ideally more.'

'They come up with all sorts of statistics,' said Mum. 'I'm working on the basis that walking is bad and ice cream is good. I'm sure one day they'll do a study to prove me right.'

Sunday 13th May

Totally surreal day.

Can't believe it.

ALEX is here.

He arrived just after lunch.

Mum and I were at the bar, debating whether to have brandies with our afternoon coffee, when Alex came strolling onto the sun terrace.

I didn't recognise him at first. I just thought some handsome, Ray-Ban-wearing aftershave-model type was at the wrong hotel. But then all the details clicked.

'Mum,' I hissed, grabbing her arm. 'It's Alex. ALEX.'

'Who?' Mum asked, squinting at brandy bottles.

'Alex.'

We both stared.

Then Alex turned around. He gave me that half-smile of his and said, 'Juliette. There you are.' As if him being there was the most natural thing in the world.

'What are YOU doing here?' I asked.

'I came to see you and Daisy,' said Alex. 'And experience a different sort of hotel – I've never seen faux marble before. Or all-inclusive wrist bands.' Alex showed me an 'All-inclusive Day Pass' band sitting above his Rolex watch.

I was too flabbergasted to be angry or sad, so ordered Alex a gin and tonic and invited him to join us on the sun terrace.

Daisy was delighted when Alex came strolling out. She didn't question why he was in Corfu, instead asking about his swimwear preferences and whether he was brave enough to attempt the 'Yellow Devil' waterslide.

Alex and Daisy chatted for a while about waterslide accomplishments. Then Daisy suggested giving Alex a 'grand tour' of the resort. She grabbed Alex's hand, pulling him towards the swimming pool and chattering about the 'all the fassies' (facilities) and 'sunbathes' (sunbeds).

'Kid's club bit smelling,' she told Alex sadly, then shouted to me: 'MUMMY! COME TOO!'

Daisy, Alex and I walked all the way around the tennis court and towards the beach.

'I've never seen a tennis court with towels drying over the net before,' Alex commented. 'Or sand this colour. Daisy – I'm delighted with this tour.'

Daisy, puffed up with her tour-guide status, started hectoring Alex to go in the sea.

'Take shoes off, Rex. Take shoes *off*!'

He did.

'Daisy is happy to see you,' I said.

'And I'm happy to see her,' said Alex, his long, tanned toes negotiated seaweed and froth. 'I've missed her. I've missed you too.'

We walked a little further, and I said, 'Alex, you know we're just friends now – right?'

'I know.'

'And you're OK with that?'

'If those are the terms, those are the terms. And I'm OK. Not great, but OK.'

'How does Bethany feel about you coming out here?' I asked.

'I imagine she'll feel fine. I don't see why she wouldn't.'

'You don't think she'll be upset?' I challenged. 'That you've jetted off to see an ex-girlfriend?'

'I don't see it as being any of her business.'

Felt really sorry for Bethany then. Clearly, Alex has terrible double standards. What woman *wouldn't* want to know their boyfriend was seeing his ex-girlfriend?

The women on that Womb Wisdom course were right – men *are* bastards.

I've had a lucky escape.

I said, 'Shall we go back?'

Alex said yes.

In the evening, Alex joined us for dinner. He only made five or six criticisms about food quality, and even declared the feta cheese 'not at all bad'. It was nice for Daisy, having Alex there. She seemed calm and contented.

After dinner, we all watched the sun set over the swimming pool, drank pink cocktails and played dominos and cards.

The 'just friends' thing with Alex seemed OK, but I was still fuming over his treatment of Bethany. To not even *tell* her he's visiting us.

Alex left for the airport at 9 pm. He had a late-night flight to London for a conference tomorrow. After that, he's off to Dubai.

Daisy was sad to see Alex go. She said, 'Miss Rex, Mummy. Had *lovely* time. Like Rex.'

'I know, Daisy,' I said. 'And we'll still see Alex from time to time. But from now on, it'll just be the two of us.'

Monday 14th May

Laura's birthday today.

We Facetimed her from beside the swimming pool, holding rum and slushie cocktails.

It was only 11 am, but as Mum pointed out, it's the last day of our holiday so we may as well enjoy ourselves and get value from the bar.

Laura was happy to hear from us. She said she wished she could be in Corfu, but baby Bear is especially demanding right now, only sleeping seven hours at night.

Seven hours uninterrupted sleep! Daisy *still* wakes at least once with some cunning ploy to get me out of my warm bed.

'Mummy! MUMMY! Can't put dress on TEDDY. TEDDY NAKED!

Mummy. MUMMY! Had a dream. A princess had a sausage in bed, Mummy. A SAUSAGE, mummy. VERY messy.'

AND she often wakes at 5 am.

Laura held baby Bear to the phone, so he could see his relatives getting drunk before lunchtime.

Mum said we should toast Laura's 'not-really-a-wedding' and pulled out an eight-euro bottle of Prosecco she'd bought at the resort shop.

We added the Prosecco to our rum and slushie cocktails, then raised our plastic glasses and whooped and cheered.

'To my little girl signing a bit of paper,' said Mum. 'And the wedding that's not really a wedding.'

Tuesday 15th May

Home.

Feels nice to be back in my own bed, but I miss having someone else doing the cooking and washing up for me.

Now I just need to do post-holiday weight loss in time for Laura's not-really-a-wedding.

Am starting a nice healthy eating routine and cutting out alcohol, with immediate effect. Although John Boy makes a good point – there's no need to shock the system. Might have a few pints of Guinness tonight just to ease myself back into reality.

Evening

Alex just phoned from Dubai. He wanted to make sure I got home safely. Thanked him for his concern, but told him to save it for Bethany.

'For goodness sakes, Juliette,' said Alex. 'What has Bethany got to do with anything?'

'Are you taking her to the wedding?' I asked.

'The subject has come up,' said Alex. 'But I think better not. I don't want to give her the wrong impression.'

'That's so unbelievably shit, Alex,' I said. 'Stringing her along.'

Alex was silence for a moment. Then he said, 'Perhaps you're right. I should talk to her. Make it very clear what my intentions are.'

'We've got to move on, Alex,' I said. 'We tried. Many times. It just isn't meant to be. We're no Zach and Laura.'

'Thank goodness for that,' said Alex. 'With this lacklustre wedding of theirs. If I ever marry you, I'll do it properly.'

'Laura doesn't want a big wedding,' I said. 'It's not who she is. She wants something low-key. It's just signing a piece of paper, when all is said and done.'

'Then I hardly know why they're bothering,' said Alex.

Asked if he was surprised about his brother's wedding. After all, it did come out of nowhere.

Alex said no. He was more surprised Zach hadn't married Laura already.

'Zach has good morals,' said Alex. 'I always found it odd he had a child out of wedlock.'

'So you think it's morally bad to have children out of marriage?' I asked.

'Yes,' said Alex.

'Your morals aren't up to much then.'

'It would seem so,' said Alex.

Asked him how he felt about the wedding being so soon – just a few weeks away now.

He said the short notice was 'inconvenient'. Apparently, it's a busy month for private jets, so he'll have to fly back to London via First Class charter flight.

'But these things are sent to try us,' he said. 'I'd do anything for my little brother.'

We had a chat about the holiday, and how happy Daisy was to see Alex.

'I enjoyed seeing her too,' said Alex. 'And it was interesting to visit a hotel with no dress code.'

'Actually, there was a dress code,' I said. 'No swimwear in the restaurant.'

Of course, Mum broke that rule, as she does every year, and ended up in a shouting match with the restaurant manager.

Wednesday 16th May

Dad keeps going on about camping. We've all said no, but he's persistent. Today, he asked if I'd like to visit Go Outdoors and stock up on camping gear 'just in case'.

'This is the time to buy equipment, love,' Dad enthused. 'Just before the summer rush.'

I think Dad was hoping the consumer delights of outdoor equipment would change my whole indoor personality.

Agreed to the Go Outdoors trip because it was raining outside, and I know Daisy loves running in and out of tents.

To be fair, Dad was right about it being a good time to buy camping equipment. There was a 30% sale on at Go Outdoors, because only an idiot would go camping during rainy, cold May.

Dad was in his element, gazing with wide-eyed wonder at fisherman's camp beds, innovative gas stoves, solar-powered compasses and other practical joys.

'Modern camping equipment is astonishing,' said Dad. 'Polycanvas is light as a feather, and these fibreglass poles are a revelation. Compare that to the big, heavy canvas tents we used to go camping in. They took two men to lift and *days* to dry out.'

Dad was, however, appalled by the more frivolous camping items on sale, top of the list being fairy lights ('a hellish waste of electricity').

'Camping is all about simplifying,' said Dad. 'Getting away from all that consumerist nonsense. If you've got some God-awful boom box belting out loud music and an electric shower set-up to wash your vegetables, you may as well be at home.'

Dad was equally dismissive of the Arctic sleeping bag ranges. As a younger man, he went camping in a thin, paisley-patterned sleeping bag, which he still owns and uses. He describes the Scottish expeditions as 'a little bracing at night', but claimed, 'all it took was a nice cup of tea and a mess tin of scrambled egg to warm you up.'

Sadly, I haven't inherited his hardy, Scottish genetics.

In the wrong conditions, I can reach levels of cold that only a hot bath and central heating can fix.

Thursday 17th May

Mum and I visited Nana Joan today.

Nana Joan needed bananas and Murray mints, because she's had a dodgy stomach since the holiday.

We took my car, because Mum and Dad's old Toyota is having its engine replaced.

Mum insisted on driving, because she hates being a passenger. My poor car has now been shouted and sworn at and thumped with an angry fist – all because Mum couldn't get used to the windscreen wipers and indicators being on different sides.

At every junction, the windscreen wipers whizzed back and forth, followed by a cacophony of swearing.

Nana Joan was pleased to see us. Her stomach was quite bad – it made gurgling noises like a blocked drain.

'The trouble with places like Greece,' said Nana, 'is the hygiene standards aren't as good as the UK. It's not a very advanced country.'

'The Greeks invented civilisation,' said Mum. 'Have you been reading the *Daily Mail* again?'

Nana admitted that she had 'glanced at a copy' and was worried about too many Polish people coming to the UK.

Mum pointed out that Nana was herself a Welsh immigrant and wasn't born in England.

'But there are so many Polish people now,' Nana insisted. 'They're setting up their own shops. It's getting out of hand. This is England, not Poland.'

Mum reminded Nana that she and twenty-two Welsh family members moved into the same street, flew Welsh flags from their windows, sang Gwahoddiad in the church every Sunday and held Tom Jones street parties every year.

Friday 18th May

Helen called round today.

It was a horrible shock, seeing her nasty beaky face trying to peer through the windows.

'What are you doing here?' I shouted, ripping open the front door. 'Halloween was months ago.'

'Juliette, I thought we could talk,' said Helen. 'Nick's very upset about not seeing his daughter. But I *do* understand how you feel about S.A.D.I.E. I hoped I could poor oil on troubled water.'

I think Helen was trying her best, because she didn't say anything about the messy house. She even put on a horrible smile when she saw Daisy eating breakfast, and said, 'Oh, hasn't she grown?'

'Who this, Mummy?' Daisy asked.

Helen said, 'Perhaps we should talk privately, away from little ears?'

Called upstairs to John Boy and asked if he could take Daisy out.

John Boy agreed and came downstairs a moment later sniffing the inside of a Nike trainer. After a quick spray of Odor-Eaters, he stuck Daisy on his shoulders and took her to the park.

'How did it all come to this?' Helen asked, when Daisy's 'little ears' had gone. 'Sadie is...oh, she's vile. Did Nick tell you what she said about my new Hermes scarf?'

Asked Helen if she had anything important to say.

'I just wondered if there's any chance, any chance at all, of a reconciliation,' said Helen, blue eyes watery and pleading. 'Nick was so much happier with you.'

I asked her if she was absolutely fucking kidding.

After a bad language wince, Helen said, 'Juliette, this family is falling apart. I know Nick made bad choices.'

'What do you expect me to do, Helen?'

'Maybe help build some bridges. I know you're good at that.'

'Nick can see Daisy whenever he likes,' I said. 'But I'm not leaving my daughter at his house while Sadie is there.'

'Juliette, I understand Sadie can be...challenging,' said Helen. 'If you'd consider getting back with Nick, I think he'd leave her.'

'Does Sadie know you're asking me to get back together with her son?' I asked.

Helen stiffened. 'You *mustn't* tell Sadie about this conversation. She is *unstable*. More than unstable.'

'Don't you think she'd find out sooner or later?' I asked. 'If I got back together with Nick?'

'So you're saying there's a chance?' said Helen, blue eyes bright and hopeful.

'No, I was just speaking hypothetically,' I said. 'There isn't a chance at all. I'm not throwing myself down that toilet again.'

Helen's eyes turned sad. 'I thought we were friends, once upon a time. The bridal dress fitting and all those chats at the old apartment. Can't you give Nick another chance, for my sake? He's grown up a lot.'

It felt rude to say that I never liked Helen and only ever put up with her for Nick.

'How many times do I have to say it, Helen?' I said. 'Nick and I are never getting back together.'

'Can't you see we're on the same side?' Helen insisted. 'Sadie is *appalling*. The way she talks to Nicholas...even Henry can't stand her. Nick tells me he doesn't see a future.'

Helen looked at me expectantly.

'Bloody hell, Helen,' I said. 'You're just not listening. Nick's made his bed. And now we've all got to lie in it.'

Helen left then, looking upset. I think she really believed she could convince me to get back with her cheating, irresponsible son. She's as delusional as Nick is.

Saturday 19th May

Bullied Althea into dress-shopping for Laura's wedding.

I needed a friend to give me the brutal, honest truth and Althea is that friend. Plus, she's surprisingly knowledgeable about designer shops.

To the undiscerning eye, Althea looks like a charity-shop hippy, but most of her clothes are very expensive. She just has a knack for picking things that *look* second-hand – in part due to alterations with cheese graters and glue guns.

Althea didn't want to come shopping at first. She had a detox hangover, having eaten nothing but organic fruit and vegetables for two days. However, I suggested a cream-topped Starbucks drink with mashed up chocolate cookies as a post-shopping treat, and she changed her mind.

Found a nice dress in the end – this lemon chiffon thing. At least, I think it's nice.

Could have done with Althea's opinion in the dressing room, but she was busy with Wolfgang.

He'd gnawed a hole in a mannequin's leg.

Sunday 20th May

REALLY need to crack potty-training now.

So sick of changing Daisy's nappy.

Attempted the Gina Ford method.

Made Daisy sit on the potty for ten minutes at a time, four times an hour.

Didn't want to hold Daisy down by the shoulders, so just ended up chasing her around holding the potty under her naked bottom.

Daisy managed a little bit of wee in the potty, and I make a big fuss about it – giving her cuddles and high fives, offering her a princess sticker and a handful of Smarties. But just like before, every other wee went on the floor.

I suppose we're sort of making progress.

There was no poo this time.

Monday 21st May

Am having a few housemate issues with John Boy.

First on the agenda is sugar. We're always running out.

John Boy has six spoons in his tea, four on his Frosties cereal and eats a spoonful if he's ever feeling 'under the weather.'

PlayStation cables are constantly strewn across the living room floor and the recycling people won't take all our waste now because there are so many Stella Artois cans.

John Boy also comes home drunk several nights a week and writes philosophical thoughts such as, 'Kids are the sunshine of life' and 'Life is short, so you may as well have a drink' on the wipe-clean kitchen cupboards in felt-tip pen.

Tuesday 22nd May

Getting a bit worried about Daisy's aggression. She's losing her temper at the tiniest, most ridiculous things.

This morning, she flew into a rage because she couldn't get her scrambled egg on the fork. She was so furious I thought she might burst a vein.

Mum says it's normal for two-year-olds to have a temper. She reminded me about my second birthday party, and the older boy I beat up for snatching my cheese and pineapple cocktail stick. It took two adults to restrain me, but Mum wasn't one of them.

Wednesday 23rd May

Nick's birthday today.

Did a Facetime call so Daisy could sing 'Happy Birthday'. Nick looked hungover, with bleary eyes and a scruffy beard. For all his talk of responsibility, he seems to be sliding back to his old self these days. I suppose he must be under a lot of stress, living with Sadie. But you would have thought, as a father of two children, he'd find a better way of dealing with things by now.

It just goes to show, people don't change. No matter what they tell you.

Afternoon

Toilet blocked.

Not sure what caused the toilet blockage, but I suspect John Boy. All those Pot Noodles.

Mum has promised to come over later with a plunger and a sledgehammer. She's happy to get out of the house because Dad keeps going on about campsites in Norfolk.

'It's verging on bullying,' said Mum. 'He just won't shut up about it.'

Don't think Mum really understands bullying. To bully her would be nigh-on impossible.

Thursday 24th May

Alex is en-route to London for Zach and Laura's wedding. He phoned me from the airport executive lounge, annoyed at the 'chaos' of charter flights.

I asked Alex if he had his top hat ready. He said because of the 'informality' of this particular wedding, he wouldn't wear his usual top hat. A three-piece suit would be sufficient.

It's weird.

We get on great when we don't have any expectations of each other. So great that it's easy to start thinking, 'Maybe things could work out.' But we've been down that road. And anyway, there's no way I'd start anything with Bethany on the scene.

Laura thinks Alex isn't ready for commitment yet. 'Men mature slower than women,' she said. 'You've just got to wait until he gets all that business stuff out of the way, and then he'll move back to Great Oakley and be a great husband and father.'

'But Zach is younger than him,' I pointed out. 'And he's already in settling-down mode.'

'Zach isn't a typical Dalton,' said Laura. 'Alex is.'

'But why should I wait?' I said. 'Don't I deserve better than someone who isn't quite ready to commit, but might be one day? And is stringing along some poor Sloane Ranger girl?'

'Of course you do,' said Laura. 'That's the whole trouble.'

Friday 25th May

It's Laura's 'not-really-a-wedding' tomorrow.

Weird to think of my big sis as a married woman.

Feels like yesterday we were cutting up Barbie dresses.

Am still a little bit hurt that Laura isn't having bridesmaids. Brandi doesn't want to get married, and Althea will never marry in a conventional way, so Laura was my last hope.

Tried to convince Laura to come over the pub today for pre-wedding pampering, but she refused even that, saying she doesn't want a fuss.

Have a slight wedding-wardrobe malfunction, in that my lemon-chiffon dress is see-through in the wrong light.

I knew something was wrong when Brandi said I looked 'smokin'.

Mum was complimentary too, telling me it was about time I showed off what God gave me.

Double-checked myself in the hallway mirror, and realised my underwear was clearly visible, including the coloured stars on my pants.

I know British consumer law is flimsy, but I thought the EU were all over this sort of thing.

Ended up wearing jogging shorts and a vest underneath, much to Brandi and Mum's disappointment.

Mum wore an outfit with lots of pink feathers and a matching fascinator.

Brandi wore a very tasteful silky dress that went all the way down to her mid-thigh and barely showed any cleavage. She looked really lovely. I forget sometimes that, under all that make-up, Brandi is very attractive.

Maybe things really are serious with 'long streak of piss' Richie. I can't think of any other reason Brandi would dress sensibly – she is certainly no respecter of formal occasions and wore fishnet tights to *my* wedding.

Dad wore the same brown suit he's had since he and Mum married in the Seventies.

To be fair, it does still fit him. I suppose it's easy to keep in shape when you live off wholemeal bread and vegetables.

Evening

Nick just phoned.

Sadie is meeting an agent in Leeds this weekend, so the house will be de-witched.

Nick asked if he could have Daisy, and I said yes.

It'll be good to enjoy Laura's wedding without having a two-year-old running around. And by enjoy, I mean get drunk.

I wish they'd put a legal limit on alcohol and parenting. Then we'd all be clear about what counts as too much. You can't drive a car after two pints of Guinness, but you can parent a child after a bottle of vodka. It seems wrong, somehow. Not the driving ban.

The parenting boozy free-for-all.

Possibly, the government thinks parents are responsible enough to set their own limits, but limits have never been my forte with addictive substances.

I'm one of those people they invented the term 'share size' for – to remind me not to plough my way through the whole packet.

Saturday 26th May

Just dropped Daisy off at Nick's.

Nick said, 'What are you all dressed up for?'

Told him it was Laura's wedding day.

'Who's she marrying?' Nick asked.

'Zach Dalton,' I said. 'The man she had a baby with.'

'Oh yeah,' said Nick. 'I'd forgotten about that. Mum says Catrina's not happy about it.'

'Catrina's not happy about the wedding?' I asked. 'Surely that's not true.'

'It's just what I heard,' said Nick, with a nonchalant shrug.

Trust Nick to be such a downer.

'Catrina must be OK about the wedding,' I said. 'She's been badgering Laura about dresses and Burt Bacharach.'

Nick snorted. 'Catrina just wants to make sure Zach Dalton's wedding cuts the mustard. That's what they're like, those Daltons. It's all about image. I bet you a tenner Catrina doesn't come.'

Told Nick he was being ridiculous. Catrina may be self-centred and narcissistic, but not to show up at the wedding...no way.

Late evening

Catrina Dalton didn't turn up to the wedding, which not only ruined Laura's day, but also means I owe Nick a tenner.

If I ever get the chance to speak to Catrina again... How could she do that to Laura? How *dare* she?

Arrived at 10.30 am for the 11 am Mayfair Dalton wedding ceremony.

Felt sad we didn't 'go backstage' to help the bride get ready, but that was how Laura wanted it – no fuss or heavy make-up or anything.

'We're just two adults making a legal commitment,' Laura told me. 'I'm putting on a dress and getting ready just like I would any other day. I don't want any of the circus.'

The ceremony room was simple but pretty, decorated with archways of country flowers, and those ivory-coloured chairs you always see at wedding receptions.

Alex was sitting on the groom's side when I arrived, frowning at his hands. Bethany wasn't with him.

Zach paced back and forth, dressed like a man trying to keep many different people happy. He'd gelled back his straggly, blond surfer hair into a weird Russian gangster look, and wore loose black jeans, leather shoes and a billowy white boho shirt with embroidery around the collar.

He looked like a hippy drug-smuggler trying to get through border control.

I sat on the bride's side with Mum, Dad, Nana Joan and Brandi.

At precisely 11 am, a three-piece orchestra started playing, 'Mr Brightside'.

We all turned and saw Laura walking down the petal-strewn aisle. She was stunning but simple, in a light-blue cotton dress with lots of strings and straps everywhere.

Dad cried happy tears, while Mum held his hand and called him a 'soft old sod'.

'She's not wearing white,' Nana whispered. 'That's a bold move. If you did that in my day, you'd get onions thrown at you.'

Zach and Laura exchanged simple vows, but Laura seemed distracted, looking around and biting her lip.

After their simple 'I dos', Laura and Zach turned to greet the room as a married couple.

Laura managed a stoic smile, then burst into tears and half-walked, half-ran out of the room, crying and shaking her head.

Zach apologised to everyone, then ran after her.

Mum, Brandi and I followed.

Laura disappeared into the lady's powder room, and Zach stood outside, knocking softly on the door and whispering, 'Darling. Please. It's OK. Really. It's nothing personal.'

Laura called back, 'How can it not be personal? It's our wedding day?'

'What's going on?' I asked.

'Laura's got herself a bit upset,' said Zach. 'Perhaps you should go in and see her. Calm her down.'

Inside the powder room, Laura was a sobbing mess.

'Oh love,' said Mum, kneeling beside her. 'What happened? Whose legs do I need to break?'

'Zach's parents didn't come,' Laura cried. 'To our *wedding*. I know they're not keen on me. And yes, I *did* send Catrina's dress designer away and refused calls from Burt Bacharach's agent. But I told her over and over again, I don't want anything fancy.'

Mum, Brandi and I gathered round, telling Laura not to worry.

'Forget about that posh tart,' Mum soothed. 'She's not worth your tears. Enjoy your day.'

'I just wanted her to give me a chance,' Laura sobbed. 'Do you know what Catrina said when Zach reminded her about the wedding? *Darling, I have a busy day planned, I'll see if I can make it.* I thought she was joking. I never thought for a moment she wouldn't come.'

'Your Grandma Eiderdown didn't come to my wedding,' said Mum, perching on a velvet stool and patting Laura's back. 'She's never been fond of me. I think because I farted when we first had tea and cakes. But on the positive side, I never had to do any of those camping trips to Scotland. You've got a good man in Zach, love. Ignore the rest of the family – Catrina Dalton is bananas.'

'But why didn't Harold Dalton come?' Laura asked. 'Am I that much of a disappointment?'

'Harold Dalton isn't Zach's real dad anyway,' Mum soothed. 'So what should you care?'

'That's just a rumour,' Laura whispered. 'No one knows for certain.'

Mum snorted. '*Everyone* knows. You only have to look at Zach. He's twice the height of his dad and blonde as a cream puff.'

It's true that Zach and Harold look different.

Zach has unwieldy giraffe-like limbs, whereas Harold is a short, compact man, with dark eyes and a broad chest.

'That may be the case,' said Laura. 'But Harold treats Zach like his own. All right, so he hasn't left him any oil paintings in the will. But he's never questioned the paternity. He's not here because he thinks I'm not good enough.'

Laura's voice rose to a desperate pitch then, and she cried harder.

'Tell Zach to have a DNA test,' Mum suggested. 'Then he can find himself a better father and your worries will be over.'

We calmed Laura down and eventually went to lunch.

There were only twenty guests, so we all shared one dining table.

Alex sat next to Zach, and I sat a few chairs away, beside Laura.

At first, Alex and Zach were talking about their Irish grandmother, and how much they missed her.

'If she were alive, she would have kept our father in line,' Alex told Zach. 'She would have made him celebrate your wedding, no matter what. And she would have brought Laura roses.'

'Yes, she loved roses, didn't she?' said Zach. 'And whisky in a cup and saucer.'

I leaned back and hissed at Alex, 'Your mother didn't come. Why didn't she come? It's awful. Laura's really upset.'

Alex leaned back and said, 'Don't blame me for my mother's bad manners. I didn't bring her up.'

'But why didn't she come?' I hissed.

'I have no idea,' said Alex. 'She didn't come to any of my school recitals, debates or presentations either.'

'That's what I said,' said Zach, leaning back too. 'Our mother is a law unto herself. Expect nothing, and you won't be disappointed.'

Then Laura leaned back and said, 'I'm feeling better now. Let's enjoy the day.'

We began our starters (seasonal salad and goat's cheese from a local farm), drank English wine (which was awful) and for a moment it felt like a normal wedding.

Then Alex stiffened. 'Zach,' he said, voice low and serious. 'Our father just arrived.'

I looked up from my organic food, and saw a small, wizened old man approaching the table, his dark eyes hard and annoyed.

Harold Dalton looked even more ancient than I remembered him, with a bald-freckly head and loose turkey neck. A scowl was etched into his forehead wrinkles – a permanent reminder of his state of mind.

It was like seeing the bad fairy at Sleeping Beauty's christening.

Zach got to his feet. 'Daddy,' he called out. 'Daddy.'

Harold's furious forehead didn't soften, but he raised a hand in greeting. He wore a smart navy suit with pink tie and shiny shoes.

'You've missed the ceremony,' Zach called. 'But you can meet my lovely new wife and make up for lost time.'

'I'm aware I missed the ceremony, Zachary,' said Harold, with a warning glance.

'Here – take my seat,' said Zach, rising and offering his own chair. 'Laura, this is my father. Daddy – may I introduce Mrs Laura Dalton.'

Harold lowered himself slowly, slowly into Zach's chair, dropping the last inch with his teeth gritted. Then he waved over a waiter and ordered himself a cold Viognier.

Laura sat awkwardly, a fearful smile on her lips.

'Nice to meet you, Harold,' she said.

Harold glowered beside her. 'I prefer to be addressed as Mr Dalton by people I've just met,' he said.

When Harold's white wine arrived, he raised his glass and said, 'Let's have a toast, shall we? To the Dalton family. May we be healthy and prosperous.'

Zach said, 'Here, here', but Alex didn't raise his glass.

'Something wrong with your drink, Alex?' Harold challenged, eyes furious.

'No,' said Alex, eyes equally furious. 'Something's wrong with the toast.'

'You don't want to be healthy and prosperous?' Harold barked.

'I want to celebrate Zach and Laura's wedding,' said Alex. 'Not the Dalton family.'

'Let's keep things calm, shall we?' said Zach.

Alex announced he was going for a walk. It must have been a long walk, because he missed the main (Welsh lamb, sautéed new potatoes and buttered spinach) and dessert (gooseberry pie with local cream). However, he returned in time for coffee (which came with a shot of British gin).

Over coffee, Harold said to Laura, 'I suppose you seem a nice, quiet sort of girl. No trouble.'

Laura gave a lovely, slightly nervous laugh and said, 'I certainly *hope* I'm no trouble.'

Harold said, 'But then Zach never was any trouble. It was his brother I had the problems with. Alex was *always* troublesome. Born that way. Takes after his mother.'

'Interesting term,' Alex replied, words clipped and furious. 'Born that way. A man is judged by his actions, is he not?'

'Yes, he certainly is,' Harold barked.

'On the subject of actions,' said Alex. 'You'll have to enlighten me. Why didn't you attend the ceremony?'

'I discussed that with Zach *weeks* ago,' Harold snapped. 'He *knew* my reasons.'

'I would have thought you'd show more respect to his future wife,' said Alex. 'And put your own beliefs to one side.'

'I'm not sitting through a civil wedding ceremony, and never will do,' said Harold. 'Zach should have done the job properly. Let's just leave it at that, shall we?'

'You've provided us with a fine example of doing the job properly,' said Alex. 'By marrying so many times. What does the Catholic Church say about that?'

'Alex, *be quiet*.' Harold took an angry little sip of wine. Then he shook Zach's hand and said, 'Zachary. The best of luck.' And off he hobbled.

Laura burst into tears and ran back to the powder room. She stayed there for the next hour, absolutely distraught.

Zach was angry with Alex, but I don't think he should have been. After all, Alex was only standing up for Laura. It was terrible that Harold didn't come to the ceremony.

Eventually, we got Laura into her special honeymoon transport surprise – a gold VW camper van – and she and Zach left for the airport, picking up baby Bear and his nanny en-route.

They're flying off on honeymoon tonight, and tomorrow they'll enjoy a mini glamping tour of Europe, including the Swiss Alps and Iceland hot springs.

Hopefully the honeymoon will cheer Laura up a bit. She did seem *very* sad, considering it was her wedding day. Thank goodness she and Zach have the money to do it all over again, if they want to.

Sunday 27th May

Laura called us from a boutique safari tent in the Swiss Alps today.

She was still very upset.

Thought she would feel better after a good night's sleep, but she can be very sensitive. It must be hard for her, being a Duffy.

The whole family talked to Laura on Facetime and tried to put things in perspective.

In the main, Laura was upset because she doesn't feel good enough for Zach's family.

Dad took a philosophical approach. He threw out a few Instagram-style snowy mountain sayings:

'We're all equal under God', etc.

Laura said it wasn't about being equal. It was about acceptance.

Dad said, 'Anyone who doesn't accept you is already beneath you.'

Laura said she didn't feel that way, and in fact felt inferior.

Dad said, 'No one can make you feel inferior without your consent.'

Laura started crying again.

Mum grabbed the phone and shouted, 'Ignore your Dad. Sod Zach's parents – they're not worth your tears. If you're good enough for Zach, the rest of them should have nothing to worry about. Drink lots of wine, eat Swiss cheese, have as much fun as you can climbing those bloody mountains.'

Laura stopped crying then, and talked about the lovely Alpine walks she had planned.

Dad asked her to take lots of photos, but I hope she doesn't. Pictures of beautiful scenery are incredibly boring.

Nice evening with the family, eating Chinese takeaway before my pub shift.

Mum ordered too much food as usual, so we couldn't cram the

mixed starters onto the table.

Luckily, Callum made a shelf using Lego brick pillars and Daisy's hardback *Alfie Gets in First* book, so we had room for the spring rolls.

Monday 28th May
Spring Bank Holiday

The Co-op had short opening hours today, so I accompanied Mum and Dad to the big cash-and-carry supermarket.

I should have known better than to go supermarket shopping with both my parents. The arguments started before we'd even got into the car.

Dad enjoys money-saving and efficient shopping, favouring long-life products that can be easily stored in the kitchen cupboards.

Mum likes any oversized food, such as T-bone steaks, catering-sized chocolate gateaux and whole roasted pigs. She also enjoys a special offer, which today included a box of 500 chocolate digestives.

Tried to tell Mum that 500 biscuits were excessive for a normal person, let alone a diabetic.

'But they're so cheap!' she kept saying.

Forgot Mum and Dad have a hire car right now (their one is still being fixed), so mistakenly loaded up someone else's old, silver Toyota.

Then I sat in the passenger seat.

Was midway through a rant about excessive chocolate digestives before I realised the elderly woman in the driver's seat wasn't Mum.

The poor woman was cowering, hands protecting her face.

I apologised profusely.

The elderly woman apologised too, saying she'd never buy so many biscuits again.

Tuesday 29th May

Callum has been told to read more at home.

Apparently, reading once a day isn't enough – the teachers are demanding reading at breakfast, after school *and* bedtime.

Talk about pressure!

Dad believes Callum's literacy problems can be blamed on the 'tedious' Learning Journey school books he brings home.

'What you need are real adventure stories, Callum,' said Dad. 'Books that take you far and away and have you fighting dragons before bedtime.'

Callum suggested Harry Potter, but Dad declared these books 'grammatically poor' and 'full of logic holes'.

He went up to the loft and brought down a selection of his own childhood books –stories about 1950s children who do things we consider dangerous nowadays.

One book was about a five-year old called 'Little Neddie' who catches the bus to town by himself, fishes by open water and camps overnight on a stranger's farm.

Dad put on his special reading spectacles and said: 'Strap yourself in, Callum. Prepare for an amazing literary adventure.'

Callum was riveted, and especially enjoyed 'Little Neddie Cooks Supper' – a story about Neddie making his own bow and arrow, then shooting a chicken to cook over an open fire.

Dad went all misty-eyed, talking about the freedom kids had in the Fifties, and how our cotton-wool generation missed a *real* childhood.

'When I was growing up, we spent all day outside,' said Dad. 'We were given a boiled egg and a slice of bread and off we went. There was none of this stranger danger – your parents only worried if you weren't back for tea.'

Mum reminisced about the polluted canal she swam in as a girl.

'There was no health and safety in those days,' she said. 'The city canal was so polluted it sometimes caught fire.'

Mum explained that on 'flamey days' they'd play hide and seek in the thick, billowing smoke. 'But we had to put a time limit on it,' said Mum. 'Or you'd faint.'

Wednesday 30th May

Daisy got out of her cot at 5 am this morning.

How did she do it? The little escape artist.

Then I put her down for her nap just after lunch, and she appeared while I was on the toilet.

Nearly had a heart attack.

'Mummy poo!' Daisy exclaimed joyfully. Then she turned it into a question. 'Mummy big poo?'

Quite clever how she's grasping language now.

Thursday 31st May

Laura is back from honeymoon already. She was supposed to be gone another five days, but she said baby Bear got 'homesick.'

Reading between the lines, I think Laura struggled with baby Bear on their adventurous, outdoor holiday. No surprise, really. I thought it was brave taking a baby on a three-hour plane ride, let alone lugging him up Swiss mountains.

Daisy was a nightmare on the short flights to and from Corfu – it's very hard to keep your temper when someone repeatedly digs their elbow into sensitive body parts (boobs and windpipe).

Mum was scathing of baby Bear's 'homesickness', saying that babies 'don't know the difference between food and bits of dirt on the floor, let alone whether they're home or not.'

I disagree – babies do get unsettled in new environments.

Daisy cried her head off the first time I took her into Tesco Metro. It was awful, because I struggle with the self-service tills at the best of times, let alone when I'm emotionally distraught. Tried to work out why my chocolate wasn't scanning, while a queue of disgruntled executives tutted and glared, impatient to buy their stress-relieving Prosecco and Pinot Grigio.

Friday 1st June

Brandi's birthday today.

We had a little family celebration with cake, sandwiches and gin.

Brandi's new boyfriend, Richie, sat with his headphones on, while Brandi drank two double gin and tonics and half a bottle of Prosecco.

It's weird seeing Brandi with someone so quiet and shy, but they seem to rub along OK.

She enjoys someone she can boss around, and Richie clearly needs telling what to do.

Saturday 2nd June

Dad called a family meeting this afternoon to persuade us all to go camping.

'The weather is warming up,' he enthused. 'Who's up for a bit of woodcraft? Fishing. Barbeques. Late-night games of cricket. Sleeping outdoors in the great British countryside.'

We all said no, but Dad was insistent.

'Every year, I get dragged to some overly-hot part of the globe and am forced to eat white bread,' said Dad. 'You all owe me a British holiday.'

Dad has never liked sunshine. His body doesn't get on with warm weather. I think it's genetic, because there's a whole album of his many blue-skinned cousins sweating and frowning in the tepid Scottish sunshine.

It's true – Dad *does* put up with hot weather every year.

We've agreed to a *very short* camping trip at the end of June – depending on the weather.

We're all hoping it will rain.

Will have to ask Althea for camping equipment. She's good for that sort of thing, since she still visits festivals every year.

Anything borrowed from Althea's house smells of patchouli oil, but I don't mind. It's a step up from stale whisky, which is what my tent used to smell like when Nick and I went to festivals together.

Thank God I never have to do *that* again.

Nick was such a little prince at music festivals. A prince and a liability, moaning about headaches and 'suspected trench foot', then getting absolutely hammered on various different drugs.

Nick, off his face, is like one of those little Yorkshire terriers barking at big dogs. He finds the biggest, scariest man around and starts insulting him.

At Reading Festival, he approached a heavily pierced and tattooed Scottish man and called him 'a big wussy girl' for wearing a kilt.

Luckily, the man wasn't bothered by the slur. He simply lifted his kilt and showed Nick the giant dragon tattoo covering his whole penis and testicle area. Then he tied a pair of army boots to his testicles.

It's a miracle Nick's only been beaten up five or six times.

Afternoon

Phoned Althea.

She wants to come camping too and suggested we all sleep together in her bell tent.

Althea is very pleased about the trip, because she's missing out on some major festivals this year. Wolfgang's estranged father plays at most of them and security won't let her in.

Althea and Wolfgang's dad aren't getting along due to visitation arguments.

'It's pathetic,' Althea says. 'A grown man, scared of a toddler.'

But frankly, I don't blame anyone for being scared of Wolfgang. He can be very fearsome and unpredictable.

Thankfully, Daisy has learned to give as good as she gets. If Wolfgang takes a toy from her, she screams right in his face. Usually, Wolfgang grunts and hands back the toy.

In the world of toddlers, I think this shows mutual respect.

Normally, I'd tell Daisy off for screaming, but the rules are different when it comes to Wolfgang. Althea and I just let the two of them fight it out these days.

Althea calls it, 'child-led parenting'.

I call it, 'the law of the jungle'.

Either way, Daisy is learning to be super tough. No one's going to mess with a kid who can tackle a boy with a blowtorch.

Sunday 3rd June

Village summer fête today.

Picked up Nana Joan and discovered she's had a fancy new hair-do. All the blonde extensions are gone, and she's opted for a silvery graduated bob.

Nana doesn't like the new look because it's 'aging', but it really does look very nice. True, we had a panicked moment in the flower tent when we lost her among all the grey heads, but practicalities aside, the new style is pleasingly age-appropriate.

At noon, there was a free 'Teddy Bear's Picnic' for the kids.

It included healthy food (brown bread sandwiches, cherry tomatoes, celery, cucumber and carrot sticks) and yellow food (white bread sandwiches, crisps, biscuits).

The yellow food was immediately snatched up by chubby fingers.

The healthy food remained untouched.

After the picnic, the kids ran races.

Callum won every race he entered and swaggered around wearing six medals.

I was impressed, until he admitted he'd entered the under-fours category.

Monday 4th June

Althea phoned in a panic.

Wolfgang has eaten a urinal cake.

'He smells like the Eighties!' Althea fretted. 'Even milk thistle and oregano oil aren't cutting through it.'

Wolfgang is in bed now, sleeping off the toxins.

Advised Althea to go to A&E.

'I don't think things are that serious yet,' said Althea. 'But if he still smells like old-lady perfume when he wakes up, I'll take him to the NHS walk-in centre.'

Afternoon

Wolfgang is fine.

He no longer smells like the Eighties and doesn't need hospitalisation.

I could hear him in the background when Althea called. He was grunting and snorting his way through a 'massive restorative vegan curry'.

Tuesday 5th June

11.30 pm

John Boy just had a night terror.

Woke up to high-pitched screaming.

I didn't realise what was happening at first, so shouted downstairs, 'Turn the TV *down* John Boy – it's gone eleven!'

Five minutes later, I could still hear shouting, so I went downstairs to investigate.

John Boy was lying on the sofa, eyes closed and gibbering: 'You've got to warn the lads. There's a bomb, a bomb I'm telling you!'

He sounded like a bad actor in a 1950s war movie.

'John Boy,' I whispered. 'You're asleep.'

John Boy wouldn't wake up at first, even when I sat him up and played a pretend piano with his hands. But after a moment, he abruptly opened his eyes.

'I let them down, Julesy,' he said. 'I let them all down.'

Then he started crying.

'Who did you let down?' I asked.

'The lads,' said John Boy. 'If I hadn't got off the tank for a piss, I never would have got blown up. They risked their lives getting me back on. They got shot at. They could have died.'

Then, just as abruptly, he fell asleep.

I tucked John Boy under a tartan blanket, wiped his tears away and put a cushion under his head.

Poor John Boy. That's the thing with men. They keep it all in, don't they?

Wednesday 6th June

Wolfgang started a new nursery today.

I asked Althea how he got on, and she said the staff were racist and persecuting Wolfgang for his ethnicity.

'What ethnicity?' I said. 'He's white British.'

Althea said racism was not always about ethnicity.

'Well what is it about then?' I asked.

Althea said that self-expression was a form of ethnicity.

Personally, I think she's making excuses for Wolfgang's feral behaviour.

Sometimes, you just have to tell kids no.

Thursday 7th June

Callum has two wobbly teeth.

He's delighted, because he's saving up for an expensive *Walking Dead* comic and thinks he can 'bank at least a tenner'.

Five pounds a tooth? This is Mum's doing.

That's the trouble with grandparents. They totally spoil kids.

Well, grandkids anyway.

When we were growing up, the tooth fairy brought us 10p if we were lucky. And if we were unlucky, the tooth fairy forgot.

Asked Callum if he wouldn't prefer a nicer comic. Something less violent.

'What about Spiderman?' I suggested. 'Or Superman?'

'Superman is lame,' said Callum. 'The *Walking Dead* has *proper* peril.'

Friday 8th June

Nick just called. He claims he and Sadie have split up again and wants to have Daisy tomorrow. But he didn't sound in the least bit upset and said 'split up' in a really odd way.

Smelt a rat.

'Why are you whispering?' I demanded.

'Whispering?' Nick whispered. 'I'm not whispering. I just have a little bit of a sore throat.'

I don't believe Nick and Sadie have split up. I think Nick's lying so he can have Daisy round his tomorrow. But then again, if he *is* telling the truth, it would be bad to keep Daisy away.

Have done the unthinkable and texted Helen.
She'll know the truth.

Saturday 9th June
Queen Elizabeth's Birthday

Texted Helen last night.

Woke up to find this reply:

Greetings on the birthday of our great monarch, Queen Elizabeth II. A certain person will be at the Gables this weekend. Regards, Helen.

At first, I was confused by the cryptic 'certain person' element of the message. Was she talking about Santa Claus or the Easter Bunny? Or even the Queen herself? But then I read *my* message and understood what she meant. My instincts were right – Sadie and Nick are still together.

Confronted Nick when he came to pick up Daisy, and he went all evasive and Nick-like, so I knew the text message was true.

Shouted at Nick, then sent him back to his wicked witch.

Daisy and I had a nice day, helping Mum do a pub barbeque to celebrate the Queen's birthday.

Mum doesn't agree with the royal family, but does agree with barbeques, so cooked a lot of meat in the Queen's honour.

There was a bit of panic when she realised she'd left the sausages in the car boot of overnight and they'd gone grey and smelt of vinegar.

'You've got enough meat to feed the entire pub twice over,' said Dad. But this didn't placate Mum at all. Barbeques are one of the few things she's image-conscious about.

'You can't have a barbeque without sausages,' Mum fretted. 'What will people think?'

Luckily, Malik saved the day by bringing a giant sausage wheel from the Polish deli.

Mum was delighted – both with the sausage salvation and the ten-inch-diameter portion.

'There's so much meat, it barely fits on the barbeque,' she said, voice brimming with joy.

Dad tried to mix things up a bit with some vegetarian options – carrot sticks, halloumi cheese, beetroot dip, etc.

Most of it was left at the end. The pub doesn't attract many vegetarians.

The halloumi cheese *was* OK, but Callum had a point – it did taste a bit like hot play dough.

Sunday 10th June

Daisy has started vandalising things.

Worried she might have emotional difficulties, due to the conflictual situation between Nick and me.

Mum says she's just a typical two-year-old. She even complimented Daisy's rebellious nature, calling her 'advanced for her years'.

'You didn't start vandalising stuff until you were nearly three,' said Mum.

Today, Daisy drew all over the dining table in permanent marker, smashed up a box of eggs and shredded my *Contented Little Baby* book with a pair of corrugated scissors.

Put on my sternest voice after the book-shredding incident and told Daisy I was going to take her toy doggy away.

Daisy pointed out, in her earnest two-year-old voice, that I'd already taken doggy away earlier, when she smashed up the eggs.

'OK,' I said, rummaging around my sleep-deprived brain for a back-up threat. 'Then you'll never have sweets again!'

Am dreading the day Daisy works out most of my heat-of-the-moment threats are unenforceable.

Monday 11th June

Had an interesting conversation with Althea today about gender pronouns.

I can't work out if the postman is a man or a woman, so I needed advice re how I talk about him/her in front of Daisy.

Do I say, 'They're bringing the post' or take a stab at gender and say, 'He's bringing the post', but risk offending a woman with a facial hair problem?

Althea is usually very good at gender-neutral language because she has so many transsexual friends. Asked what she'd do in the circumstances.

'Use the universal "she"', she said. 'And if a man gets offended, tell him to stop being sexist.'

She was in a rallying mood, because she'd just confronted a bigot at the supermarket.

The 'bigot' had complained about a shirtless football fan.

Althea shouted at the bigot about freedom of expression and the right to nudity. Then she shouted at the shirtless football fan for his racist British Bulldog tattoo, and the fact he was buying 'shit-quality' Carling lager.

Buoyed up by these small victories, Althea is emailing the supermarket about body prejudice. And also their poor selection of gluten-free cakes.

Tuesday 12th June

Shift in the pub tonight. I really don't mind working there at the moment – I'm sort of like an agony aunt/wise old woman of Africa. Everyone tells me their problems.

I've got some stock phrases now.

'Life isn't always fair.'

'Women are complicated.'

And most important: 'Whatever it is, you'll have to tell me tomorrow. It's closing time.'

Wednesday 13th June

Visited Nana Joan today to help with her new iPad.

It's quite nice helping older people with technology. They believe the younger generation are computer geniuses, just because we can move our contacts from one phone to another.

Made the iPad text big, so Nana could read her emails. It took a while for her to understand the 'no keyboard' concept, but we got there in the end.

She had a few emails from old friends, and also a random message from a would-be scam artist:

Hello,

I'm pleased to write you after I came across your profile when I was searching for an old friend that bears the same last name with you on Facebook.

I am glad to see you on there and you caught my attention, I sincerely appreciate your good looks. I am a widower living alone. I have been thinking seriously about us being friends. I will really appreciate knowing you. I will tell you more about myself when I get a feedback from you.

God bless you,

Regards

Christmas Sunday

Nana had already replied:

Dear Mr Sunday,

Thank you for noticing my good looks. So few people do, now I'm getting older, but I like to think I've still got it.

Women are beautiful no matter what their age, and if you've got it, flaunt it.

You sound like a cheeky chappy.

Perhaps you'd like to send me a picture and we can go from there?

Joan

Told Nana not to reply again.

Deleted the email, but worried now. I always thought those scam emails were transparent to everyone. But I don't think the older generation understand how easy it is to message random people.

Thursday 14th June

Alex called.

He said he'll be back in Great Oakley this week, overseeing some urgent renovations on the Dalton estate (new swimming pool and spa area), and asked if he could see Daisy and me.

Said no.

I understand he still wants to see Daisy from time to time, but coming round the house is a bad idea. It's too close for comfort.

Friday 15th June

Fish and chips at the pub.

Nana Joan joined us. She gave Callum and Daisy five pounds each, folded up in little jewellery boxes, and shared her saveloy sausage with them. Then she raged about Carmen Akawolo and her perfect white teeth.

Nana and Carmen *have* made a tentative truce. They've both promised not to hit each other, if the following terms are met:

+ Carmen stops giving banana puff puffs to Nana's boyfriends.

◆ Nana stops driving her electric wheelchair over Carmen's flowerbeds.

Saturday 16th June

Sadie and Nick have split up again.

It's real this time – Helen has confirmed it.

Nick phoned early this morning, saying he had no breakfast cereal or toilet roll and had been left alone with a screaming infant.

Felt extremely sorry for Horatio and agreed to come over and help out.

'Can you bring a loaf of bread?' Nick asked. 'And some milk. And laundry tablets – the hypo-allergenic ones. And fabric softener. And toilet roll – soft toilet roll. And some recycling bags.'

Told him to sod off and do his own shopping – the Co-op is only down the road.

When Daisy and I arrived at the Gables, Helen was there, mooning over her little prince. She was re-arranging Nick's cupboards, talking about the 'impossible order' Sadie had put things in, and making Nick some 'real Columbian coffee.'

Had forgotten what a nightmare Helen is as an in-law. The first time I met Nick's mother, she walked in on Nick and me in bed together.

The second time, Nick and I went round to Helen and Henry's house for Sunday lunch and an 'official introduction.'

Helen said, 'You must be Juliette. I didn't recognise you with your clothes on.'

I said, 'You must be Helen. I didn't recognise you when you weren't sticking your big nose in your son's bedroom.'

It went downhill from there.

Sunday 17th June

The weather forecast predicts sunshine for the next fortnight, so it looks like the family camping trip will be going ahead.

We'll be leaving Nana Joan behind, so I visited her old people's home to sort out medicine.

Nana is on blood-pressure medication (which she claims has increased since Carmen Akawolo joined the old people's home), plus anti-inflammatory tablets for her arthritis and a few other general old-person bits and pieces.

Retirement seems to necessitate a good handful of daily prescription meds. At Nana's care home, pill containers are common enough to be a fashion accessory. This year, the trend is English garden designs and country flowers. Last year, it was renaissance paintings.

Nana was quick to mention that Carmen Akawolo had a 'flashy' gold pill-container box with 'garish' flowers painted on it.

Monday 18th June

What is it with the British weather?

One day chilly, the next BOILING hot.

Summer arrived this morning, and we're totally unprepared for it.

Dad had to rush out and buy a giant parasol for the pub garden, and he and Callum spent the morning cementing it into the ground.

Worried about Daisy in the burning sunshine, but not sure which sun cream to buy.

When I was growing up, we only ever used sun cream on holiday. Even then, it was Factor 8 or 15.

Nowadays, everyone uses Factor 50 on their children – a level of protection that mimics concrete walls.

Seems a bit extreme. I mean, surely Daisy needs *some* sunshine. Need to obsessively Google.

Tuesday 19th June

Have just been terrified by Superdrug and Boots the Chemist websites.

Apparently, ALL sun exposure increases the risk of skin cancer.

Ordered Factor 50 lotion, baby sunscreen lip stuff and a sunhat with neck panel.

Mum laughed when I informed her of my safety-conscious purchases.

'Kids need a bit of sunshine,' she chortled. 'Sun cream is all a big con.'

Phoned Laura and Althea for alternative perspectives.

Laura said life is about balance. She advised using a little sun cream in very hot weather but going without if it's a mild day.

Althea said sun cream was a capitalist plot and should be avoided. Her philosophy is to let Wolfgang gain gradual sun exposure, so he can build up his own natural protection.

'There's no way I'm covering him in chemicals, the long-term effects of which are unknown,' Althea declared. 'For all we know, Ambre Soleil causes bowel cancer. The human body is designed with its own sun protection. It's called melanin.'

But Wolfgang's skin is naturally darkish like Althea's. He's never going to have any trouble in the sun.

With the exception of Callum, our family have that terrible, pale English skin that goes red in May.

Brandi calls Callum's orange-brown skin his 'all year suntan' and claims he'll save a fortune on sunbeds and Fake Bake when he's older. Callum sees advantages to his skin tone too, claiming that as a 'black man' he'll be more likely to be picked for premier league football teams.

None of us has the heart to tell him he's not very black.

Wednesday 20th June

Helen asked me to lunch today at the village deli.

Suspected she wanted something because Helen has never, ever invited me to lunch – even when Nick and I were together. But I was intrigued, thinking she must have some important news/gossip about Nick and Sadie.

I rarely visit the village deli, because they hate children and you can get a cheaper lunch in the café if you're not fussed about olive quality. But went along with it, because I know Helen is as flexible as a table leg.

Agreed to meet Helen at 12.30 pm, but Daisy and I were a little late (Daisy's fault – she refused to put on socks).

I could tell Helen wasn't happy about our time-keeping. Her lips were pursed when we arrived, and she made a patronising comment about the *difficulties* of motherhood and punctuality. Still, she tried her best to be nice, forcing a vulture-like smile onto her thin lips, and requesting a high chair for Daisy.

The deli owner snapped about the cost of child facilities, and told me if I needed to change Daisy, I'd have to leave.

There were no child meals, so Daisy made do with wholemeal toast and unsalted butter.

I had homemade beans on toast, which were disappointingly worthy and sugar-free.

Helen decided to 'live a little' and try an organic celeriac and beetroot soup, with toasted pumpkin seeds and crème fraiche. (Although she regretted her choice, because the beetroot horribly overpowered the subtle taste of the celeriac.)

Asked why Helen wanted to meet me. She said she wanted to

see Daisy. Asked why, if that were the case, Helen never, ever got in touch to see her granddaughter.

'For goodness sakes, Juliette,' said Helen. 'Are you always going to rake over the past? Why can't you let things go?'

Told her there was a lot to rake over.

Then, out of nowhere, Helen started crying.

It was the strangest sound I ever heard – a cross between a squawking bird and a donkey.

I didn't know what to do. It was like seeing Margaret Thatcher or Hitler cry. You want to be compassionate, but at the same time you feel they've brought their problems on themselves.

'It's OK,' I said, trying for a kind smile. 'Whatever it is, I'm sure it can't be that bad.'

But knowing Nick, it could be.

'I just can't *bear* it,' Helen snapped, becoming angry. 'Something has to be *done*.'

'About what?' I asked.

'*Sadie*. She's ruining Nick's *life*. Horatio is passed from pillar to post. Sadie doesn't want the responsibility of motherhood. Nick and I have to pick up the pieces. I've had Horatio five times this week. Can you imagine? I'm close to retirement age. I need a *break*.'

'Well what can I do?' I said. 'This is all down to Nick.'

'You can help me, Juliette,' said Helen. 'Nick still loves you. If only you'd take him back.'

'We've been through this,' I said. 'It's not going to happen.'

Helen ate her soup with ferocity then. After some angry spooning she said, 'You know, I expected more of you, Juliette. I thought you wanted a family.'

'I have a family,' I said. 'And we're doing just fine.'

Thursday 21st June

Got home from Nana Joan's to find John Boy on the roof, hopping around on one leg, trying to replace some broken tiles and clean out the blocked guttering. His prosthetic leg was propped up by the side of the ladder.

Was nervous about John Boy hurting himself – especially when he admitted there were loose tiles everywhere and he wasn't sure if he could get down. Got really worried when he starting talking about 'army rolling' off the roof and landing on his shoulder.

Mum and Dad were in London seeing Laura, so I couldn't phone them for help.

Was so panicked I phoned Alex, knowing he was in the village for his 'essential maintenance'.

Alex answered on the first ring and said he'd be right down. He arrived within five minutes, his fancy MG squealing as he pulled onto the grass. Then he leapt out of his car and looked up at the roof, shielding his handsome face from the sun.

'Hallo there,' Alex called up the ladder. 'That's a little dangerous, don't you think?'

John Boy hopped along the roof and shouted down, 'Mate, you're talking to a man who got shot at for a living.'

'Do you need a hand down?' Alex asked.

John Boy refused help at first, so Alex climbed on the roof. The pair then postured over building knowledge.

I'm not sure either of them really knew what they were talking about, but they were trying to outdo each other with terms like 'render' and 'soffit'.

When they'd finished word posturing, Alex helped John Boy down, then came in for a cup of tea and a Jaffa Cake.

Daisy was delighted – about both Alex and the Jaffa Cakes.

'I really appreciate you coming,' I told Alex. 'I hope Bethany doesn't think it's too disrespectful, but honestly I had no one else to call.'

'Why do you keep bringing Bethany up?' said Alex.

'I'm just trying to be considerate,' I said. 'I wouldn't want my boyfriend seeing their ex all the time.'

'You have a boyfriend?' Alex asked, looking angry.

'No,' I said. 'I'm speaking hypothetically.'

'Bethany isn't my girlfriend,' said Alex. 'She has no claim on my time.'

'You've broken up?' I asked.

'We were never together,' said Alex. 'Is that what you thought? That Bethany and I were seeing each other?'

'It's what she told me,' I said.

Alex stood up then and began furiously pacing. 'She said that?'

'Yes,' I said. 'Outside the church when I was stalking you.'

'That is *totally* unacceptable,' Alex barked. 'To imply...what did she say exactly?'

'That the two of you were 'doing well' or something like that.'

I've never seen Alex look so angry. 'That is *absolutely* untrue,' he shouted. 'A total fabrication. Bethany is a family friend, nothing more. She was accompanying my mother to church, not me. It was *outrageous* of her to suggest we had any other sort of relationship.'

Alex stopped pacing then and said, 'No wonder you were so unreasonable.'

'You're one to talk about being unreasonable,' I said. 'You believed that terrible rumour.'

'And I apologised.'

'But you still *believed* it. You were that jealous.'

'And you believed I was seeing Bethany. *You* were jealous too.'

'She told me you were together,' I said. 'What did you expect me to think?'

'I would expect you to think the best of me,' said Alex. 'And that

I wouldn't move on so quickly.'

I suppose he had a point.

'So what do we do now, Juliette?' Alex asked.

'I honestly don't know,' I said. 'I'm a bit sick of going round in circles.'

'Maybe we could spend some time together. No expectations.'

'We've been there before,' I said. 'We're a car crash.'

'There's a lot to think about,' said Alex. 'You need time.' Then his phone bleeped and he said he'd better be getting back. The infinity pool dado rail had arrived, and he wanted to make sure it was installed the right way up. Apparently, few people understand which direction the grain must run in.

Friday 22nd June

Callum's school sports day.

Mum, Dad, Brandi, Nana Joan, John Boy, Daisy and I attended for moral support.

Callum's house were the underdogs, so Mum volunteered for the parents' events to win points.

Mum single-handedly won the tug of war through brute strength and intimidation, shouting the All Blacks' Haka rugby chants before taking up the rope. Three would-be tug-of-war mums scampered back to their picnics at the sight of Mum slapping her elbows and bellowing.

When the tug of war started, Mum easily pulled the remaining five mums over the line, dragging their flailing bodies a final victory metre.

Callum was extremely proud of her.

'She's just awesome, isn't she?' he said.

Saturday 23rd June

It's Nick's visitation day, but he hasn't been in touch.

Waited at home until 11 am, in case he came here to see Daisy. He didn't, so we went to the pub for family brunch.

I don't know if Nick is still with Sadie, or what's going on, but I'm definitely not chasing him. Let him sort his life out, then come to us.

The family brunch was good – we had a chat about camping, working out who got the extra bed with Mum and Dad in the caravan (John Boy) and what we're going to eat (mainly sausages).

Mum has already bought hot dogs, marshmallows and five catering cans of baked beans. This provoked a family discussion (argument) – are baked beans healthy or not?

Laura informed us that tinned baked beans are full of sugar, and offered to make us a healthy, homemade version.

This resulted in a lot of swearing.

Even Dad said, 'Oh come on love, it's a *holiday*.'

'Baked beans *can't* be unhealthy,' said Mum, looking distressed. 'They're a vegetable.'

'The beans themselves are a good source of fibre and protein,' said Laura. 'But they're also full of salt and sugar.'

The mention of salt intake started another row, with Mum exploding about the two frozen pizzas Dad gave away to one of the neighbours yesterday.

This was a double insult, as far as Mum was concerned. First, the pizza she wanted to eat was gone. Second, Dad gave it to the neighbour who steals pint glasses from the pub.

Told Laura about the Alex/Bethany confusion.

'I always thought it was strange Alex got a new girlfriend so quickly,' said Laura. 'He's not that sort of person. He's very loyal.'

'And jealous,' I said.

'Perhaps,' said Laura. 'But isn't that better than indifferent?'

Sunday 24th June

Althea phoned this morning to rant about hair removal. Specifically, she wanted to complain about hair removal adverts, and lack of hair therein.

'The women in those razor adverts always hold a Gillette quadruple blade razor to a leg that's already been shaved,' she raged. 'Since when did female body hair become so repulsive that we can't even show a woman authentically removing it?'

Althea's feminism is a bit like her vegetarianism, in that she does shave her legs and spends too much money on clothes (self-expression!), just like she'll occasionally eat a bacon sandwich from a burger van. But her heart is in the right place.

She is custom-decorating wellies for camping next weekend. I'm not sure what she'll come up with, but she mentioned silly string and Lady Gaga.

She offered to make me a pair of fun, crazy wellies, but I politely declined.

'Oh yeah,' she said. 'I forgot. You've got wellie trauma, haven't you?'

She's right about that.

The last time I wore wellies was at Glastonbury festival, pre-Daisy. I bought a cheap, leopard-print pair from eBay, which fitted extremely snuggly on the calves. So snugly that they got completely stuck.

The combination of slippery mud and an air vacuum created a lock-tight bond that even the strongest, fattest, soberest man at the festival couldn't break.

I had to keep the boots on for two days, sleeping with my feet outside the tent.

After the festival, Althea cut me free with her tin snips.

The relief was incredible.

I suppose my calves just aren't willowy enough for standard boots, but I resent paying three times as much for custom-sized ones. I mean, half the population are over size 14 now. It can't be that bloody specialist.

Althea and I had a laugh, remembering my two-day welly prison and all the drunk men lining up to pull my boots free.

'It was like the sword in the stone,' Althea reminisced. 'But without King Arthur.'

Althea had to go then. 'Wolfy's got hold of the Gorilla Glue,' she explained. 'He's smashing the tube on the floor and making ape noises. This could get messy.'

Monday 25th June

Have already started packing for the camping weekend, even though it's five days away.

I'm not usually this efficient, but experience has taught me that preparation is key when it comes to the great outdoors.

As a feckless, drunk twenty-something, it was OK to forget a sleeping bag and tent pegs. But now I have Daisy, I need to be organised. Responsible.

Took me AGES to write the camping list. I don't know what's happened to my memory. I just can't seem to retain information these days. Maybe it's because I'm so tired all the time.

Having said that, I remember lots of pointless things that have absolutely no use at all. For example, I know every word to the *Sesame Street* and *Family Ness* theme tunes.

John Boy helped me get my old festival camping gear down from the loft. It consisted of a dented aluminium frying pan, a tobacco tin containing a tiny rabbit's dropping of dried-out cannabis, a huge lantern that takes all day to charge up, a velour inflatable pillow that was never comfortable (even before the puncture) and a mouldy air bed. I also found a large hunting knife sheathed in leather, lent to me by Mum for cutting streaky bacon.

As I packed up the car with old, crap camping equipment, Mum came over to drop off a spare sleeping bag. She offered to lend me a hand ramming things into the car, and I gratefully accepted.

'What's this?' Mum asked, spotting the tobacco tin on the breakfast bar. 'John Boy's not smoking again, is he?'

Told Mum it was Althea's old cannabis from years ago.

'That could be just the job for my back pain,' said Mum, popping the cannabis ball into her mouth. Then she noticed the hunting knife and told me off for owning a dangerous and possibly illegal weapon.

'That's a ten-inch, double-sided blade,' she said. 'If the police catch you with that, you could do time.'

Pointed out that Mum had given me the knife.

Mum gave the cannabis a thoughtful chew and said, 'Oh yes. I remember now. For the streaky bacon.'

Not sure I'll sleep very well on this camping trip.

The Go Outdoors website makes camping look so cosy, showing families snuggling up together in tents. But Daisy can literally do a 180-degree turn whilst sleeping, smacking me in the face several times in the process.

Tuesday 26th June

Nick and Sadie have both changed their Facebook statuses to single and put up new profile pictures.

Sadie's profile is now a black-and-white shot of her pulling a fedora hat over one eye, cheekbones tilted to catch the light.

Nick has a sad picture of himself on a country path. He's changed his wallpaper to a shot of him and Horatio.

Knowing Nick and Sadie as I do, I'm not ruling out a passionate, romantic reunion – possibly captured by *Hello* magazine. But the mutual status change *is* a big deal.

Maybe they really mean it this time.

Evening

Nick called round after tea.

Wasn't surprised to see him.

Helen was looking after Horatio so Nick was, as usual, childfree.

For once I didn't lecture him about parenting copping out – he really did look and smell terrible. Invited him in.

John Boy took one look at his distraught, tear-sodden face and threw him a can of Stella Artois.

Nick broke down at this kind gesture and took a seat on the sofa, crying and sipping from the frothy can. His high-pitched, womanly sobbing woke Daisy up, and she toddled downstairs to tell us she'd heard an 'angry lady ghosty'.

Nick cried even harder when he saw Daisy and cuddled her for a long time.

Daisy accepted the cuddle, then turned the situation to her advantage. 'Sweets Daddy?' she said. 'Daddy ice cream?'

Which I thought was quite an advanced form of social manipulation.

We let Daisy sit with us for a bit, while Nick behaved like a schizophrenic lunatic.

One minute he was laughing with relief, telling us how pleased he was to be free, how much better things would be for Horatio and Daisy. How Sadie was an 'effing nightmare', and he could finally close the door on the worst few years of his life. The next minute, he was sobbing about the betrayal. Hadn't she loved him? Had it ever been *real*?

Seemed a bit mean to mention karma while Nick was in tears, so just gave the occasional pitying noise and let him go on.

Learned lots of things I'd rather not know – one of which being that Nick and Sadie haven't had sex in over six months.

Apparently, Sadie *said* she was too tired. But she *wasn't* too tired to have sex with an actor ten-years younger than Nick, with a naturally brown beard.

Nick tentatively suggested that we might give things another go, now the Sadie nightmare was over.

Told him no way.

He cried again.

Ended up feeling *really* sorry for Nick.

That's the thing about karma.

It always happens when you don't care any more.

Nick stayed way too long and ignored all hints to leave.

In the end, John Boy took him to Mum and Dad's pub for a few pints.

They're still not back, so I hope Nick doesn't feel too ill tomorrow.

It could be a very messy night.

John Boy lives the army machismo drinking culture, ridiculing any male who doesn't have a whisky chaser with their pint of strong lager. And Nick likes to get drunk.

Wednesday 27th June

Helen came round this morning with baby Horatio.

The sun was boiling hot, but Helen wore a long-sleeved white blouse tucked into tight black jeans, completing the look with a billowy chiffon scarf.

She told me once, during the village sailing regatta, that women over thirty shouldn't show bare flesh, no matter what the temperature. It was an implicit criticism of Mum, who wore a nautical-striped Lycra bandeau top that threatened to spill boobs every time she waved at the boats.

Asked Helen to what I owed the *unexpected* pleasure of her visit – with great emphasis on the word 'unexpected'.

'Please don't ask me to get back together with Nick again,' I said. 'I've told you and I've told Nick a hundred times now. It's not going to happen.'

Helen whisked a confused-looking Horatio out of the pram (he's so blonde – like a Nazi prison guard) and held him to her cheek.

'I was at a loose end with little Horry,' she said, 'And I thought Daisy and her half-brother should get to know each other better. Spend a little quality time.'

Invited her in, thinking the whole time: *What do you want Helen? Come on. Out with it.*

She took a seat at the breakfast bar and slagged off Sadie for twenty minutes. Then she asked if I had any filtered water.

Horatio wriggled on her lap as Helen bad-mouthed his mother. His squinty blue eyes assessed his captor, sizing up the potential for a jailbreak. But Helen clamped her claws tight around Horatio's chubby forearms.

Helen told me again about the Hermes scarf 'episode'. Then she detailed an ugly facelift argument, and I learned about Sadie's disrespectful attitude to good-quality Fired Earth tiling. Finally, Helen turned her rage on Sadie's lack of parental responsibility. Apparently, Sadie walks out on Nick regularly, leaving Helen to pick up the pieces.

'For a *mother* to abandon her *son*...'

I asked why Nick wasn't taking care of Horatio today.

Helen said Nick had a stomach bug and was convalescing.

Considered dropping Nick in it and telling Helen about his bender with John Boy last night, but knowing Helen, she wouldn't believe me anyway.

'I expect Nick's immune system is very low,' Helen said. 'He's under so much *stress*. And I am *too*. I feel like the world is closing in on me. I can't take Horatio anywhere *I* want to go.'

Helen has been barred from the village deli apparently, because Horatio threw up last time they visited.

'So I can't even get a decent cup of *coffee*. And Horatio is too young to sit still in restaurants, let alone a Royal Ballet performance.'

While we were talking, Horatio threw up over his little sailor suit.

'Oh, *Horry*,' said Helen, holding Horatio at arm's length. 'Not *again*.'

With great dexterity, she dived into her patent-leather clutch bag for a slim packet of wet wipes, whilst keeping Horatio away from her clothing.

'I'm certain he has a dairy allergy,' she said, dabbing at Horatio's clothes. 'It's just not normal for reflux to go on this long. He's a year and a *half* now. And he doesn't *sleep* at night.'

Apparently, Horatio sleeps in the second guest bedroom at the far end of the house when he stays with Helen, so she can 'put as many doors between us as possible'.

'That sounds a bit dangerous, Helen,' I said. 'You should be able to hear him cry.'

'They call it *survival*, Juliette,' said Helen, angry and wild-eyed. Then she asked if we could have a 'play appointment' with Horatio this morning. 'It would really help to ease my stress,' said Helen. 'Horatio vomits much less when there are other children around. I suppose they're a distraction for him.'

Had no intention of spending the morning with Helen, but decided it would be nice for Horatio and Daisy to have time together. After all, they are half-brother and sister.

'OK,' I said. 'How about this? You leave Horatio with us today, and the kids can play together.'

Helen's face crumpled with relief.

'Would you? *Thank* you, Juliette. I appreciate it. We are all *family*, after all. We help each other in times of need.'

I snorted at that. 'When was the last time you helped me out, Helen?'

'That's unfair, Juliette. I've been caught in the middle. You haven't made things easy.'

Told Helen to leave before I changed my mind about having Horatio.

'Yes, I should be going.' Helen checked her slim, gold watch. 'Would it be OK – you know, I have a lot of errands today. Perhaps I could pick him up after supper?'

'Don't push it, Helen,' I said. 'Pick him up at four o'clock. I'll see you then.'

'I can give you an allowance,' said Helen. 'If you need to buy him lunch or have things dry cleaned.'

'It's OK,' I said. 'He is family, after all.'

'I'm so glad you see things that way,' said Helen. She looked like she was about to say something else. Something kind. But she only managed, 'Juliette. If you need to wash his clothes, you will use a low setting, won't you? And don't tumble dry. That outfit is from Fenwicks.'

Horatio gave me lots of big baby smiles when Helen left.

'Bugger,' said Daisy.

'Brother,' I corrected her.

We put Horatio in the bath and let him splash around for a bit, while Daisy blew bubbles over the water. John Boy wandered into the bathroom while we were doing this, did one of those loud roary man yawns, wee'd at length in the toilet, cleared his throat and spat in the sink. Then he noticed us all watching.

'WAHEY!' John Boy shouted obscurely, staring at the little blonde baby in the bath. 'Who are you, mate?'

John Boy reeked of beer, so I'm guessing he and Nick had quite a session last night.

Horatio stared at John Boy with his little peepy eyes.

'He's Nick's son,' I said. 'Horatio.'

'Morning, mate,' John boy said. 'Don't shit in that bath, will you? I cleaned it yesterday.'

'My bugger,' said Daisy.

'Oh, your brother, is he?' said John Boy. 'Shall we make him a bacon sandwich with golden syrup, Daisy-waisy? I'll put the grill on.'

Daisy nodded in happy agreement.

'Love you, On Boy,' she said.

'I love you too, mate,' said John Boy, ruffling her hair. 'Bacon sandwiches all round, yeah? And then we'll have a little play.'

Couldn't be annoyed at John Boy's noisy bodily clearing after that. Agreed to a bacon sandwich and felt very lucky to have him living with me.

Late evening

Just finished my pub shift and VERY tired.

It was hard work looking after two kids. Lucky Helen kept her word and picked up Horatio at 4pm. Otherwise I'd have been wiped out.

Horatio is at that age where he has a toddler body but a baby brain. He doesn't understand things like not opening fridge doors and smearing peanut butter all over himself.

On the positive side, Horatio and Daisy entertained each other. Daisy had a great time pretending Horatio was a Baby Annabelle doll, and trying to stuff toy milk bottles into his mouth.

John Boy was helpful too – he loves kids and enjoyed chucking Horatio around and teaching him how to commando crawl.

'I should crack on and start my own family, really,' said John Boy. 'I was planning on this year, but then things went tits up with Gwen.'

'Don't you think you're a bit young?' I asked.

'I'm twenty-*three*,' said John Boy, like this was totally ancient. 'I need to get a move on. As soon as I find someone to marry, we're gonna try for kids on our wedding night.'

John Boy then went on to describe his ideal wedding day. He plans to wear a white suit (no shirt) and ride a white horse like Prince Charming. His girlfriend will be dressed like Stephanie Seymour in the Guns and Roses 'November Rain' video.

I hope John Boy does find a nice girl. Someone who appreciates what a good person he is and doesn't find tattoos too scary.

The pub was a bit rowdy tonight – I think due to the summer heat and the Cranberry cider Dad was trying to get rid of.

Even Mum lost her cool at kicking-out time, shouting at Mad Dave to 'get the fuck out now', and eventually giving him a cautionary belt around the head with an open hand.

I think she's a bit stressed about camping this weekend. She has a phobia of running out of food and is worried the small campsite honesty shop won't meet our requirements.

Mum also claims to have post-traumatic stress after our last family camping trip (over twenty years ago) when we ran out of eggs.

'It wasn't the end of the world,' I said, after the fifth time she mentioned it. 'We had bacon sandwiches without a fried egg. So what? Hashtag-first-world-problems, Mum.'

'Don't come all high and mighty with me,' Mum fired back. 'You were as upset as any of us not to have a fried egg. *And* you kicked off because you only got one rasher of bacon.'

Really need to discuss tent/sleeping arrangements with Althea.

Althea might not be coming camping now, because a 'cowboy hat man' she met on Tinder has invited her to Morocco this weekend.

If Althea doesn't come camping, she will lend me her bell tent. However, only she knows how to set it up – so she'll have to give me detailed instructions. Knowing Althea, she will deliver these in mantra form.

Thursday 28th June

Woohoo!

Althea is coming camping with us.

The Morocco trip is a write-off because the Moroccan authorities are cracking down on foreign tourists who smoke cannabis.

Pleased that Althea is coming because she brings a lot of joy on camping trips with her hippy love-in collection of rainbow wind socks, bunting, hula hoops, etc.

Asked Althea about sharing the bell tent, but she says Daisy and I can have it all to ourselves. She's bought an old transit van, which she's converted into a camper, complete with sensory area.

Afternoon

Have just returned from Althea's house. Had to drive there to pick up the bell tent and other useful bits and pieces – enamel cups, etc.

Forgot how much I hate driving in London.

Why is everyone so angry? You pause for three seconds at a green light to stop your daughter throwing Ribena on the floor and BEEEP!

Cycle couriers whizz straight across every junction, no matter what the traffic lights are doing. Saw one cycle courier ride straight into the side of a double-decker bus, then go flying. Instead of bursting into tears, as I would have done, the cyclist leapt up and started punching the bus doors.

Althea was enjoying the sunshine in her big, rambling garden when I arrived. She'd Rasta-braided her curly hair for the camping trip and wore a loose elephant-print smock like an African guru.

Wolfgang was in the branches of a giant fir tree, wearing wings made from real feathers, screeching and pretending to be an eagle.

A dig around Althea's garage revealed her bell tent was inhabited by a family of rats, who had eaten significant portions of essential canvas.

Althea kindly offered me a patchwork quilt to lay over the holes, but in all honesty the tent is uninhabitable.

Will have to visit Go Outdoors during peak season and buy a new one.

Why didn't I buy one with Dad back in May?

I am such an idiot.

Afternoon

All the decent tents in Go Outdoors were at top price – over £70.

That's what comes of buying tents in summertime.

I only want a little dome tent! I don't care if it has a hook for my lantern and tough Teflon technology.

The only tent I could afford was a child's tent with dinosaurs on it.

Daisy is delighted, but I'm worried the two-man tent is too small because 'two-man' is only ever really 'one-man' once luggage, pillows and shoes come into play.

Arguably, Daisy is only half a man. But as previously outlined, she wiggles around like a demon. I'll be lucky if she's still in the tent come morning.

Go Outdoors is rigged for weak-minded parents like me, because they offered a matching dinosaur sleeping bag with the tent at a 10% discount.

It was *very* cute.

Daisy got all excited and said, 'Sleepy dinosaur, Mummy. Happy.'

She's certainly using words to good effect these days.

Splashed out another £20 on a matching dinosaur sleeping bag.

Also threw in a jumbo bag of M&Ms on sale by the till.

Like I say, shops are rigged for weak-minded parents.

Evening

Arg!

Along with the duvets, sleeping mats, crates of beer and bags of jumbo marshmallows, I couldn't fit the little tent and Daisy's new sleeping bag in my car.

John Boy tried to help, kicking things into place with his prosthetic leg, but it was no good.

My car is designed for carefree twenty-somethings who chuck a small dome tent, single sleeping bag and crate of beer in the car for a festival once a year.

Now I know why people buy roof boxes, which, before, were a mystery.

Have been forced to choose between thick, warm bedding and a bed.

Admittedly, I could leave the beer and Prosecco cool box and have room for an air mattress, but that's not going to happen. In life, you have to prioritise.

Have opted for bedding and packed two yoga mats instead of the luxurious flocked double air bed Mum and Dad lent me.

Like Mum says, on a good camping trip you'll drink yourself unconscious. And kids sleep through anything.

Daisy is very excited about camping. That's because she's never been before. When she realises that, along with the toasted marshmallows, there is a lot of physical discomfort, arguing about tent poles and cold, late night dashes to dark toilets, she may change her mind.

Friday 29th June

Camping today.

Am trying to put on my cheerful hat, because I can recall *some* nice times on family camping trips.

Fish and chips around the campfire. Mum's super-duper hot chocolate with whipped cream and crumbled up cookies on top. Bacon sandwiches in the morning. Bacon sandwiches for lunch. Sometimes for dinner too – who doesn't love a bacon sandwich?

Unfortunately, bad memories also linger.

Thin 1970s camp beds and even thinner 1970s nylon sleeping bags, fierce wind, rain and thistles making a mockery of Dad's 'storm-proof' tent, Mum snoring through thin canvas walls.

Mum has won a campsite record before – causing FOUR neighbouring campers to sleep in their cars.

As soon as we arrived at the campsite, Daisy ran around like a lunatic, shrieking, cavorting and singing inappropriate songs, occasionally helping herself to Wotsits and chocolate biscuits from Mum's giant food suitcase.

Put my tent up surprisingly quickly, but then Dad passed his critical eye over it, saying I hadn't pegged it out symmetrically, lashed the storm guy ropes or put the pegs in at a 45-degree angle for 'maximum strength'.

Let Dad re-do the whole tent, while Mum and I opened the Prosecco and set up the barbeque.

John Boy, who was already on his second can of Stella Artois, said, 'Just stick all the charcoal self-lighting bags on, Aunty Shirley. You want a proper tear-up for that many sausages.'

Like idiots, we followed his instructions.

Half an hour later, we had flames as high as the caravan, and the campsite fire warden sprinting across the field, shouting and waving.

The warden insisted on dousing our barbeque with three buckets of water, but the flames refused to be quelled. The barbeque was like one of those mythical beasts that reform over and over.

Eventually, John Boy starved the fire of oxygen by squirting his shaving foam over it. But obviously, no one wanted the sausages after that.

Mum suggested getting fish and chips or Domino's pizza.

Dad accused Mum of intentionally ruining the barbeque so she could order a takeaway.

Mum was incensed, saying they'd been married over thirty years – didn't he know her well enough to realise she'd never intentionally ruin sausages? Then she stormed off to the caravan, slamming the door so hard it came off its hinges.

Dad roared that he'd *warned* Mum about the dry rot around the doorframe.

Mum roared back, 'Fuck off!'

They're trying to fix the caravan door right now, but it doesn't look promising.

Althea still hasn't arrived, which is a shame because she would cheer Mum up with her colourful camping gear and The Doors, Pink Floyd and David Bowie MP3s and booming speaker system.

Evening

Alex is here.

He's turned Christian Grey and stalked me.

I'll be honest, being stalked feels great. However, I'm keeping things friendly, not romantic. I've learned my lesson re falling down that rabbit hole again.

Alex arrived in a Land Rover (which he called a 'Landie') borrowed from one of his many farm-owning friends, plus some army-style cooking equipment and a set of cricket bats.

'What are you doing here?' I asked him. 'How did you find us?'

'I came to spend time with you and Daisy,' said Alex. 'And Laura told me where you were.'

'This is verging on stalker-dom,' I accused. 'Do you have a Red Room in that big house of yours?'

Alex didn't seem insulted by the stalker accusation, simply

saying, 'Whatever it takes,' in a mysterious voice.

Said I couldn't handle cryptic crossword clues with Mum swearing in the background about 'sodding dry rot'.

'Are you staying the night?' I asked Alex.

Alex said yes – he planned to knuckle down and sleep in the Landie.

Apparently, Alex is very used to roughing it. His London boarding school regularly drove the boys out into the wilderness and left them with nothing more than a rucksack of equipment and an ordinance survey map.

'We were expected to navigate twenty miles of dense woodland, build a fire, pitch our tents, then cook a roast dinner,' Alex told me. 'We had no adult help whatsoever, and anyone who got hyperthermia was given a jolly good talking to.'

John Boy, walking past with a pint-sized can of Stella, said: 'Sounds like the army. You must have had a great laugh.'

Alex said yes – there were 'japes' to keep the lads' spirits up. Like bundling the effeminate boys in grey blankets and kicking them down hills. Or pouring pepper into boys' underwear so they'd be in agony and couldn't sleep.

John Boy was impressed by Alex's traditional army mess tins and canvas bags, calling them 'well smart'. He offered Alex a can of Stella Artois, and the two proceeded to have a manly chat about surviving the great outdoors.

I suspect Alex would have preferred an expensive whisky in a spotless glass, but he accepted the beer and drank straight out of the can.

When Daisy came running over for more Wotsits, she waved enthusiastically at Alex, hopped onto his lap and ate crisps between thumb sucks. It looked so natural – her sitting with him, all cosy and comfortable.

I, on the other hand, was awkward beside Alex, taking large

glugs from my enamel mug of Prosecco, not at all sure what to make of this new development.

Brandi, Callum and Richie arrived mid-afternoon in Brandi's pink Mini, car windows down, horn beeping cheerfully. Richie sat in the passenger seat, knees together, head bent over his mobile phone. He was dressed in classic music-festival attire: sawn-off denim shorts raggedy around the knee and a Red Hot Chilli Peppers t-shirt.

'Would you like a pint of real ale, Richie?' Dad called out, patting a metal beer keg draped in damp tea-towels. 'I've brought one of my favourites from the pub beer cellar. It's called Golden Oldie.'

Richie mumbled something. Brandi played the role of interpreter: 'He only drinks Smirnoff Ice.'

Fortunately, the pint offer wasn't wasted, because John Boy accepted on Richie's behalf, and downed the Golden Oldie in seconds. Then he had a shot of Aftershock, took off his prosthetic leg (which was giving him a rash in the heat) and went off to chat up some twenty-something girls at the other side of the campsite.

We heard whoops and screams as John Boy hopped around with one of them on his back.

Evening

Nice evening around the campfire. The fire itself took a while to get going, but we got there in the end – despite the damp wood. The poor fuel-quality was Dad's fault, because he refused to pay 'a king's ransom' for bagged firewood from the honesty shop.

Alex offered to pay, but Dad wouldn't have it.

'Five pounds for a bag of firewood!' said Dad. 'That is quite literally burning money. Wood grows for free! Who's up for a foraging mission?'

Dad took Daisy and Callum for woodland foraging and returned with a poor collection of green twigs. Then all the men fought over lighting the fire.

Alex managed it in the end. He used petrol from the Landie fuel tank.

Once the petrol had burned off, we were able to get more sausages cooking – luckily, Brandi had two packets of Wall's sausages in her little pastel-blue cool box, along with a six-pack of Smirnoff Ice (for Richie) and various mixed cocktail cans.

As predicted, Mum came out of her huff when she smelt food cooking.

Mum was as surprised as everyone to see Alex.

'What are you doing here then?' she asked.

'I came to see Juliette and Daisy,' said Alex.

'Don't mess her around again,' said Mum. 'Do you want a pint of ale? Bob's bought a keg.'

Alex said yes, he'd love a pint of ale.

We had a little game of cricket while Dad made sure the sausages were absolutely, completely cooked *all* the way through and Mum shouted at him for being 'bloody obsessive'.

Then we all sat around to eat.

Alex *did* make some tentative requests for 'Dijon mustard and possibly a few rocket leaves', but he ate the crap, cheap sausages without complaint and made lots of nice comments about hearty food and good company.

Late evening

Althea finally arrived at 7 pm.

She and Wolfgang came careering across the field in her customised transit van, beeping her horn and flashing her headlights. They were later than usual because they'd stopped to pick fresh strawberries at a local farm.

Apparently, it took rather a while to show Wolfgang how to pick single strawberries.

Althea offered us five cardboard baskets of strawberries for a 'midnight feast', several of which contained entire plants, complete with roots and leaves. She gratefully downed the plastic pint of ale Mum gave her, then single-handedly erected her huge events shelter, raggle-taggle of bunting and fish wind socks, cauldron tripod and hammock village.

We all tried to help, but Althea is militant when it comes to her artistic vision. The event shelter 'altar' had to face east, and the bunting hang just so.

When she had finished, she put on a floppy Liam Gallagher sun hat, accepted another pint of ale, sat in her Mexican hammock chair and asked Alex what he was doing here.

'I came to see Juliette and Daisy,' Alex replied.

'We're just friends!' I said, in a high, embarrassed voice.

'Alex,' said Althea. 'Do you want to be *just friends* with Juliette?'

Alex looked at me, all stern. 'No,' he said.

'Jules,' said Althea. 'Do you want to be just friends with Alex?'

'No,' I admitted. 'But it's not going to work out.'

'The past is gone,' said Althea. 'All you have is now. If you both want it to work, there must be a way. WOLFGANG, STOP JUMPING OVER THAT FIRE!'

'We're too different,' I said.

'So it's just a sex thing?' Althea asked.

Alex barked, 'Absolutely not.' He stared at the fire, looking all angry and brooding.

Then Dad strolled over swinging a cricket bat. 'Alex, do you fancy a *sunset* game of cricket? Callum? Richie? John Boy? Who's up for a thrashing?'

'What's this sexist bullshit?' Althea demanded. 'Only asking the men if they want to play.'

Dad explained that Mum, Althea and I were all inappropriately dressed for sports, referencing our 'dangerous footwear' (flip flops).

'It's a sprained ankle waiting to happen,' said Dad. 'I won't have a visit to Accident and Emergency on my conscience. Not on *this* trip.'

Callum was keen to join in, but Richie opted out of the game after a few minutes. It was for the best. I've never seen literal butterfingers before.

After the game, we all sat around the fire drinking and chatting.

Then Alex and Dad went for a 'nice walk in the woods', so I was able to question Mum, Brandi, Althea and John Boy about the latest Alex-related developments. (Richie was there too, but might as well not have been – he had his headphones on and was playing Angry Birds).

'I got it wrong about his girlfriend,' I explained. 'He wasn't seeing that Bethany girl and he wants to try again. What should I do?'

'Go for it,' said Althea. 'You'll grow as a person.'

'He's less of a twat than I thought,' said John Boy. 'He got the fire going, and I like his camping set-up. He's come all the way out here to see you. That's good. It shows he's keen.'

'He's really fit,' said Brandi.

'He could be worse, love,' Mum conceded. 'I mean, look at Richie over there. At least Alex can look you in the eye and tell you if he wants sausages or not.'

It was Daisy's comment that really got me. 'Love Rex, Mummy,' she said.

Now I'm back in confusing 'will they, won't they' no man's land.

Things are easier when I'm sure we have no future.

Am writing this by lantern light with Daisy sleeping beside me.

Alex is sleeping in the back of the Land Rover on a wool blanket – which he said was reminiscent of his boarding school days.

Better go to sleep now.

Someone – Mum I think – just screamed 'put that sodding light out.'

Saturday 30th June

I've done something crazy. Possibly stupid. Either way, my life is about to change big-time.

Daisy woke at 6 am.

This meant I woke up at 6 am too.

Bloody sunshine.

I'd forgotten about the curtain-less qualities of canvas.

Took Daisy to the toilets and was struck by the sparkly green grass and rolling fields.

Lovely to be part of nature like this. For a moment, I understood Dad's love of camping and sleeping in the wild. Then we reached the horrible, concrete toilet block with its pathetic lukewarm showers, and I remembered why I hate camping.

Daisy and I went for a wee and brushed our teeth (I didn't risk the showers, instead using John Boy's 'army bath' technique of liberally spraying deodorant).

When we came out of the toilets, Alex jogged past. He'd already been for a three-mile run and picked up bacon from the campsite honesty shop.

'Did you sleep well?' he asked.

'Quite well,' I said.

'I didn't,' said Alex. 'I've had a lot to think about. There's always a lot to think about with us, isn't there?'

Daisy said, 'Bacon!'

'I was wondering,' said Alex. 'If I *could* move back to Great Oakley next year, would it make a difference?'

'A difference to what?' I asked.

'Well, would you consider living with me?' Alex asked. 'In Great Oakley.'

'You'd move to our backwards village?' I said. 'With its low-quality olives?'

'Yes,' said Alex. 'I would move back. If I thought it would give us a chance.'

'I mean…I suppose, well, it would give me something to think about.'

'So you'd consider living with me?' Alex asked.

'I didn't say that.'

By the time we got back, Mum's fluffy, pink head was emerging from the caravan, toothbrush in mouth.

Dad was already outside, hands on hips, taking in big lungfuls of countryside air.

John Boy, Brandi and Richie were slumped in camping chairs nursing enamel coffee cups, looking pale and hungover.

'Good morning, everyone,' Alex announced. 'I'd like to ask something.'

John Boy lifted his tired face and said, 'If you want to know who accidentally pissed on your mess tins, it was me. Sorry.'

Alex frowned. 'No. It's not that. First of all, I wanted to ask if anyone wants a bacon sandwich.'

There were agreeable noises.

'And there's something else.' Alex put the bacon on Dad's tripod camping stool. 'Something more important. I have a question for Juliette.'

Alex turned to me, dropped to one knee and pulled a jewellery box from his pocket. He took my hand, brown eyes serious.

I stared at him. 'What are you *doing*?'

'I've asked your father's permission,' said Alex. 'I have a ring with me.'

'Alex.' I shook my head, tears coming. 'You just *can't* ask me this.'

'I can,' said Alex, flicking open the ring box.

Inside sat a beautiful antique-looking ring with a small square diamond.

'This belonged to my Irish grandmother,' said Alex. 'She said I

237

should give it to someone lovely. I'm keeping that promise. Juliette, will you marry me?'

I looked at my family.

Dad and John Boy were grinning at us, John Boy giving a thumbs up. Brandi seemed confused, like when she has to add numbers in her head. Mum was alternating between surprise and frustration, trying simultaneously to watch and open a pack of bacon.

Daisy was smiling.

I thought about Alex. How, despite his occasional coldness and jealousy, he never gives up on me. And how he cares about Daisy and made a real effort this weekend with my family. I thought about Alex moving back to Great Oakley, and what a sacrifice that would be for him.

Blurted out, 'All right. Yes – yes, I'll marry you.'

Alex's lips twitched.

'All right?' he said. 'Or yes? Which one is it?'

Yes,' I said, nodding. 'Yes. I will. I'll give it a go.'

Alex slipped the ring on my finger, and we smiled at each other.

John Boy started singing, 'We've got to fight fight fight fight, fight for this love. Because heaven is worth fighting for.'

Then Dad cleared his throat and said, 'You've got the wrong hand there, Alex. It should be the *left* ring finger, not the right. The Romans believed the vein on the left hand ran straight to the heart, so that's where the tradition –'

'Belt up, Bob,' said Mum. 'Now what about this bacon sandwich?'

Thank you for finishing my book.
If you have a minute, please review
on Amazon and GoodReads.

Suzy xx

What to read next?

BOOK IV:
The Bad Mother's Christmas

Here's a taster...

The BAD MOTHER'S CHRISTMAS

SUZY K QUINN

Lightning Books

BAD

MOTHER'S

CHRISTMAS

SUZY K QUINN

Saturday 30th June

Late evening

So I'm engaged to be married.

Again.

I wonder how many marriage proposals happen on family campsites with coin-operated showers?

Probably not many.

Feel weirdly nervous, which I don't think is the usual reaction of a blushing bride. I want to marry Alex, but, but...

Rather ominously, Alex and I are sleeping apart on our first night as an engaged couple because my 'two-man' tent doesn't really fit two people.

I'm sleeping with Daisy, who is flailing around in her dinosaur sleeping bag like an interpretive dancer.

Alex is lying on cold, grey boarding-school blankets in the back of his Land Rover a few metres away.

Does he know I'm freaking out?

I did *sort* of broach my feelings over the campfire.

'Let's hope we can build a happy family together,' I said. 'Despite our differences.'

Alex said 'hope' was a pointless word. 'We won't hope,' he said. 'We will succeed because we make every effort to do so.'

That freaked me out even more.

It's not marrying Alex that's the problem. It's the 'building a happy family' part.

How can we do that when Alex's mother and I don't get along?

Sunday 1st July

Morning

Woke up at 5 am to find Mum and Dad arguing in hushed voices over a whistling kettle.

Their sticky-up morning hair made them look like angry punk rock stars – Dad the white-haired scarecrow guitarist and Mum the pink-haired lead singer.

'It's consumerism gone mad, Shirley,' Dad whispered. 'Camping is about downsizing. Appreciating nature. The simple things.' He jabbed a knobbly, sunburnt finger at a nearby luxury motor home. 'A big van like that is just an utter waste. Who needs a dishwasher on a campsite? And an electric orange juicer is just ridiculous.'

'You're being very selfish Bob,' said Mum, hands on hefty hips. 'Not everyone enjoys nature. All I'm asking for is somewhere to watch Netflix when it rains.'

As Mum and Dad argued in hissy voices, the motor home's hydraulic door whooshed open and a deeply tanned, white-haired lady popped her head out.

'Would anyone like some homemade hollandaise sauce?' she asked. 'We can't store it – our fridge is too full of fresh crab and oysters.'

Behind her, an elderly man could be seen removing buttered kippers from a halogen oven and delicately adding sprigs of parsley.

'A spot of hollandaise sounds wonderful,' said Mum. 'It'll go a treat on our bacon sandwiches.'

Within five minutes, Mum had befriended the white-haired lady and invited herself on a grand-tour of the luxury motor home.

When Mum clumped back down the motor home steps she'd learned the couple's life story.

'Rita and Paul bought that van with Paul's redundancy money,' she told us. 'Their daughter just moved out, so they've got an empty nest. Rita has a grown-up son from a previous marriage; he got kicked out of the army and has a drink problem. He lives with an older woman – two kids of her own – in a bungalow with bad damp and last year they had mice.'

Mum went on to describe the motor home in detail: its shower room, fridge freezer, two king-sized double beds etc.

'Rita's offered to make you a celebration cake for your engagement, Juliette,' said Mum. 'She's got her own little baking pantry on board with four sizes of cake tin. She can do you a three-layer cream Black Forest gateau with kirsch cherries.'

'Who on earth needs a cake to celebrate getting engaged?' Dad demanded. 'Isn't love enough?'

None of us said anything, but we were all thinking the same thing.

A three-layer cream Black Forest gateau sounded *very* nice.

Mid morning

Just finished breakfast. Alex has gone for a run in his ninja black jogging gear.

Still freaking out about being engaged.

I thought a good night's sleep might sort me out, but I didn't have a good night's sleep because Daisy was horizontally cartwheeling in her sleeping bag.

Was too nervous to finish my egg and bacon sandwich this morning, or Mum's 'brunch' offer of tea and biscuits.

Mum gets worried when people don't eat and she kept shoving her hand on my forehead, asking if I had a temperature.

'Your curls have gone all flat,' she said, tugging at my limp blonde-brown strands. 'That's a sure sign of illness in your case. Unless you've been over-bleaching it again. You didn't let Brandi do your highlights did you?'

Assured her that I wouldn't be that stupid. At least, not again.

My platinum blonde, hair-extended little sister aspires to turn everyone into slutty Barbie.

'My hair is flat because I couldn't rinse it properly,' I said. 'I ran out of 50 pences in the shower. I'm fine Mum. Honest.'

But I wasn't being honest because I'm not that fine.

Feel *really* nervous.

Late morning

Minor argument over lunch.

Althea is my best friend and a welcome camping companion, but no one likes aggressive veganism. Softly softly is a better approach. True – Mum *has* bought 'fucking obscene' quantities of meat, but there are gentler ways to change peoples' minds.

Of course, Mum should never have claimed red meat was a health food. This sent Althea into full activist rant. With her Che Guava t-shirt, ample form and main of curly black hair, she cut a dynamic figure, raging and pointing at Mum's buckets of sausages.

'Who needs seventy sausages for one weekend away?' she shouted. 'Have you ever seen a commercial pig farm? It's piggy Auschwitz for innocent animals.'

Mum looked every bit the guilty meat-eater in her red chef's apron, giant BBQ fork held aloft.

'There are a lot of us here, love,' said Mum. 'I only brought 10 sausages a head. Anyway, *these* sausages are totally free-range. The pigs had a good life before their intestines were pulled out and stuffed with meat. I bought them from a local farmer, Porky George. He's a lovely fellow and very kind to his livestock.'

'No meat farmer is truly kind,' said Althea. 'Do you know how these pigs were slaughtered?'

Mum said the pigs were read bedtime stories. Then cuddled to death.

Afternoon

It started thundering and raining heavily after lunch, so we're all holed up in our tents or caravans, sleeping or reading until the storm passes.

Dad is in his element, wearing all his hiker waterproof gear and talking about survival skills and the great outdoors.

The rest of us are wishing we were Rita and Paul, snug in their motor home, drinking tea from real china mugs and watching *The Weakest Link*.

8 pm

We're supposed to be barbecuing sausages for our evening meal, but Dad still hasn't managed to start the BBQ because the coals are damp.

Rita and Paul were kind, offering to share their Quattro Formaggi pizza, garlic bread, green salad and red wine in real glasses.

Sadly, Dad declined for all of us, saying we'd rather do 'real' camping, thank you very much.

We're all still furious with him.

Evening

Separate beds again for Alex and me. Am still freaking out.

I want to marry Alex, but I'm also scared.

When Nick and I broke up, I thought my world had ended. But I stayed strong for my little girl, and, through grit and determination, bought a house of our own with two flushing toilets and a fridge full of cash-and-carry cheese cake.

Life isn't perfect, but it's stable. And stable isn't bad, given the time I've had in the last few years.

A wedding isn't always a fairytale ending. What if Alex and I can't make it work and mess Daisy around even more? She's had enough upheaval.

There's a lot to get my head around. And a stomach full of sausages to digest.

Monday 2nd July

At last!

A good night's sleep.

I moved Daisy to Mum and Dad's caravan last night due to excessive windmilling. It was for Daisy's own good: if I got accidentally slapped in the face one more time I would really have lost my temper.

Alex crept into my tent in the early hours of the morning, saying he wanted to watch my face as the sun came up. He looked very handsome in the dawn light, with his glinting brown eyes and tousled black hair. However, due to my tiny tent he ended up with elbows and knees in uncomfortable places.

When he finally left to make me a morning coffee, it was a huge relief. His elbow had been on my boob the whole time.

After breakfast (coffee and more sausages), Alex was a gentleman and helped everyone pack up. He and my cousin John Boy made a good team, tossing tents and sleeping rolls into the backs of vehicles, but then John Boy's leg stump swelled up and we had to force him to rest on Mum's deluxe padded camping chair.

John Boy didn't want to rest – he usually carries on with physical activity until he's in agony, then unstraps his prosthetic leg and anaesthetises himself on vodka. But with the sun out, he was happy to take off his shirt and tan his tattoos whilst Callum and Daisy decorated his prosthetic leg with Disney stickers.

My tent was easy to take down, but getting it back into the bag was trickier. Alex spent a red-faced half-hour trying to wrestle armloads of slippery dinosaur fabric into an umbrella-sized bag.

Callum and Daisy got a chant going.

'Rex, Rex, Rex!'

It was quite cute seeing the two cousins getting along, because they've been fighting a lot on this trip.

Callum is getting the blame for the fighting, which is unfair. My seven-year-old nephew may look like a ne'er-do-well in his skull t-shirt, black jeans and bright-orange trainers, but he's actually been very gentle with Daisy, and she did *ask* him to squirt the water gun.

Daisy, on the other hand, plays the sweet and innocent two-year-old card with her adorable blonde brown curls and big blue eyes. But she is a silent assassin, scratching, biting and stamping Callum whenever adults are looking the other way.

As Callum rightly puts it, it's looks prejudice – something he'll use his public profile to tackle when he's a premier league football player.

Eventually Alex used his 'Landie' to drive over the crumpled tent fabric, squashing the puffy nylon fabric into neat, flat folds. He looked heroic in the Land Rover, with muscular arms spinning the wheel back and forth, and Callum was impressed – calling Alex 'Rex and his Monster machine'.

Callum likes adults who scare him, and he followed Alex around after that, calling him 'mate' and 'lord'.

Alex offered to come back to the cottage and help me unpack, but I said no – I wanted to spent a bit of time alone to process this huge life change. Actually, I didn't say 'process'. I said 'celebrate'.

'I'd rather hoped we'd celebrate together,' said Alex.

'Just give me time,' I told him. 'It's a lot to think about.'

I'm freaking out, freaking out!

Tuesday 3rd July

Back at the cottage. Should unpack the camping stuff but too tired right now. Daisy is napping and cousin John Boy is in his bedroom too, changing his bedsheets and scrubbing the wooden floor with a wire brush and soap.

John Boy offered to change my bedsheets and scrub my floor too, but I said no. John Boy pays me rent. He shouldn't have to do my domestic chores too. And anyway, my carpeted bedroom floor would be ruined by a wire brush.

Too tired to cook tonight, so phoned Mum and Dad and suggested we all have a Chinese together.

'I'm not walking all the way up to your house,' said Mum. 'I've been camping all weekend.'

'It's only a five-minute walk,' I said.

'But it's uphill,' said Mum. 'You should come to us.'

The country track between the cottage and Mum and Dad's pub isn't really uphill. It's just a slight gradient. But I didn't bother arguing because I'm happy to do the takeaway at Mum and Dad's. It means I can have a pint of Guinness with my egg-fried rice and cashew chicken.

John Boy is coming for the takeaway too. This is good because he'll carry Daisy on his shoulders there and back.

I know it's only a five-minute walk, but it is a *little* bit uphill on the way home.

10 pm

Back at the cottage after the Chinese takeaway.

I toyed with asking Alex to come over, but decided against it. I really do need thinking space. Also, takeaway Chinese isn't really Alex's thing. He regularly flies to Shanghai, Beijing and Hong Kong, and gets annoyed at English attempts to 'ruin' good cuisine.

I was in a world of my own as Mum unloaded the silver-foil

cartons and she ended up shouting: 'Bloody hell Juliette, pay attention and tell me if you want egg-fried or special-fried rice before these spring rolls get cold.'

Embarrassingly, I started crying. This was unexpected for everyone – me included.

Mum felt terrible then, and emptied all the spring rolls on my plate. The rest of the family hugged me and asked what was wrong.

'I don't know,' I said. 'I have no idea why I'm crying.'

'It's a big decision, isn't it love?' said Dad. 'With you and Alex. Lots of changes. Where you live, who pays for what, and Daisy will have a new step family. Those Daltons have their problems, don't they? It's a great big step into the unknown, marrying into that lot.'

Cried even more then.

'It'll be fine love,' said Mum, ruffling my hair so curls fell all over my face. 'If Catrina Dalton gives you any trouble, she'll have me to answer to.'

Which is pretty much what I'm afraid of.

Wednesday 4th July

Texted Alex last night to apologise for being 'a bit off' since the camping trip camping.

He texted back to say he had no idea what I was talking about.

That's the nice thing about Alex's dysfunctional upbringing. His assessment of 'weird and distant' is decidedly different to mine. A few days apart is normal to him.

He is going to 'swing by' later to talk wedding plans, so I'd better tidy up the house, take out the recycling mountain etc.

John Boy is very good on the domestic front, crushing all his Stella Artois cans in the recycling container to save space, but my wine and Guinness bottles are more conspicuous.

Where will Alex and I live when we get married?

I can't imagine Alex living here.

And I can't imagine living at the Dalton Estate, with its housekeeper, acres of grounds, swimming pool, horses…and visits from Catrina Dalton.

What will become of us?

Afternoon

Phoned Althea to stress about marrying Alex.

'My life is messy enough already,' I said. 'And Alex's mother and I aren't getting along right now. I can't bring Daisy into another dysfunctional mother-in-law situation. Two messes do not make a tidy.'

'Families always have issues,' said Althea. 'As long as you've got the love, you can make anything work. Wolfgang's dad is an idiot, but I love him so it works. Think positive. One big, happy blended family.'

'I just can't imagine getting on with Alex's mother,' I said. 'Not after what she did to Laura.'

'Think that way and you'll set yourself up for failure,' said Althea. 'You've got to visualise success. Imagine you and Catrina Dalton bonding and having a lovely time. You can do anything with visualisation. This week, I pictured Wolfgang playing peacefully with other children. And the universe delivered. He shared his flapjack with another kid yesterday.'

Further probing revealed that Wolfgang had actually rammed an unappealing beetroot and carrot flapjack into another child's face. But I suppose it's one up from stealing the other child's food.

Maybe Catrina and I *can* get along. It's possible.

But possible isn't the same as probable.

Evening

Alex just dropped by for a glass of wine, but he's gone now. He has a meeting in Edinburgh tomorrow and is catching the overnight train.

'Say the word and I'll cancel,' said Alex. 'I promised I'd be around for you more and I mean it. We're newly engaged. The company can survive without me for one meeting.'

I did not say the word.

I still need thinking space and don't mind Alex being away.

This is not a good sign.

However, I did suggest doing a celebratory meal next week.

'Excellent,' said Alex. 'I'll bring Champagne.'

Champagne feels very official.

Almost too official.

Still – have been cheered by Althea's positivity. Anything IS possible. Catrina and I can be friends. I just need to work out how to make it happen.